The Light of Souls

AlyH4x

Book One from the Arcadian Archives

For those who desperately wish for a more magical world...this is for you.

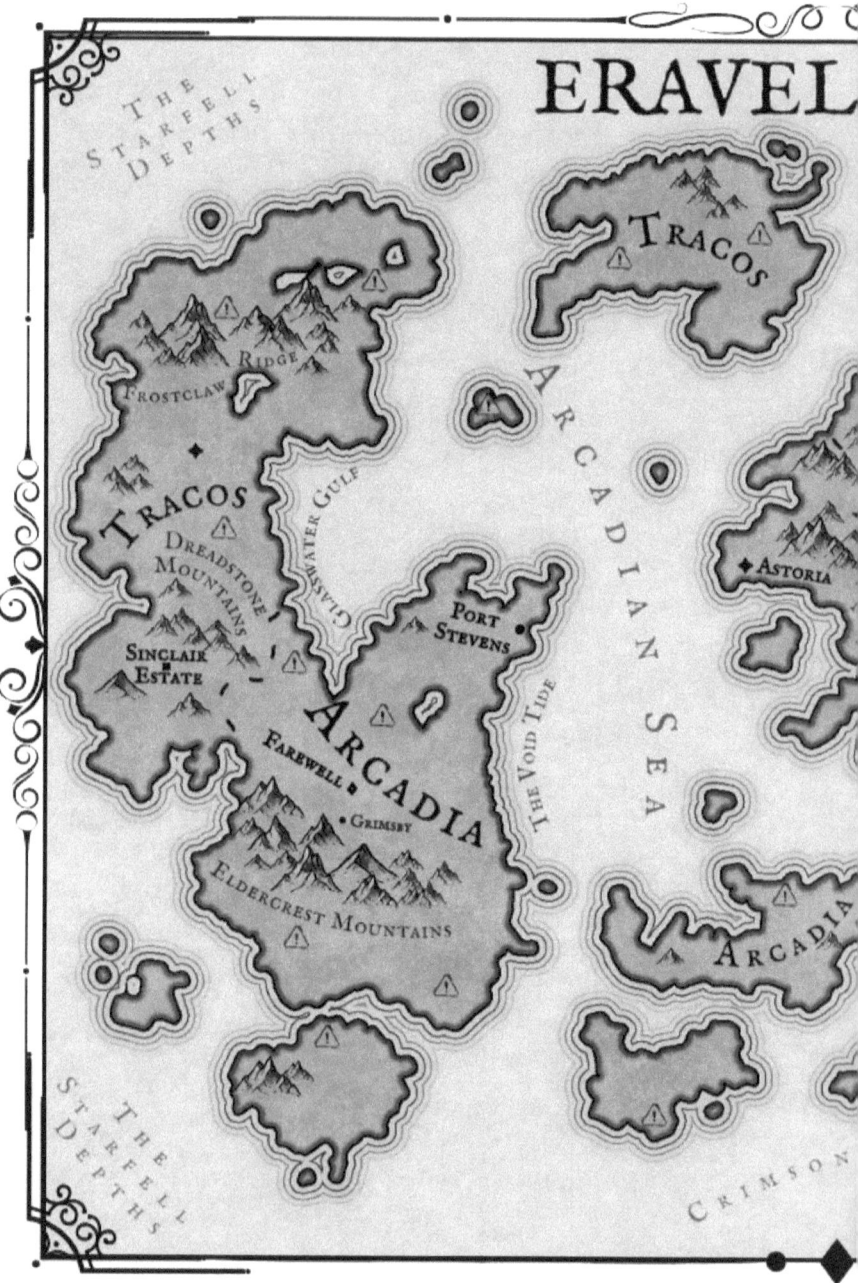

ERAVEL

THE STARFELL DEPTHS

TRACOS

FROSTCLAW RIDGE

TRACOS

DREADSTONE MOUNTAINS

SINCLAIR ESTATE

GLASSWATER GULF

ARCADIA

FAREWELL

GRIMSBY

ELDERCREST MOUNTAINS

PORT STEVENS

THE VOID TIDE

ARCADIAN SEA

ASTORIA

ARCADIA

THE STARFELL DEPTHS

CRIMSON

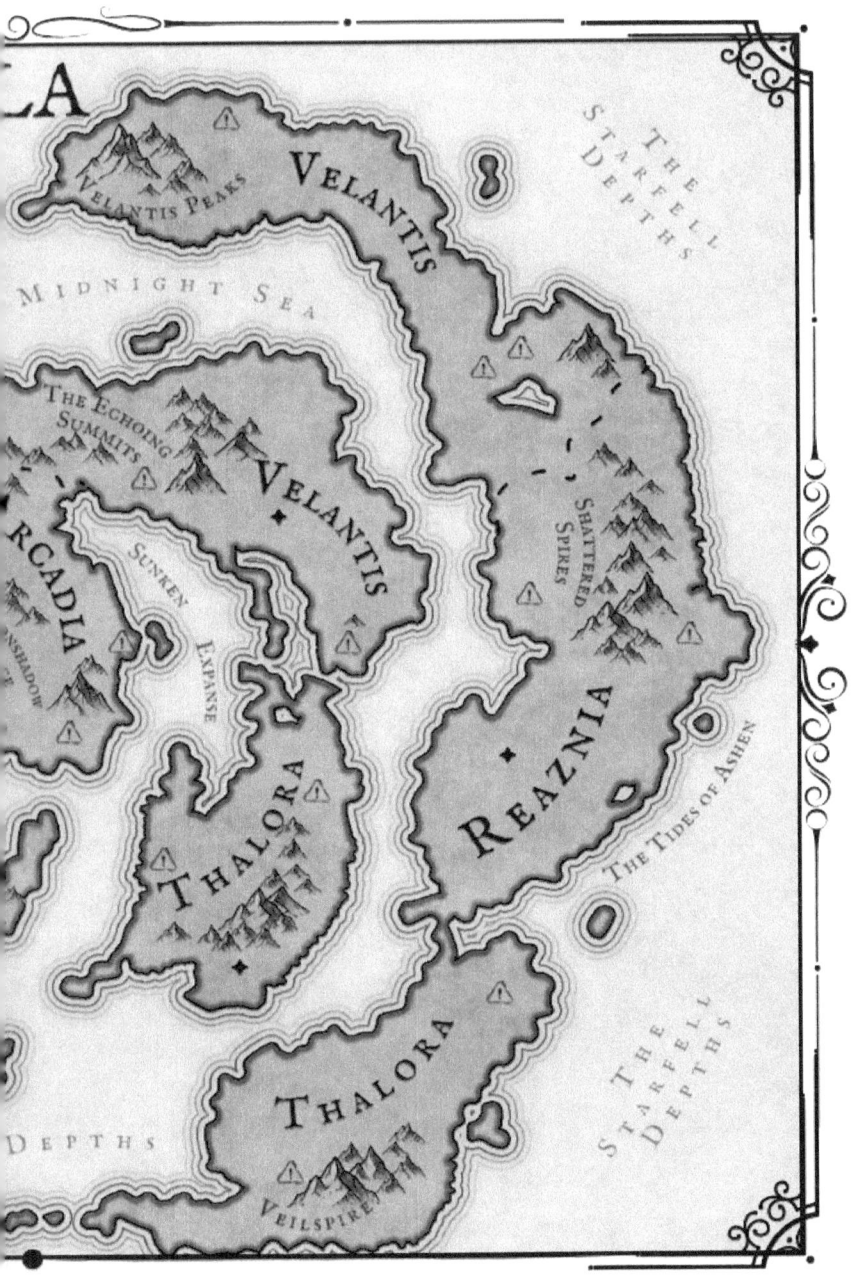

LA

VELANTIS PEAKS

VELANTIS

THE STARFELL DEPTHS

MIDNIGHT SEA

THE ECHOING SUMMITS

VELANTIS

VELANTIS

SHATTERED SPIRES

RCADIA

NSHADOW

SUNKEN EXPANSE

THALORA

REAZNIA

THE TIDES OF ASHEN

THALORA

DEPTHS

THALORA

THE STARFELL DEPTHS

VEILSPIRE

1

BLUE EYES

The cold wall of the abandoned fortress pressed into the back of the young woman who regretted straying from her set path and now faced rather unideal circumstances. Long blonde hair spilled out from under the heavy cloak, still drying from the light rain shower earlier. Piercing blue eyes, the color of secluded mountain waters, watched the danger slowly eliminate the short distance between them.

Before her, prowling low to the ground, was a creature she had not seen before... If she could even call it a creature. Red lights radiated from what would be eyes, if the beast were living. The slender metallic frame was modeled after a wolf, with sharp teeth and bladed claws primed for tearing apart its prey.

Of the many questions racing through her head, how she was going to prevent the mechanical beast from sinking those teeth into her flesh took all her focus. The light pack she traveled with held rapidly depleting rations and a book, but nothing that would aid in defending herself.

Moments before finding herself in this precarious situation, she made the decision to stray from her path, with some wild idea of investigating the obnoxious whispering that pestered her for the last stretch of her trek. Completely oblivious to the danger that lurked nearby, she followed the enticing calls that beckoned her. The voices could not be ignored, especially not after she caught a glimpse of the structure hiding amongst a camouflaged cliffside.

The building must have been a remnant of the old ways, perhaps even built in the Era of Silence, long before magic had swept through the world of Eravella. The structure itself was carved inside the rocky walls, parts of it barely visible amidst the encroaching foliage. Though centuries had passed since its construction, the structure still bore the hallmarks of its former glory, its angular contours a testament to a bygone era of technological prowess.

The exterior, perhaps at one point designed to blend seamlessly with the rocky cliffside, now stood as a stark contrast to the surrounding wilderness—a silent sentinel guarding the secrets within. An attempt was made to seal the entrance with steel plates, but enough of a gap allowed her to peer inside. Cautiously, she peeked into the darkness, hoping to find the source of the infuriating whispers that continued their quiet call.

The low growl was the first indication she was not alone. The beast approached slowly, ensuring she had nowhere to go, its advance pressing her up against the wall. The unintentional side effect of living under the same roof of one of this era's most feared mages is that every other threat paled in comparison. So, when the beast leapt at her, she wasn't exactly scared but rather upset for not identifying the dangerous possibility sooner. There wasn't much she could do other than brace herself for the impending impact and even less time to react when suddenly a man stood in between her and it.

The grind of metal on metal rang out and the creature was forced back. As the man's sword came into view, the steel of the blade turned a bright red. A wave of heat warmed the air. The sword engulfed in flames. With a single, decisive motion, the man struck at the beast, his sword slicing through the air. The blade found its mark, burying itself deep into the pulsating core on the creature's chest, sending it staggering sideways, until it fell over, motionless. A black liquid seeped from the wound, creating a dark puddle on the old, ruined road.

Waiting only long enough to ensure the beast would not get up again, the man whipped around to face her. His green eyes narrowed as he towered over her. "These ruins are off limits to tourists." His commanding tone grew colder as he spoke, "You shouldn't be out here. You're clearly not equipped to handle mechoids."

She tore her eyes away from him to examine the steel body of the creature once more. In the crumpled heap, the red eyes were now empty black holes, and parts of the exposed circuits sparked from where the blade severed the connections. The metallic frame showcased writing of a dead language– *LYNX PROWLER* – a testament of the old ways.

The shock quickly dissipated. She had only read about mechoids and certainly didn't expect to see one so close. These mechanical creatures, relics from the Era of Ascension, were the very creations that had triggered the Great Ruin, nearly wiping out humanity. The proper thing to do would have been to thank the man for his assistance and potentially saving her life, but instead she blurted out the first question that came to mind. "A Prowler?"

She regretted the question instantly for it only seemed to solidify the man's uncertainty of her. Slowly, he placed the sword into the holder on his belt, his eyes traveling across her to appraise her.

"You're lucky that one didn't choose to pounce sooner." There was a sharp edge to his tone that suggested annoyance, as if he was more bothered by her question than he was with disposing of the beast. Still cautious of her, he let his eyes leave her for another brief scan of the area.

Taking him in fully, she guessed he must have been older than her by at least a few years. He wore the light armor of a guard, the lower half of his head shaved but leaving a longer length of dark brown hair toward the front that looked as though he styled it simply by running a hand loosely through it. The man's eyes were a shade green, deeper than most of the surrounding forest, and they concentrated on clearing the area before turning his attention back on her.

As he moved to close the gap between them, she noted a silver emblem fastened to his armor, depicting a shield with a crystal-like gem at its core. The implication of the badge put her more on edge than the presence of the sword sheathed at his side or whatever magic he was capable of. He finished his apparent appraisal of her, raising an eyebrow, "Alright, what are you doing here, Blue Eyes?"

In her recent liberation, she encountered very few other people, all of whom she barely conversed with, let alone explained the extraordinary circumstances that placed her there. While it was unlikely this man could know her origins, she knew better than to place her trust in just anyone. To him, she was nothing more than an annoying lost traveler, and all she needed to do was play the part so she could be on her way again.

"I'm traveling to a nearby town," she offered, doing her best to keep a cool and calm voice despite her heart pounding. "I must have chosen the wrong road to follow." With her back still against the wall, the whispering continued to call from behind her, making it difficult for her to focus on the unconvinced face before her.

"Are you heading to Farewell?" he asked.

She gave a quick nod. Seeming to have expected as much, he turned, pointing back toward the road she strayed from. "Farewell is a good stretch that way. I'm just wrapping up my patrol. I can take you back," he offered her a polite, yet condescending smile. "Ensure you don't find yourself taking the wrong path again."

She contemplated taking him up on the offer. Seeing the mechoid in person actualized the danger she must have been in while roaming the forest. However, the slight smirk he gave her only deepened her distrust of him, and she was not interested in answering any more of his lingering questions. Avoiding any potential annoyance, she showed him the same polite smile, "I'll be fine on my own, thanks." She started to move, intent on getting past him. "I'd rather not follow a strange man in the forest."

He held out a hand to stop her. "Well, I'd rather not let some reckless civilian be mauled to death because she thinks she can handle herself." He shook his head, showing he had already made up his mind, then he shifted to a more formal tone. "This isn't a safe area. I'll guide you back to town."

"I'm not interested," she repeated coldly, pushing past him. "Save yourself the trouble."

He didn't try to stop her, but she heard him mutter, "I doubt I am."

His gaze followed her as she pulled the hood of her cloak more tightly around her and continued back to the paved path. Once she was far enough away, she risked a check over her shoulder, ensuring she was not followed. Finding nothing to arouse her suspicion, she cursed her foolishness and set her focus back on her task. After all, it was only her life at stake.

With enough time and distance, the whispering

eventually faded away, and the quiet was a welcomed change as her mind whirled through a cascade of thoughts. She was far past the point of no return. In fact, she reached that point the moment she stepped outside of the estate grounds that had been her personal hell for over eighteen years. Despite her exhaustion from walking for days, she struggled to obtain the sleep she desperately needed to keep going, only managing to gain short bursts of restless sleep. She suffered from both the paranoia that someone would find her while she slept and from the painful reminders of exactly *who* she was running from.

Her escape started nearly two weeks before. Knowing delays were inevitable, she devised a plan so she had a full four days to create as much distance between her and the estate before it was discovered she left. Her assumption proved to be correct when on the evening of the fourth day, she felt the sudden jolt in her body seizing up as every nerve in her being burned. This was a sensation she was far too familiar with, and it remained impossible to grow accustomed to the way it drained her body and mind. It was unavoidable the moment *he* found out she was gone, and she had to do her best to recover quickly and get on the move again to maintain her advantage. Now leagues away from the only place she had known, she headed for the strange new town, feeling more scared and alone than she had ever felt in her entire life of isolation.

As the dense forest gave way, she found herself standing on the edge of a vast clearing, where orderly fields stretched out toward the imposing walls of Farewell. From her vantage point, the road ahead seemed to be a direct path leading to the city gates, beckoning travelers like a guiding hand. Clusters of buildings nestled around a hill, their rooftops forming a jagged silhouette against the horizon.

Even at this distance, she could discern the winding path of a well-trodden road snaking its way up the hillside.

As she approached the city, her attention was overtaken by the sharp bark of a dog, cutting through the air like a warning bell. Turning toward the source of the sound, she watched as a black and white canine burst out of a nearby farmhouse. She braced herself for a confrontation, but to her surprise, the dog's demeanor was anything but hostile.

Instead of lunging at her, the dog crouched down low, its tail wagging furiously. With cautious curiosity, she watched as the playful creature circled her, its movements exaggerated and joyful. Tentatively, she extended her hand, offering it as a gesture of peace. The dog, sensing her openness, approached with enthusiasm.

A small chuckle escaped her as the unexpected interaction unfolded. After a brief sniff and an affectionate lick, the dog seemed to have found a new friend.

"Scout!" a voice called and was shortly followed by an older woman stepping out onto the front porch of the farmhouse. She wore an apron adorned with a charming apple pattern. "Scout! Now stop that, leave her alone," the warm voice called again, and the dog responded with another bark as it continued to circle between her legs. Laughing, the woman addressed her, "Good evening, dear. Seems Scout has made a new friend out of you."

Trying not to trip over the playful pup, she couldn't help but offer a chuckle. "That's alright, he seems friendly enough."

"I wondered what had gotten him all worked up."

The woman's white hair was pulled back into a neat bun, her features time-worn but graceful. Watching her with shimmering silver eyes, she used a cloth to dry her hands. "You've must have come a long way, are you heading into town?"

"Yes," she stammered, caught off guard by the question and wondering just how disheveled she must look to prompt the comment. "I'm hoping to meet someone in town. I'm told they run the Farewell bookstore."

"You'll find it in the Pioneer Plaza." The old woman gestured toward the town entrance. "It's at the other end of town, one of the shops that looks on the old pioneer statue. Just walk straight through; you can't miss it."

Thanking the woman, she turned to Scout who stared at her expectantly. Smiling, she reached down and patted him before making her way into the city, leaving the disappointed pup behind.

An archway built into the stone wall allowed passage into the protected city. The name "Farewell", engraved proudly amongst the stonework, welcomed travelers into a bustling plaza. Like many towns in the Era of Resurgence, Farewell retained the remnants of the advanced technologies from the time before the collapse. Lampposts still flickered to life with a soft, steady glow. Buildings showed signs of technical infrastructure – old wiring systems running along walls, pipes and draining networks, integral to the city's infrastructure, intertwined with the architecture.

She travelled along the busy shops, doing her best to avoid colliding with the crowds of people traversing the area while she took in the various store fronts and street vendors. Taking her time to walk the streets, she browsed the shops that lined the path. Most of the establishments made it easy to discern the wares sold within by utilizing signs or displaying the goods in the shop windows. Although, she noted there was an oddly rough-looking shop where the windows were deliberately fogged and prominently featured a large wooden silhouette of a hen above its doors.

Despite feeling overwhelmed, she found it easy to blend in among the townsfolk, most of whom were preoccupied with their own evening routines. Though often she would pass by random strangers offering her a nod and polite greeting, only to do a full-on double take when they made eye contact. It was odd for everyone to seem so warm and go out of their way to greet a total stranger, but on second thought, perhaps that was normal for people living within a city.

Following the instructions from the old woman, she traveled through the streets, finding her way across the lively town until coming into another plaza which housed the promised statue at its center. The plaza itself mirrored a similar archway that led out of the city, allowing for one to travel right through the city, if needed. In contrast to the former plaza's centerpiece—an ancient and imposing tree—this plaza featured a tribute to the town's history. The metallic man held a pickaxe over his shoulder and his gaze set toward the horizon beyond the archway that led out of town. Most of the buildings surrounding the area were adorned with banners, giving off the impression that this was the main entrance into Farewell.

Nestled snugly between two towering structures, a quaint wooden sign proudly proclaimed the establishment as *"Farewell Stories,"* with the mantra *'When one story ends, another begins,"* etched below in elegant script. Through the crystal-clear display windows, she caught sight of a young woman engrossed in her work, leaning over a desk scattered with papers.

She adjusted her bag and retrieved the hard-backed book that had led her to the doorstep of the old bookstore. The cover displayed *Forgotten Roads*, with the author's name proudly presented on the cover. It was both the key to her freedom and a stark reminder of the mysteries shrouding her existence. Even in her exhaustion from the many long days of traveling, she battled to steady her pounding heart.

Anxious to discover if it was all worth it, she decided not to prolong the event any longer and pushed the door open.

A little bell chimed above her, catching the attention of the young woman at the desk. Close to her age, perhaps slightly younger, the woman's bright silver eyes complimented the enthusiastic smile. Long brown hair, which gave off hints of red when in the light, was thrown into a loose braid. The woman stood from the desk, standing shorter in height compared to her.

"Evening, what can I do for you?" the woman asked, the friendly voice suiting her. Returning the greeting, she held on to the hope she would get the information she needed.

"I'm looking for Malcom Burton."

"Yes, he's upstairs." The woman's gaze fell upon the book clutched in her arms. "Oh, I see you have one of his books! He'll be glad to hear he has a fan from out of town. Hold on, I'll grab him!" The woman's energy level seemed to rise with every word. There was no time to offer any affirmation before the woman disappeared up the stairs. With the woman gone, to distract herself, she scanned the many shelves that displayed the shops inventory. It was a fruitless endeavor, as she was too focused on listening for the footsteps above her.

It was only a short time she had to wait before she heard the woman's descent on the stairs.

"He's coming now," the energetic woman reassured her, finding her way back behind the desk. The sound of a slower descent on the stairs shifted her eyes onto the man as he came into view. His face was a canvas of joyous wrinkles, hosting a perpetual smile. Silver eyes gleamed through speckled glasses beneath a crown of tousled, snow-white hair. He paused when catching sight of her, adjusting his glasses to mask the puzzled expression. "Hello," he said warmly, "I hear you are a reader of my books." He spoke with a soft, gracious tone. "Would you like me to sign your copy?"

Unexpectedly, she found herself in a stunned silence.

Taking her for being shy, Malcom attempted to address her again, using a warmer voice than before. "My dear, you must have come a long way to meet me." He eyed her condition curiously. "The least I can do is sign your book." He reached out and gently pulled the book from her, laying it flat on the nearby desk. He pulled out a pen from his shirt pocket, opening the book. "What's your name? I'll make it out to-" He stopped abruptly, finding there was already writing behind the last page of the book, by now realizing it was his own writing, written for her mother. It was a passage in dark blue ink she'd memorized from reading it so often.

My dearest Amelia,
There is no greater gift than being able to watch you grow
into the wonderful woman you've become, and I will forever
be thankful for the opportunity to have been by your side
through it all. In this next chapter, you will continue to
reward this world with your kindness and passion. I look
forward to hearing of your adventures when you return.
May the goddess bless you, and the stars guide you.
Your forever guardian,
-Malcom Burton

When the author finished reading his note, he returned a puzzled expression back onto her. With the message playing in her mind, she was reminded once more of her purpose, and the daze seemed to wear off.

"My name is Avery," she said, finding the strength behind her voice. "I've come here because I do not know anyone else whom my mother trusted."

It was Malcom's turn to be shocked into silence, staring at her with wide eyes. "Gods," he said breathlessly, taking his glasses off to rub his nose. He turned to the woman behind the desk, the confusion showing plainly as she took the scene in.

"Leah, let's close up shop for the day. I would like to hear what this young lady has to say."

2

A LIFE DEBT

Two years ago...

"Langston was finally able to check into Poyer. Our suspicions were correct, he was taken in by that oaf, Oshie," a man with a shrill voice reported, standing beside an oversized desk stained black to match the dark furniture in the room. Adjusting glasses sitting on his thin nose, he continued reading from the screen of the glyph, a sleek, palm-sized device that provided access to the data at the touch of a fingertip.

"Langston confirmed he survived the interrogation, so we can assume he squealed to make a deal." Avoiding any indication he noticed Avery's arrival, the man carried on delivering his news. Avery lingered awkwardly in the study doorway, awaiting direction from the figure seated behind the desk, who was absorbed in listening to the report being delivered.

Sitting comfortably, as he always did in his chair, Theodore Sinclair let his molten gold eyes rest on Avery as she did her best to look uninterested in the conversation. In the unsettling silence, Theodore's looming presence cast a shadow over Avery, his watchful gaze anticipating her every move since he assumed the role of her guardian all those years ago. Long black hair framed his narrow face and aside from his sunken yellow eyes, he had not changed over the years.

Theodore aged much more gracefully than his secretary, Jarek Rogi, who despite being younger than Theodore, bore many signs of age. Jarek's graying hair was thinning and shined from whatever it was he used to keep it flat. His voice cracked annoyingly as he droned on his report, a stark contrast to Theodore's unwavering demeanor. Avery could only assume that Theodore tolerated him, because like so many others, Jarek worshiped Theodore like some sort of God.

Silently, Theodore indicated the chair across from him, watching Avery as she settled herself into the seat. Avoiding his gaze, her own eyes skimmed over the bookshelves adorning the walls. Although she was often summoned to his study, she always found some oddity to focus on rather than his cold stare.

There were many curiosities displayed on shelves throughout the room. Despite there already being another dedicated library in the estate, the study contained its fair share of books, all of which required permission before touching. Historians would riot had they known there were so many relics of the old ways that filled the shelves. Technology and other artifacts once used in the long dead society were nothing more than decorations and trophies that Theodore collected over the years. Perhaps Avery would have found them fascinating had they not been stored in the one room she despised most.

Rarely did Theodore call upon Avery for an occasion that resulted in anything good for her. Jarek's presence worsened the experience, as he maintained the impression that Avery was not worthy of being in the same room with either of them. Continuing to ignore her presence, Jarek momentarily raised his eyes from the glyph to briefly gauge the effect the news imprinted on his master.

Theodore masked any annoyance well behind a bored expression. "How unfortunate," Theodore started with his usual indifferent tone. "I cannot say we failed to foresee this. However, I anticipated we could expedite the operation in Cernonia with his connections. I suppose that cannot be helped now."

The absence of his intense gaze made it easier for her to study his features, attempting to get her own impression of his mood. Already there was an uneasiness when moments before her dinner was interrupted by the estate butler to announce that her presence was wanted in the study. However, she could not recall doing anything that would have prompted Theodore to reprimand her.

The unsettling feeling only worsened as the two men discussed their affairs. It was seldom for her to be present when business was discussed, and it didn't seem the two would stop on her account. Theodore reached for the short glass in front of him, swirling the mixture as he spoke. "Reach out to Vivian, have her take care of Poyer. We will have Langston take his place. They trust him there, and we will rework our plans for Cernonia."

Nodding, Jarek traced down the note. "What of Poyer's son? Liam, I believe is his name. Shall I make that connection?"

"Yes, do so. He is quite young. I doubt he will be as useful, but with his father out of the picture we may be able to use him down the road with enough resources." Theodore suggested dryly, taking another sip from his glass and shifting his eyes back onto Avery. Jarek took down another quick note before returning to his own desk. "I agree, my lord. It will be the best chance we have to maintain our influence within that circle."

The fear of the repercussions slowly seeped away as Avery resolved her intent on reading Theodore's features for some glimmer of reason. Not only were the two men discussing business, but she knew replacing a contact within their operations could only mean one thing. With Theodore's full attention on her, clearly it was intentional for her to hear it. Everything Theodore did served a purpose, and as he watched her closely, she understood why; he was doing his own appraisal of her reaction to the information. Seeing she had given up on pretending not to listen, he directed the conversation at her, as if she was conspiring alongside him. "Poyer will set a good enough example for them. I'm sure he expects protection from the Duke, but he will soon learn he has poorly placed his trust."

Doing her best to not let her own thoughts on the matter become plain, Avery tried to keep the air of disinterest, but the slightest narrowing of Theodore's eyes told her it was not working.

"Do you have something you'd like to add to that, Avery?" he asked, and the question was enough to finally convince Jarek to take in her existence. A pang of irritation grew in her from both their eyes resting on her. While Theodore's tone suggested interest, she knew better than to express her distaste for his work. Without removing her gaze, she shook her head, forcing a toneless voice.

"No, you have demonstrated on several occasions that my thoughts are irrelevant on matters that concern your operations."

Jarek made a sound like a laugh, nodding approvingly. "If that isn't the wisest thing she's said, my lord."

Avery refrained from glaring at the assistant and kept her focus on not provoking Theodore. He drummed a hand against his chair impatiently, contemplating whatever plagued his mind. The anxiety grew inside her the longer he took to gather his thoughts. If his mind was not already made up, then whatever it was, would surely be impactful to his affairs. Slowly replacing the glass on his desk, Theodore broached the subject, "I have decided you will start playing a more active role and study under Jarek. I need you to be prepared to take over his duties."

Feeling the weight of his words setting in, Avery did her best to seem unfazed by the news despite it being the very thing she was dreading.

"I didn't realize he was to be replaced, although I cannot say I am surprised."

Riled by the comment, Jarek waved the glyph accusingly.

"It's that attitude right there, my lord. These delicate matters cannot be entrusted to someone who refuses to take it seriously."

Unamused by their banter, Theodore ignored both comments, expanding upon his thought, "Jarek is needed elsewhere once we reach a milestone in an upcoming project. I will need someone to remain here to take over his responsibilities while he is away."

There was a rising panic in Avery as she continued to project her indifference. She said nothing, for everything she thought of in the moment would definitely send her past the dangerous waters she was already swimming in. Theodore accepted her silence, apparently settling his mind on the set course as he spoke, "What you have heard here today is the result of one of our contacts failing to meet our expectations. Poyer has decided to trust the Arcadians to protect him. Eliminating him will strengthen the hold we have within Arcadia's capital."

Finding her self-restraint faltering, Avery raised an eyebrow. "It seems rather counterproductive to gain trust by murdering the people you wish to influence."

Unmoved by the comment, Theodore only shook his head slightly. "As Jarek mentioned, there is a delicate balance in the way we handle our cards. In order to play the game, sometimes you must sacrifice your own players."

The suggestion did not sit well with Avery, and she could not help narrowing her eyes at him. "I have no desire to play a game where lives are used as the pieces."

Without turning his head or taking his eyes off her, Theodore addressed Jarek with the slow wave of a hand. "Leave us."

Jarek nodded, bowing his head and navigating around the desk to exit the room, managing to give Avery a smug sneer as he passed. When the door closed, Avery's hands tightened on the arms of the chair, her body tensing in anticipation of what was to come. His yellow eyes were studying her again.

Calmly, Theodore adjusted himself in his chair, leaning upright on his desk. "I will rephrase my previous statement so there is no misunderstanding." He clasped his hands together, his eyes boring into her. "You will start studying under Jarek to learn how to handle his responsibilities during his absence. You have come of age, and it's time you start engaging in the role in which you are here to fulfill."

Fighting the fire growing inside her, she forced herself to hold back the worst of the responses that came to mind. "I find it strange you cannot find another replacement who is more qualified and eager to do your bidding."

There was a flash of annoyance on his face before resuming his bored demeanor. "You are foolishly attempting to upset me with the false hope that I will change my mind and instead punish you for remaining difficult. It is a waste of your time and energy. I have already made up my mind. You *will* learn how to fulfill your responsibilities here, and I will not repeat myself again. I do not suggest you try to test me, Avery."

She bit her tongue, knowing the sharp edge in his tone was more dangerous than she was willing to fight against.

Theodore always got what he wanted. After all, the Blood Tyrant was known for destroying entire cities if it meant he was closer to his cause.

When she continued her silence, the smallest glimmer of a smile touched his face. He reached down, pulling out a drawer in his desk, revealing from within a hard-covered book. He placed it on the desk, then pushed it toward her. "This was one of your mother's favorite books. Amelia brought it with her when she came to work for me, and it has been in my possession since."

A chill swept through Avery as she stared at it. She did not move from her seat until Theodore nodded, permitting it. Carefully, Avery lifted the book from the desk while Theodore continued in a slightly lighter tone, "You may have the book. I don't enjoy the story myself, but perhaps you will find it more palatable."

The friendly tone made Avery's stomach turn, and she tried not to look disgusted by his attempt to appeal to her. Again, his eyes narrowed, reading right through her façade. "It would be wise to consider this next chapter of your life as an opportunity to make it far more comfortable. It must be rather exhausting to constantly choose to take the path containing the most resistance." He waved a hand toward the door, dismissing her. "You may go. Send Jarek back in."

Without a word, Avery left the study, carrying the book in her arms. Jarek was waiting in a chair in the corridor, scrolling through his glyph until he heard her approach.

"You should be honored," he spat at her. "Many people would kill to be in my position."

Avery rolled her eyes at this, giving him the smirk she had been withholding. "I highly doubt that. I imagine you would have been replaced long ago if there was anyone out there that eager."

Jarek's face deepened a shade of red as he strode over

to her, pointing a finger venomously. "You think you're so clever. You need to accept your place and start being useful for once in your life. Lord Sinclair has given you more than you ever deserved."

Avery's lips curled, her own anger surfacing as he aimed his frustrations at her. "Tell me, does this hostility of yours come from the knowledge that Theodore believes an eighteen-year-old could do your job, or is that just a coincidence?"

The comment was enough to cause Jarek to shake with anger, baring his teeth at her, "Why you-" he sputtered, but Theodore's voice rang out from behind, demanding his secretary's presence. Jarek pursed his lips, flustered. In a moment, he composed himself, donning another sneer. "I don't know why I bother trying to get through to you. Knowing the traitorous blood that runs through you, there just isn't any help for you." He moved to return to the study, catching Avery's glare as he passed her. Jarek understood she was forbidden to utter any word that pertained to her parents and there was nothing she could think of in the moment that would not violate that rule. Deciding he was not worth the trouble, she continued down the corridor, gazing down at the book that once belonged to her mother.

◆ ◆ ◆

The book now rested in Leah's lap, opened to the note Malcom wrote some time ago. The curtains were drawn shut, and the sign outside was flipped to indicate the shop was closed. Avery was shown upstairs to where the author and his assistant called home. The staircase led directly into a room shared between a kitchen and a small sitting area that surrounded a fireplace.

Nestled in the corner, a writing desk sat facing so it could take in the wide view of the room and out beyond the long paned windows. Many papers scattered its surface, displaying long written pages in black and blue ink. Seated next to the fireplace, Avery placed her tea glass down beside the small plate of cookies provided to her. While she was hungry, she could not imagine trying to eat anything with how twisted her insides felt. Malcom stared down into his own glass, giving Avery time to process her thoughts.

"Thank you for the tea." Avery attempted to ease into it. "I know I am a complete stranger to you, but you must understand, I don't know where else to go."

Malcom shook his head, giving her a sympathetic smile. "You have not bothered me in the slightest. Although, I haven't heard anything from Amelia in almost thirty years. You say she is dead?"

Avery nodded, noticing a sadness wash over the cheery expression of the author. "She died when I was around two. I know very little of her." She indicated the book. "It appears you knew her well."

"She came to me when she was four. Her parents were killed by mechoids, and there was no other family to look after her. I lost my own daughter at the time, and it was only right to make sure she was raised well." A soft expression emerged as he spoke, "She was a magnificent young lady."

Avery's face softened in return, "Please, if you don't mind, tell me more about her. Why did she leave Farewell?"

"Amelia was of age, one of the brightest mages Farewell had seen in quite some time. She dreamed of getting out into the world to learn from other mages and discover more about herself." He paused, pushing himself out of his chair with a grunt, making his way to the writing desk where he pulled on some drawers. Rifling through the contents, he continued, "We never knew much about her parents, and that was one of the first things she wanted to look into. Ah- here it is!" He pulled out a small photograph, bringing it over to Avery. "Here is Mel a few days before she left."

She took the outstretched photo. A much younger version of Malcom smiled brightly up at Avery, his arm over the shoulder of a young woman. Wild long brown hair framed an elegant but lively face that housed the most beautiful violet eyes. Breathless, Avery wanted to burn the image to memory, only having seen a few other photos of her mother in the estate.

"She was ready to take on the world." Malcom's eyes travelled back to the book. "But I never heard from her again. Not even a letter."

The sadness was returning, but Avery pressed him for more. "Did she know of Theodore Sinclair?"

The question seemed to startle the old man; he shook his head vigorously. "Surely you don't mean Lord Sinclair of Tracos?"

Avery froze, his recognition of the name and the slight fear in his stunned gaze reminding her of the danger she was in. Malcom seemed to read Avery's startled mind. He sighed, shaking his head. "I feared she might have gotten mixed up in that. We were on the verge of war in those days."

Avery nodded, not wanting to dance around the subject. "She was working for Theodore before she died."

Malcom furrowed his brow at this, but it was Leah who gasped. "That can't be right. I've heard such good things about Amelia, why would she work for him?"

Avery shrugged, "I don't know. It was only through the message you left in that book that I found out she knew someone outside of Theodore's network."

"You've been in Tracos then?" the author asked.

"Yes, under Theodore's guardianship, continuing to serve the life debt owed by my mother."

"Gods, a life debt?" Malcom pulled off his glasses to rub at his eyes. He replaced them, giving Avery another long look. "How old are you?"

"I've just turned twenty over the winter," she said. Aware of the author's growing astonishment, she appealed to him, "I understand I am unloading this on you, and I don't have any answers for you either. I fled the Sinclair estate in hopes of getting some answers about Amelia. I don't know if I have any other family, or if you might know who my father was?"

Malcom's eyes widened. "Your father? No, as I've mentioned my dear, I have not heard from Amelia after she left."

The cold familiar chill of uncertainty swept over her body. "Then, I do not know what to ask of you. To be honest, I did not know if I would make it this far, and I was hoping to gain some glimmer of information that I could act on."

"I want to help you, Avery..." The author's voice trailed off, and he moved his gaze to the floor as he thought. He was quiet while he contemplated, and after a moment, he suddenly looked determined. "We should talk to Harvey. He has more experience with these types of things." He slowly eased himself off the chair once more. "I can take you to him." The author looked Avery over, "Or maybe I can bring him here. Give you a chance to freshen up first."

"Oh," she stammered, and unclenched the tight fist she didn't realize she was holding. "Do you trust him?"

There was no hesitation, only a reassuring nod. "I trust him with my life."

"Alright." Cautiously, she nodded. She knew how dangerous it was to take others into her confidence, knowing how well-connected Theodore was, but there were no other alternatives. "I will see him."

With her agreement, the author did not delay in leaving the small shop, promising to return shortly with the company. In the meantime, Leah offered to get Avery a change of clothes and a chance to wash up. Casting a critical gaze at herself in the mirror, she couldn't help but understand why the man in the forest had regarded her with suspicion. While she had always been slender, her cheekbones seemed more pronounced than usual, and her eyes betrayed the weariness of many sleepless nights. The mess of blonde hair was tied back in a poor attempt to contain it. There was no doubt she was long overdue for a thorough wash.

A neat stack of clothes awaited her after she finished removing a majority of the forest that clung to her.

"Oh, good they fit!" Leah said, inspecting the outfit she had thrown together when Avery emerged from the washroom. "I was worried they might be too small. How do you feel?"

Truly feeling a bit better now that she was washed and managed to untangle her hair, Avery returned a grateful smile. "Much better, thank you."

The ladies were now seated on a cushioned alcove in Leah's room that looked out upon the town square. Plants of varying species were draped around to frame the window. A sizable stack of books rested on a table next to where they were taking in the view of the plaza. To pass some of the time, or to avoid the stifling silence, Leah created conversation about herself and her time with the author.

Malcom was something of a father figure to Leah. He had taken her in after losing her mother to illness at eight years old. Growing up with a love of books, she was well read and bonded with Avery over a few titles that shared their interests. There was a slight hesitation from Leah whenever they started on a new topic, but whatever held her back melted away the more the two talked. It was a refreshing experience for Avery, as she couldn't remember having such a pleasant conversation, especially considering the circumstance.

Lights from the building directly across the way flickered on, showing the maroon and silver banners slightly fluttering as a breeze passed through.

"That's the guild hall," Leah pointed out, following Avery's line of sight.

"A guild?"

"Yes, Farewell's guard is run by the guild, and they hold a seat on the council."

"Who does the council report to?"

Leah thought for a moment, "I suppose they would reach out to the capital if there were a need. Like most cities in Arcadia, Farewell operates pretty autonomously."

The distant chime of the shop doorbell rang, and the sound of muffled voices became clear. They listened as the footsteps made their way throughout the store and upon the stairs. Malcom spoke quietly as he led the others, "Let's just try to limit our questions and give her some time to breathe."

There was some more hushed discussion as they reached the top. Avery rose from her chair, finding Malcom looked far less grim.

"Avery, you look refreshed!" he said cheerfully. "I'd like you to meet my friends here. This is Professor Harris Colleymore." He indicated the man with dark brown hair just above his shoulders. He wore a simple dress suit, and large rimmed glasses that made his brown eyes even larger as he stared wide-eyed at her. "And this is Harvey Carter, he runs the Big Hen up the road."

Unlike the professor, Harvey fixed her with a gaze from his narrowed silver eyes. His grey hair was kept short, and his neatly trimmed beard framed his face. He wore an expression of someone who certainly didn't want to be there, and she guessed that the faint scent of a cigar lingering in the air emanated from him. Neither of the men broke eye contact with her.

"Haven't seen those since working overseas." Harvey's deep voice cut off his sentences gruffly.

"Yes, they are definitely striking," the professor agreed, blinking a few times to ensure he was seeing clearly. Malcom stepped forward, indicating the company. "Avery, I've briefly explained to Harvey what you've shared with me. He suggested bringing along the professor, a longtime friend of ours. Harvey-"

"It's amazing you even made it this far from the looks of it," Harvey interrupted, sounding anything other than amazed. "We're supposed to believe you made it all the way here from Tracos?"

Anticipating the resistance, she addressed him calmly. "If I were to say otherwise, it would be a lie."

"Is that so? Then tell me, why would Lord Sinclair keep some kid around to do his work?"

Malcom jumped in again, "Hold on, Harvey, don't just-"

"No, it's alright," Avery said quietly. "You're right, it doesn't make sense. I can't answer you, because I don't know. The only thing I've been told was that I was under his guardianship to serve a life debt."

Harvey made another sound like a grunt, but his gaze was still on her, his eyes seeming to search right through her.

"What kind of work did he have you do?" the professor asked calmly, although he could not mask the concern in his gaze.

"Mostly secretarial work. I handled the intake of ledgers from many of his operations and managed some of the communication between him and his contacts. Recently, he seemed to think I'd make a good successor of sorts. It was his intent to get me more involved than I wanted to be."

"How'd you manage to leave?" Harvey asked bluntly.

"I gained his trust over time. He and I have never seen eye to eye, but I needed him to trust me. I waited until he was to be away from the estate long enough that I could get a head start."

"Well, you're out of Tracos now, it will be much harder for him to get to you," Harvey said, sounding as though he was dismissing the whole ordeal.

"You don't understand. He doesn't have to be here to get to me."

The whole room went silent as all of them took in her words.

"Would you please elaborate?" the professor asked. "Help us understand your situation."

"I cannot explain it well, but Theodore still has a hold on me. He doesn't have to see me or be near me, but he is able to do something that causes my body to seize up. I cannot stop it."

Avery found her own eyes were fixated upon Harvey, watching as he stared at her unconvinced. He stepped forward, and it was the first time Avery realized he was using a cane to walk. He held out a hand to her. "Let me see your arm!"

Briefly, Avery looked down at his extended hand before shifting her gaze to Malcom. The author motioned for her to indulge him. Slowly she extended her hand, letting Harvey grab it in cold and calloused hands. His eyes stared down at her bare arm, flipping her wrist over and occasionally angling it around in a surprisingly delicate manner. He looked up, eyeing Avery suspiciously, "When's the last time you used magic?"

Alarmed by the abrupt question, she returned the suspicious stare. "Never, I can't use magic."

"What?" Harris stammered from behind Harvey. "You

must be joking?" He rose out of his seat to advance toward her. Startled, she pulled her arm away, taking a step back from Harvey.

"I'm not a mage. Theodore gave up on that a long time ago," she said defensively, now glaring up at Harvey.

"How is that possible?" the professor breathed, searching Harvey for answers. The old man's cold eyes looked like they had seen too much in one lifetime.

"She's got a vessel, but it's empty and damaged."

Malcom stepped up, trying to calm the others. "Perhaps this is the result of whatever Theodore did to her."

The professor pursed his lips. "It's not a condition I've ever heard of."

Harvey made an unpleasant noise, shaking his head in disapproval. "Not being able to wield magic only makes her chances worse."

The professor shrugged as he studied Avery, still having difficulty understanding what he was looking at. "I may be able to teach her. I just can't imagine how she hasn't learned yet."

Avery gave her attentive gaze to the professor. "What do you mean? Why is that so hard to believe?"

Harris paused a moment, frowning. "Because you have an overwhelming aura. Harvey and I could feel it before we stepped inside the shop."

"My…aura?" she asked, and she watched as Malcom exchanged a worrisome look with the professor. Her stomach knotted again, and her mind was racing through her memories. Theodore had been furious when she failed to show signs of being able to use magic, often speaking about how her mother was a very powerful mage. He went as far as bringing a strange man into the estate to look her over, hoping to find out what was wrong. After the man conducted his tests, he spoke privately to Theodore and never again did he try to push her to use magic. She was forbidden from asking about it.

"It sounds like we need to get her to the Mage's Council in Astoria," the professor suggested. "Maybe we can get her protection under the Knights."

Avery tilted her head, trying to follow the logic. "The Mage's Council?"

"Whatever magic Lord Sinclair is using on you is beyond that of something typical or even something rare. We are talking about something outside the realm of anything within a normal mage's capabilities. The Mage's council in the capital may be able to understand it better. They would have knowledge of the forbidden magics." He was looking to Malcom, continuing to explain, "The Lunar Knights at the very least will be able to keep her safe from Lord Sinclair."

Harvey made another undesirable sound, scoffing at the suggestion. "If she can even make it there."

Becoming annoyed by the old man's condescension, she ignored him and looked to Malcom. "How far is the capital from here?"

Before the author could answer, Harvey cut in once more, "The distance isn't the issue, there are a lot of mechoids between here and the port that you'll need to take on in order to get to Astoria. Not to mention if Lord Sinclair decides to start sending people out to find you, you'll be dealing with a lot more than just surviving the trip out there." He shook his head disapprovingly. "It will take months to get her sorted, she won't last long."

Avery glared up at the old man, giving him the same blunt tone, "You make it sound as if I have a choice."

Harvey gave one last grunt before turning on his heel and heading for the stairs. The sudden departure stunned the other two men. Harvey made it to the stairs before

Malcom finally found his voice to call after him, "Harvey, we need your help!"

The old man did not look back, shouting over his shoulder as he descended the stairs, "Have her come to my place in the morning. Early!" He did not wait for a response. They heard the bell ring above the shop door, signaling that he had exited.

"I think he likes her," Harris said with a quick smirk. "Mal, I'll hunt around the store for some books I want her to read. You said you had a place for her to stay?"

Avery jerked her head in Malcom's direction. "You do?"

She realized the small shop did not offer much space, but she hoped to stay at least for the night until she could become more acquainted with Farewell.

Malcom, seemingly reading her mind, maintained his cheerful demeanor. "Of course, if you'd feel more comfortable staying with us, you're more than welcome to. Though, I imagine you'd prefer your own space. There's a wonderful woman who lives just up the road. I'm certain she'd be willing to lend you her spare room while you're here." After some consideration, Avery agreed, knowing she was continuing to stake her life on Malcom's judgment, but she was grateful for yet another glimmer of hope that he provided.

3
THE EXTRA ROOM

"Where to start?" Professor Harris Colleymore muttered, returning to the table with a handful of books he selected from downstairs. Malcom and Leah exited the snug living area to procure some necessities to tide Avery over until she could establish herself. The professor waved Avery over to the small table, inviting her to sit down. Over the course of two cups of tea, he quizzed her, striving to unravel her reservoir of knowledge.

"Really, nothing on the core magics?" he asked, unable to hide his fascination, "and what of mechoids? Surely you've been given material on those...no?"

She did her best to keep up with the rapidly fired questions, every so often trying to read from the notes the professor took down on spare parchment he procured from Malcom's desk. Harris notably paused in his line of questioning, adding careful consideration to his wording. "What kind of secretarial work did Lord Sinclair have you do?"

"I was learning how to manage his connections and maintain the ledgers for a few smaller projects. I've become rather proficient in deciphering the language of the old ways. Much of the communication between Theodore and his contacts is written in a ciphered variation of the dead language."

"Oh." The professor pressed on, displaying a clear desire to gauge her comfort level with the questions. "Of course, I'm familiar with Lord Sinclair's presence in Tracos and his authority within their..." he struggled for a word before settling on one, "...their council. However, I'm unclear as to what role he serves the Traconian empire."

Avery nodded her understanding. From an outside glance it would be hard to know how the cunning Lord maintained his influence, as most of his operations depend on the secrecy of those involved to produce the right results. Although Tracos shared a boarder with part of the Arcadian territory, the two kingdoms were anything but neighborly. The Traconian empire was least popular among the five kingdoms. That tends to be what happens when you threaten violence at any mention of a political dispute. It was well-known that Emperor Shauxion gave little thought to peace, despite his self-proclaimed aversion to 'needless bloodshed'. It was hard to take the words at face value, knowing that the same man tasked Theodore with razing one of its own cities for fear the Arcadian's *may* have developed a connection with one of the barons.

Hundreds, maybe even thousands of innocent people were killed to set the example.

Avery had to push the unpleasant reminder out of her mind, adjusting herself to address the professor's comment. "The empire uses Theodore's assistance whenever the need arises for infiltration or strategic removal of certain obstacles."

"Obstacles, as in resources?" he asked.

"Resources, information, and often times, people." She listed it out, noting the concern settling itself on the professor's expression once more. It was a stark reminder of the dangerous implications with her involvement in such things. A knot continued to tighten in her chest as she proceeded. "Theodore has slowly been trusting me with the intricacies of his network, but even then, I'm only given bits and pieces. It's rare for anyone working under him to know more than they need to."

The crease in the professor's brow betrayed his attempt to conceal his concern by switching the focus of the conversation. "From what I understand, Theodore is a well-studied mage, I'm surprised to hear you have spent so much time living among a mage without picking up on how it works."

"It wasn't as if I was raised as his daughter," she said, disgusted by the very thought of it. When she was younger, she often wondered what it would have been like if Theodore treated her as if she was his own kin. Perhaps she would not have resented him so much for his work, and perhaps she could have lived more comfortably within the estate.

Unluckily for her, the Blood Tyrant seemed unable to stand the sight of her. She had known the hatred in his stare since she could remember, which made for a rather cold and isolating childhood. She was indifferent to the professor's question, offering Harris a small shrug. "I was specifically prohibited from learning about it when Theodore determined I could not use magic."

"Ah, well..." Harris sputtered, the words catching in his throat.

Without waiting for him to speak, she took the opportunity of the silence to ask her own burning question. "Earlier, you mentioned something...You said that I had an... aura?"

Harris continued his silence for a moment longer, picking up his tea and taking a sip before finding the right way to frame it. "It's actually quite extraordinary that you don't know. You see, since I am a mage myself, I can feel your presence without you needing to be too close. It's almost as if I am feeling the vibrations of your body reacting to the elements around you. The stronger the mage, the stronger the vibrations."

Avery's expression mirrored the concern evident in the information. "But I don't feel anything."

"Which only makes it stranger," Harris agreed. "From what I feel, you should be a very strong mage. Especially for your age. The fact that you haven't had any formal training and yet your body has such a strong reaction must mean that you were born with it. Yet, not having any notice to it yourself..." Harris trailed off once more, lost in his thoughts.

"So then, people are born with the ability to use magic?" she asked.

"Yes, some are, but there are those who can learn to use magic if their vessel is strong enough. While those who are born with it can more naturally wield it, one must study magic and learn to control it."

While grappling with the information, Avery's mind buzzed with questions. Yet, Theodore's stark voice sliced through her thoughts, reminding her of the impossibility of it.

"I don't think I will be able to learn how to use magic, Professor Colleymore," she said quietly. The professor's shoulders drooped slightly hinting his initial enthusiasm waned. He leaned back, observing Avery's solemn expression as she continued, "I don't mean to offend your capabilities as a teacher, but I find it difficult to believe if there were a way for me to wield magic, Theodore would have found it already. He was absolutely convinced I wasn't capable, and I've only seen him change his mind in the most hopeless of cases."

Harris regained his smile, letting out a small chuckle. "I

have never met a mage with an aura quite like yours, Avery. I agree with Malcom. This condition of yours must be the result of whatever it is Lord Sinclair did to you. I would like to give it a try and see if we can't help tap into that power of yours." He set his empty tea glass down with an enthusiastic thud, the hopeful energy returning, "Besides, part of learning to wield magic is knowing it is within you to begin with."

Harvey – the old, disgruntled man whom Malcom trusted, and who seemed to know what she was up against – his earlier criticisms echoed in her mind. Yet, the prospect of wielding magic to aid her journey to the capital intrigued her. Without a more promising option, she decided, "I'm willing to learn whatever is necessary."

With her assurance, Harris provided Avery with his recommendations on which books to study, helping Avery pack them into her bag as Malcom rejoined them. With Leah's help, Malcom threw together another pack of spare clothes. He addressed them, looking up at a large wall clock above the fireplace. "We should get you over there soon, so you can settle in and get some rest." Handing Avery the newly packed bag, Leah also extended Amelia's copy of *Forgotten Roads*. Thanking her, Avery grabbed the book, finding another book stacked beneath it. She flipped it over to read the title, *Treasures of the Graveyard*, with the author's name, Grey Highcroft, marked neatly at the bottom. She recognized the author, brought up in discussion when Leah and Avery waited for Malcom to retrieve Harvey and Harris.

"You mentioned you only read the first two installments of this series," Leah said, growing a shade of pink, "I know Harris has given you a ton to read, but you may want a break from that…" she started speaking faster, but upon noticing, she shrugged sheepishly and attempted a calmer approach. "If you ever want to talk about them, feel free to drop by!"

She met Leah's eyes, a genuine light in her own. "Thank you, Leah! I think I would like that."

The stars were in full view in the night sky as Malcom led Avery through the city. The old author kept polite conversation, pointing to the different buildings in the town and discussing the residents that lived within them.

"Some of them will remember your mother too!" he added enthusiastically, however upon seeing Avery did not share the same joyous expression, he tampered down his tone.

"Mr. Burton," she said, attempting to mask her own anxiousness with a brave, reassuring look, "I don't think it's a good idea for many people to know who I am. The fewer people that know about me, the less likely Theodore can find me. I need all the time I can get before making the trip to Astoria."

Malcolm resumed his grave expression from before, thinking the matter over, "I suppose you are right." He let the silence fill in, his mind clearly at work. "You have my word that we will do our best to keep it to ourselves and keep you safe."

She thanked him, at which point he stopped her. "There is no need to thank me, and please, Avery, don't feel the need to be so formal with me. Malcom or Mal is just fine."

Malcom led them through Farewell, and to Avery's surprise, they exited the town altogether. She was about to ask about their destination, when she caught sight of the farmhouse again. Lights illuminated from the windows of the lower floor, and the sound of Scout's barking grew clearer as they approached the edge of the farm. The door opened to let the dog bolt out. He found the pair of them without issue, wedging himself through Avery's legs. The old woman reappeared still donning the apple patterned apron from earlier, showcasing a few new flour stains from what could only be assumed was a day full of baking. The sweet smell in the air told her as much.

Upon recognizing the company, the old woman's eyes brightened, a look of delight spreading across her face. "I was wondering if I would see you back here tonight." She opened the door wide and beckoned them to come in.

Malcom followed inside, addressing the old woman, "Cecelia, this is Avery. She's traveled a long way and is looking for a room to board for a bit while we get some things settled. Can you-" he started to ask but stopped mid-question when Cecelia brushed past him.

"You're already looking better, dear. Have you eaten?" She led Avery to sit down at a large round table that could seat six. The woman turned to get busy in the open kitchen, which was only separated from the room by a large counter that provided extra working space. Malcom searched Avery in surprise by the woman's seamless familiarity.

"She gave me directions when I came into town," Avery offered.

He grinned. "Well then, Cecelia, will she be able to stay here?" he was asking the room as the old woman did not stop for him.

Cecelia waved a hand in the air, clearly annoyed at the question. "Yes of course, Malcom. What do you think I'm going to do? Have her sleep in the streets? For crying out loud! You would think you would know better than to ask me such silly questions. Now go and move her bags into the back room."

"Yes, ma'am!"

Malcom disappeared through a hall that led out of the kitchen. Cecelia placed a plate of bread in front of Avery with some butter, waving her back into the seat when she tried to get up to help. "No, you stay here and work on some of that bread."

The mere smell of the bread convinced Avery not to argue, and she finished the first slice by the time Malcom rejoined them in the kitchen. "Harvey agreed to have her come by his place in the morning," he said, reaching down to give Scout a pet.

Cecelia raised her head from the vegetables she was chopping, slightly tilting her head in Malcom's direction. "Oh good. It's about time that old bull started doing something useful again."

"Avery," Malcom started to say, regaining her attention. "If you need anything, please don't hesitate to ask me." He smiled, but the old author looked tired. A bit of guilt settled in her stomach, reminding her how much they were already doing for her.

"Thank you, sir. I appreciate it."

He winced slightly at her words but clasped his hands together as he addressed Cecelia.

"Well, I'll be off then. Let me know if there is anything I can-"

"You can quit your worrying and go get some rest," she commanded. Malcom chuckled and left through the kitchen door.

Before long, Avery finished some more bread and the plate full of various cheeses and vegetables as the older woman puttered around the kitchen. Scout placed his head in Avery's lap, giving her eyes that tried to tell her he was never fed. The soft clinking of dishes being washed filled the silence in the farmhouse.

"Do you live alone?" Avery asked, catching Cecelia's eye.

"I do. I have some farm hands that come every day to help with the crop and animals."

"There aren't too many houses outside of the walls. Isn't

it safer in the city?"

"Sure, but I prefer it out here, lived here my whole life." She pointed up to a small portrait that hung on the wall near the table. "My father was the Guild Master up until he passed. Helped shape much of Farewell."

Other pictures were scattered along the walls, depicting many smiling faces in various settings, each adding a warmth and personality to the space.

"Did you know a woman by the name of Amelia?" She found herself asking, and her muscles tightened involuntarily, bracing for the impending reprimand that did not come.

Cecelia didn't look up from the sink. "Mel? Of course, there isn't much that goes on in Farewell I don't know about. When you're around as long as me, you get that kind of position in life."

Finding a cloth to dry her hands, Cecelia moved out of the kitchen to pull out a chair, sitting across from Avery at the table. "She was as wild as could be… you could tell she was going to make waves wherever she went. Knew how to follow her heart that one." The old woman surveyed her patiently. Her gentle demeanor and soft, understanding eyes offered a sense of calm.

Avery waited, expecting the old woman to begin her own line of questioning, but the questions never came. Seeing that Avery did not wish to speak, she flicked her eyes up to the wall clock, speaking softly, "This old lady needs to retire for the night. Feel free to come and go as you please and let me know if you need anything."

"Oh." Avery stood from the table. "Are you sure?"

"Is there a problem, dear?"

"No, ma'am. It's only, I feel like I owe you an explanation."

"What a funny thing to say, I've only just met you, how could you possibly owe me anything?"

"I wonder the same thing from you, isn't it odd that you know nothing about me and yet offer me a room?"

Cecelia gave a laugh, leaning in a bit closer to Avery. "Believe it or not, this is one of the least strange things I've done." She patted Avery's arm. "You should get some rest, my dear, if I know Harvey, he'll expect a lot out of you tomorrow."

"Really? I'm rather convinced he expects me capable of very little."

"Oh, I'd wager this whole house he must see something in you. He wouldn't have bothered if he really didn't want to."

The old woman chuckled again, bidding Avery good night before she climbed the stairs and out of view, leaving Avery with more questions.

Through the short hallway, toward the back of the house, Avery found her bag and books stacked on a soft bed with a grey checkered blanket. The room itself was much smaller than her quarters back at the estate, but there was something cozier about it. A wooden stand sat beside the bed, crafted from the same rich, dark wood as the dresser and bookshelf positioned beneath the window.

Wrestling to open the overpacked bag, she went through the contents, finding Leah was more than generous with the amount of clothes she loaned to her. The drawers of the dresser were found to be empty, and Avery debated unloading the bag completely. An uncomfortable feeling crept through her, knowing she had no immediate or foreseeable way of repaying the generosity she received that day. With so much on her mind, she opted to leave the contents in the bag and settled for unpacking the books that Harris assigned onto the nightstand.

Continuing to avoid her thoughts entirely, she grabbed the first book Harris assigned, titled *Vitality of Vessels* by

Laura Playa. Slipping under the covers of the bed, she stared at the cover of the book, her mind shifted through the various conversations from the day. A part of her had been drained from the experience, yet she was fueled by the prospect of learning more about her mother, and about how she could rid herself of Theodore. She managed to get through several chapters before sleep finally took hold, providing her with the first good night's rest in weeks.

◆◆◆

Avery awoke early the next morning, not knowing exactly when Harvey was expecting her. The farmhouse was quiet. Even Scout was not around to greet her when she emerged from her room and slipped outside. The sky was still producing the morning gradient of the sunrise as Avery walked back into town, passing the same shops from the previous day until approaching the fog-stained window of the establishment she assumed to be the Big Hen. Trying the door, she found it locked and perched herself against one of the pillars on the stoop to resume reading the book while she waited.

Some time passed before her reading was interrupted by the clicking sound of the door unlocking. Harvey Carter opened the door, wearing the same disapproving scowl as before. Without a word, he motioned for her to enter with the quick inclination of his head. She closed the book, passing by him as she crossed through the door seal.

The lighting cast a dim glow, barely illuminating the dozen or so tables scattered throughout the room, allowing ample space for patrons to navigate. Avery anticipated that once the tavern filled up, the atmosphere would become lively and vibrant, but for now, the only sounds were the soft hum of the lights and the echo of Harvey's cane striking the hardwood floor.

Standing in the center of the room, Avery awaited

direction, busying herself with taking in the tavern. Harvey reached the bar top, taking to a stool so he could sit and face her with his back to the bar. They shared a long silent pause, his unconvinced eyes focusing on her. As Avery's tolerance waned, she directed a steadfast gaze at him.

"Will you also be teaching me how to use magic?" she asked.

"No." He barked at her, his narrowed gaze still drilling into her. "We may get to that. But first, we need to straighten a few things out." He brought his cane in front of him, resting both of his hands on it. "For starters, how the hell did you make it here from Tracos?"

Without hesitating, Avery obliged him. "I gained the most ground on the first three days after leaving the estate. I made my way on foot to a nearby town where I sold some relics Theodore wouldn't miss for the credits. I needed to secure a transport over the kingdom border to Delrey. Once I was in Delrey, I managed to find a transport that would take me as far as Grayden, and I found out the hard way that there aren't any transports into Farewell, at least not from where I was. So, by the morning of the fourth day, I ventured the rest of the way on foot, gaining as much ground as I could each day, and trying not to freeze at night."

"Without running into any mechs?"

Avery shook her head. "Not until the day I arrived here. A guard was on patrol in the area and took care of it."

He raised his eyebrow slightly. "Is that so?"

She narrowed her eyes. "I gain nothing by lying to you."

Harvey grunted; his cold eyes unmoved. "So, then we can expect Theodore will trace you back here any day now?"

"Not if he is too busy chasing false trails."

He grunted again, and Avery took it as her cue to explain, "Over the last few months, I fixed a few items on the ledgers to make it appear as if I was arranging transport and lodging in the Reaznia territory. We use a similar technique when trying to manipulate the Arcadian's systems. It's extremely hard to spot unless you know to be looking for it. Theodore will think I fled to Reaznia. By the time he finds out I came to Arcadia instead, he won't be able to track where I used the credits."

There was another long pause before he fired the next question at her. "What is it you're after?"

"Excuse me?"

"What's your end game here? What's your plan?"

"To go to the Mage's Council, isn't that what you-"

"What is it you want? Protection?"

She aimed another deliberate glare at him. "There is no protection from him. Not for me."

"Then what is it you're after?" he repeated, sounding harsher than before.

"I don't know," she snapped at him. "I didn't think I'd get this far." She felt her body shake slightly and forced a calming breath. "I'm just trying to get a fighting chance."

He pushed himself from the stool. "Follow me," he ordered, reaching behind the counter.

Using a door found at the back of the tavern, they walked out into a closed off courtyard. A tall wooden fence surrounded the area with an overgrowth of vegetation that seemed to thrive in the absence of care. A small shed stood nearly abandoned at one end of the courtyard and a table with benches pulled up on either side looked to be the only part of the yard that got used. The rest of the area was wide open and could have fit several of the tables inside the tavern.

Harvey walked out into the center of the area before he turned to face her. The object he obtained from under the counter turned out to be a longsword, which he held out for her to take.

"You ever wield a sword before?"

She grabbed it, her hand sinking with the weight, causing her to nearly drop it. The old man scoffed, shaking his head, "Don't bother answering, I can tell just by the way you're holding it you've never wielded anything bigger than a butter knife." He perched himself on the nearby table, folding his arms over his chest. "You ever read about battles and sword fights?"

He watched her nod and then barked at her again, "Well, they're crap. Those stories try to tell you that a sword fight is like a dance where two opponents match each other's movements, but it doesn't work like that. When you're in battle, there is no choreography; there is no chivalry. Your opponent will do anything and everything to take you out. All that stands between you and your fate is the relationship you have with your sword, your reflexes, and with any hope, some luck on your side." He pulled out a cigar, seeing that he had her full attention. "Now pick up the sword like you mean it."

She raised the sword again. "You'll teach me how to use a sword?"

"No." He bit down on his cigar, his unapproving glare on the hand holding the sword, "I'm going to teach you how to survive."

Harvey started her off with a few basic swings to gauge where she was at, and it was clear from the constant shaking of his head he was not impressed. Her stamina and strength were poor. Within a few swings, Avery's breath was heavy, and the weight of the sword was already taking a toll on her right arm as she struggled to run the drills. After enduring several rounds of it, Avery could barely hold it up.

She swiped at the invisible opponent in the air, her form getting worse with every attempt. Harvey was quick to point out her mistakes, and it was clear he was not gaining any confidence in the plan to get her to Astoria. In the next swipe, she lost her footing and nearly toppled on the ground. Cursing under her breath, she picked herself back up, clenching her teeth as she looked down at the sword. Her body was already starting to ache, and her heart galloped in her chest, her lungs threatening to burst with every shallow breath she took. The impossibility of her task was dawning on her.

The deep sinking feeling she was hiding down under the false hope of freedom slowly crept out and clouded her thoughts. She thought back to the creature that attacked her when she arrived at the outskirts of Farewell. If that man had not been there, she would have been dead. Harvey was right, it was a miracle she made it all the way to Farewell.

Yet, the journey to Farewell had once seemed impossible, and she had managed to make it. This time, she wasn't alone. With Harvey's guidance, she could grow stronger, train harder, and learn to protect herself in ways she hadn't before. Reaching the capital wasn't just about escaping; it was a chance to discover how to sever Theodore's cold grip from her life. The thought of it stirred something deep within her—a flicker of determination reigniting into a flame. She knew the path ahead was daunting, but it was far better than having no path at all, no plan for reclaiming her freedom. For now, that hope was enough to keep her going.

The old man watched in silence as she battled some of her inner demons.

"You done?" He puffed at his cigar, as if mentally estimating her odds.

"No." She took a deep breath, tightening her grip on the sword. "I think I'm realizing I'm only just getting started." She kept her eyes forward, determined to see it through.

Harvey grunted, puffing at his cigar, "Alright then, let's go again." He waved at the air gesturing for her to proceed with the drill. For a fleeting moment, Avery swore she caught the corner of his mouth twitch up in silent surprise.

4
THE CORE MAGICS

They retreated into the Big Hen after Harvey decided Avery had enough for one day. The smell of fresh cooking replaced the previous lingering odor of stale beer. A bear of a man emerged from behind the swinging kitchen doors. Hidden behind thick, dark hair, he raised an eyebrow at Harvey, who addressed the newcomer with a glare. "Make her a plate. Pack it with meat."

The tavern's chef took in Avery as she sat on the stool at the bar Harvey indicated. Without saying a word, the chef disappeared behind the kitchen doors.

"Jaune will fix you up with some food," Harvey said, nudging his head in the direction of the kitchen. "If you want a chance at getting to Astoria, we need to get you conditioned and up to speed as quickly as we can."

Although her muscles were already throbbing from the sudden overexertion, she nodded her head, determined. "Same time tomorrow, then?"

Harvey grunted, which almost sounded like a laugh, then dove into an overview of the drills he would be running her through every day. By the time he finished, Jaune brought out a plate of food, piled high with various types of meat. The appetite she built up from the training hit an all-time high. She thanked Jaune, who provided her with a surprisingly graceful bow of his head before ducking back into the kitchen.

Much like Cecelia's cooking the night before, the food was warm and filling, and she tried to remember if she had ever tasted anything like it. The Sinclair estate preferred simplistic and quick meals, unless company was expected, but Avery was rarely allowed to attend those meals.

As she savored what was left of her plate, she caught Jaune's curious stares from time to time when he bobbed in and out of the kitchen to help Harvey prepare the shop for the day. She gave Harvey a questioning glance when the chef returned to the kitchen once more.

"It's the eyes," he said, catching the interaction. "...and he can tell you like his cooking."

"My eyes?" Avery clarified.

He nodded, moving to sit on the stool to take the weight off his bad leg. "We don't see many blue eyes around here."

"I've noticed an abundance of silver eyes here," she said, not giving any weight to the thought, but upon noticing the old man watching her more intensely, she re-evaluated the information. "Is there some significance to that?"

Harvey shook his head. "It might be to some."

"But, not to you?"

"I've learned it doesn't matter."

"Why would it matter in the first place?" she asked, puzzled by his sudden indifference.

The tavern door opened, and both turned to see Professor Colleymore making his way in.

Harvey gave him a nod, redirecting Avery's question. "I'm sure he can tell you all about it."

"Oh, Avery, you're already here," the professor said enthusiastically. "Perfect, we can go as soon as you finished eating."

"Where will we go?" she asked, watching Harvey pour Harris a mug of coffee.

"My lab at the research facility. It is a bit of a hike up the hill."

Avery polished her plate, giving the professor enough time to enjoy his morning caffeination before beginning their trek.

"How was training with Harvey?" the professor asked, making polite conversation while they walked.

"It was...unusual," she managed to say. "Although I'm sure I will think much differently tomorrow when the soreness sets in."

Harris laughed, not denying her point. "I'm sure you are right."

"Harvey mentioned you could tell me about silver eyes. I've noticed people seem to be fixated on the color of mine," she said, recalling her interaction with the strange guard in the forest.

"Ah, yes, I suppose now is as good a time as any to begin our lesson. You'll learn more about the history of mages from *Vitality of Vessels*, as the author covers what we know about magic in today's era."

"Yes, I started reading it last night. It's curious, as it reads more like a story rather than a reference text." She eyed the professor. "Some of it seems... hard to believe."

Harris nodded, agreeing, "Much like yourself, I find it hard to understand. Many of these stories have been passed down for generations. There is of course... disagreement with how the first mages of our world came to be. My mother, for example, tells similar stories, and I've learned there are some nuggets of truth and reason in the retelling of our history." He gave a soft chuckle. "But I am getting ahead of myself. Let's start with what you've read thus far."

Avery nodded, the concept of reporting on her studies was not foreign to her. "The Era of Silence came to an end when the gods awoke from a long slumber, introducing to the world the gift of vessels. Vessels were what allowed humans to wield the essences of the world, like elements, and bend them to their wills. That is how magic came to be."

"Yes!" Harris beamed. "And you must remember, in that era, the Age of Ascension, Eravella thrived on innovation. Even before vessels were introduced, humanity was already rapidly developing tools and systems. Technology, in many ways, dominated the world. Communication was instant and ubiquitous, with powerful, intricate systems woven into nearly every aspect of life, making almost anything accessible at one's fingertips. We know there were many wars won by whichever side produced the latest and greatest advanced weapons. That is, of course, how mechoids came to be." Harris paused to catch his breath, winded from the incline. "Shortly after the gift of vessels came, people attempted to innovate, immediately finding ways to integrate magic into their beloved technology. Many believe this was the beginning of the rapid end of the second era."

"The Great Ruin," Avery acknowledged, her tone reflecting her understanding.

The professor nodded. "The gods were not pleased with this, demanding humankind to cease the progression at once. There was a disruption within the balance that magic brought to the world. The people revolted, ignoring their gods' demands. In turn, the gods decided to turn their backs on humanity once more, leaving them to deal with the consequences. Without the help of the gods, humankind fell to their own creations, wiping out their own race and much of what wildlife remained."

"The gods rescinded their gift, and humanity was left to die," Avery added quietly.

About halfway up the hill, the professor veered slightly along their path to stroll past a small resting area. A small bench overlooked the waking city, high enough to see over the rooftops and into the plaza that housed the old Farewell tree and the Big Hen. Avery could see clear into the courtyard where she trained with Harvey. Harris paused to take in the view with her.

After a few moments of silence, Avery searched the professor with a questioning glance. "Yet, mages still exist today?"

He motioned for them to continue up the long-curved road. "Right, according to the stories, Fayne, the goddess of nature, couldn't help but check on her beloved humans. Fayne helped in the creation of humankind and felt guilty for abandoning them once more. She stumbled upon several places throughout our world where humans survived against all odds. Fayne, along with her sister, Halo, the goddess of the sun, convinced the rest of the gods to return to the aid of their creation. This time, however, their council learned from their previous mistakes. Instead of giving to all, the gods and goddesses chose champions. Finding those of like mind and heart to bestow their gift. That is why Mages from a long line of magic wielders will often have a distinct eye color. It's attributed to which of the gods or goddesses may have blessed the lineage. Those with silver eyes are a reminder to us that the gift can be taken, while colored eyes remind us to consider our blessings."

"Seems cruel either way," Avery said bluntly. "If there was a time without vessels or gods, where would humanity be, had the gods not intervened in the first place?"

There was a curious smile that brightened the professor's face. "My mother would say we cannot dwell in what could have been, for when we focus on our past, we cannot truly see our way forward."

Nearly reaching the top of the hill, a sprawling complex

stood out amidst the more traditional architecture of Farewell, its sleek lines and vast expanse of glass windows reflected the morning sunlight in dazzling patterns. The sheer scale of the facility became more apparent the further they walked. The main building was several stories high, with smaller structures branching off from it, creating a campus of buildings.

Harris avoided the main entryway, where towering glass doors awaited to welcome any visitors, and instead led her inside one of the smaller connected buildings. After a short maze of hallways, the professor opened a door and showed Avery into a decent-sized office. The room was partially what she expected out of an office, with a large desk and shelves containing many books. A whiteboard with various diagrams and some notes written in the language of the old ways were drawn in blue marker. A table across the room housed mechanical parts of varying sizes, with tools and other metallic bits in bins, labeled to describe the contents.

Harris made his way in, pulling off his cloak to hang it by the door.

"What is it you teach here, professor?" Avery asked, translating the language written on the board. The diagram showed some sort of power core, and the notes indicated there was potential for tracking mechoid activity.

"Sadly, I haven't done much teaching these days. However, when I'm not filling in for the director, I am the head researcher for the discovery and containment of relics. I'm fascinated by the technology of the old ways, and find this work gets me closest to it." He glanced at a stack of documents on his desk. "That is, when I'm not dealing with other matters." He sighed heavily.

"Well it can't be helped, let us turn our attention to how you may wield magic." He grabbed a pen from the white board and tossed it to her. "I think we should start with defensive magic. These will be used to block and even repeal magic being targeted at you. Go ahead and throw the pen at me."

Avery obliged and lightly tossed the pen to the professor. A thin flash of light appeared, creating a force that sent the marker flying back toward her. "Now, the different areas of magic are like the different muscle groups. You have to train each area for it to get stronger." He waved his hand again, summoning the marker back to return to his hand. He used it to draw three circles on the board. "Though there are many areas of magic, we'll be focusing on the core artillery magics or "dueling" magics as they are often referred to. Offensive Magic, Defensive Magic, and Elemental Magic." He wrote each of those words in their own circle. "Each of these play upon the other, and it is rare to only utilize one without the other." He highlighted the area where each of the circles connected. "Now, the magic you saw me use was of course defensive magic, as I am avoiding the marker by blocking it. However, I am also able to force it back to my opponent, which makes it offensive."

"But how is it elemental?"

The professor tossed her the marker. "Try throwing it again."

Avery repeated the act. Another bright light appeared, this time taking on a dark blue hue, sending the pen back to her. A sharp cool breeze touched her.

"Essentially, I use my vessel as a means of guiding the essences of the world around me and bend them to do what I need." He summoned the marker back to his hand. "The second time I deflected the marker, I concentrated on using ice properties. Aside from that, there is electric, fire, air, water, and terra, to cover your basics. Mages are known for more advanced magics such as clairvoyance, celestial and so on." He jotted them down on the whiteboard as he listed them.

When he finished, she took in the whole list. "And you can do them all?"

"No, I don't stray from the basic elements. I've advanced in the electric domain. There are some mages out there who can handle them all."

The lingering thought of Theodore crept into her mind as she tried to make sense of how it all fit together. "Professor, is blood magic a type of elemental magic?"

Harris looked surprised at this question. "Yes, it's a form of very advanced magic. In fact, it is a part of another domain." He walked up to the whiteboard, adding it to the list.

"Demonic magic?" she asked, reading it.

"Yes, Demonic magic is dark magic, and the practice is forbidden in this kingdom."

Avery sat soaking it in, keeping her eyes on the whiteboard. It didn't surprise her to hear, but somehow the thought made her more anxiously aware of the looming danger she had put herself in.

The lesson continued, with Harris explaining more of the history of mages and a small exercise where she sat in an awkward silence while attempting to focus on her breathing and the elements around her. The result was as expected, with her being no further able to produce any glimmer of mage ability. At least she did find the information fascinating, and she was eager to learn more on the subject so long forbidden.

Once they finished for the day, Harris offered to walk her back to Cecelia's, but she insisted she could make her way back on her own. In truth, Avery wanted to take some time to think and was not ready to head back to the farmhouse just yet. She followed the road back down the hill, heading toward Pioneer Plaza, her thoughts festering on the day's lesson. Passing the bookstore, Leah could be seen through the window of her alcove, tending to some plants. When she spotted Avery, she set down the water jug with a swift motion and waved eagerly, gesturing for her to come inside.

"Oh yeah, Demonic magic is nasty stuff!" Leah scrunched her face in disapproval as Avery recalled the conversation a little later. "There have been plenty of mages that have found ways of contributing to a greater cause with its practice. Though, it's generally forbidden unless you work under a council with the right permissions. It's very dangerous magic."

Leah's invitation brought forth a comforting respite, accompanied by the soothing warmth of a steaming cup of tea. As Avery recounted her day, she found solace in the familiar embrace of the bookshop, grateful for Leah's genuine interest and attentive ear. The two shared meaningful conversation, basking in the camaraderie of the moment. However, Avery's attention was soon drawn to movement outside the shop. Across the plaza, a gathering had formed within a building adorned with Farewell's distinctive silver and maroon banners. Two guards were posted outside the door, greeting people as they trickled in.

"Looks like there is a meeting at the guild hall tonight," Leah said, observing what stole Avery's attention.

A man appeared from within the guild hall, addressing one of the guards at the door.

"Do you know that guard there?" Avery pointed. "The one talking to the man with the maroon sashes."

"Yes," Leah nodded, giving Avery a surprised look. "That's one of the captains of the Farewell guard." She faced Avery, teeming with anticipation. "Do you know of him?"

"No," she replied firmly. "I encountered him in the

forest before reaching Farewell. He intervened just in time to save me from a Prowler."

Leah's jaw dropped and her eyes widened in alarm, "He did *what?*" she demanded, forcing Avery to recall the event.

"I can't believe it!" Leah laughed once Avery finished. "Do you know how many women would dream of getting rescued by that man?"

Avery joined her in peering out the window, puzzled by the notion. Honestly, she found the whole situation humiliating and found the guard's persistence annoying.

"Captain Adler is the best swordsman in Farewell, and probably this side of the Arcadian Sea." Leah continued to gush, "His team takes on the more dangerous field missions, especially any going out into the dead zones." At Avery's curious glance, Leah gave a sheepish smile. "My friend, Mindy, is a close friend of his. I've heard a lot about him."

They observed and conversed as the remaining members arrived at the guild hall. Captain Adler, accompanied by the man adorned in the sashes, whom Leah had identified as the Guild Master, eventually joined the others inside, leaving the plaza in a tranquil state.

Avery rose from her seat and stretched, sensing the weariness creeping into her muscles. Despite her fatigue, she knew there was still a considerable amount of reading to be done for the professor, and she hoped it would shed light on some of her lingering questions.

It was well into evening by the time Avery mounted the porch to the farmhouse. Cecelia prepared a stew which they shared while Avery gave her the highlights of the day. Scout's fluffy head found its way into Avery's lap as she finished with a heavy sigh. "I have so much to learn. I've always thought I was well read, but I've never realized how much Theodore has kept from me." Cecelia did not say anything but pursed her lips and hummed an agreement.

A small flicker of concern washed over Cecelia's eyes, but she smiled regardless.

"You have already proven yourself very capable just by getting here. Don't forget that." The old woman reached for the empty dish, batting Avery's hand away when she tried to help. "Now, you go and rest," she said, shooing her to the backroom. "And make yourself at home dear. That room is all yours until you don't need it anymore."

Managing to give Cecelia one last thanks before being banished from the kitchen, Avery retreated to the backroom. Unloading the book from her pack, she glanced around the room. The unpacked bag was still upon the dresser where she left it, and Cecelia's kind words hummed in her mind. It was reassuring to know the old woman did not mind her occupying the room, and it was a small relief to not worry about finding a place to sleep while she worked out her next steps.

With some lingering uncertainty hanging over her, Avery knew she had a lot to accomplish and limited time to do it. Harvey's morning lesson pestered her thoughts as she unpacked her clothes into the dresser, determined to improve during their next training session. She remained awake well into the night, delving into the pages of Vitality of Vessels. As the hours passed, a surge of pain served as a stark reminder that Theodore's looming threat continued to grow with each passing day. The relentless ache pulsed in time with her heartbeat, like icy tendrils clawing at her ribs. She clenched her jaw, trying to breathe through it, but the sensation only intensified, whispering warnings that her time was running short and the darkness he promised was inching closer, no matter how far she ran or how hard she fought.

5
ROUTINE

The days grew warmer as the summer months approached. Avery found refuge in her routine, growing stronger with every passing day. Over the course of several weeks, she developed a disciplined schedule. Each morning began before sunrise, running the perimeter walls of Farewell before arriving at the Big Hen warmed up. She pushed herself at every instruction from Harvey, not struggling nearly as much to keep the sword up for the duration of the training. The lessons morphed from practicing with wooden swords to wielding one of Harvey's old iron blades. It was heavier, and although it was not battle ready, mistakes and missed blocks carried a heavier consequence.

Another element added to Avery's training was in the form of a rough ex-sailor named Logan, who owed the tavern owner a favor. He and Avery sparred while Harvey observed and barked corrections at her. The exercise proved to be taxing, both physically and mentally, and Harvey had no interest in giving her any breathing room.

The progress in her mage ability was stagnant. She met with Harris every few days to continue their lessons, typically in the form of lectures by the professor. Despite her inability to produce magic, the meetings were still informative, as Avery delved deeper into the intricacies of artillery magics and mechoids. Frustration simmered within her as she learned more about vessels. From the books and lectures, there seemed to be no indication as to why Avery was unable to harness her own vessel. Nor could she uncover more about what Theodore did to her that granted him control over the bouts of pain. Unfortunately, the professor could not provide any reference books on demonic magics, leaving her with no choice but to wait until she could journey to the Arcadian capital to seek further answers.

However, the professor provided her with lectures on the history of Arcadia, helping her understand more about the way the kingdom was run. Harris explained that unlike Tracos, where barons oversee territories under the direct command of the ruler, Arcadia operated with a more democratic system. Various factions participated in decision-making, though the Queen still holds ultimate authority, ensuring that the kingdom remained unified. Arcadia, the largest and arguably the most powerful kingdom in the world, spanned across three continents.

Avery had learned the basics of Arcadian history – albeit reluctantly – from Jarek when she first began her studies under him, though his teachings were limited. She knew that the Silivus royal family had ruled Arcadia since the dawn of the Age of Resurgence, establishing the kingdom alongside the Vanguards, another strong family who swore to protect the lands. The professor elaborated, explaining that the strength of Arcadia lies in the bond between the Silivus and the Vanguards, who were blessed by two goddesses. This alliance has remained strong for generations, solidifying the foundation of Arcadia's power. Queen Eleanor Silivus came into power after the passing of her husband, King Allyen, several years earlier. The Arcadian military was commanded by Duke Alekzander Vanguard, the sword of Arcadia, and watchful eye over the various rankings of guards stationed throughout the kingdom.

Although intrigued by the information, Avery chose to focus her energy on more practical studies, saving discussions of Arcadia's history for her chats with Leah. Most of Avery's evenings were spent at the bookshop, partaking in discussions about books and the ongoings of Farewell with Leah. The two became fast friends as they spent the time overlooking the plaza, enjoying tea and company. Avery would return to the farmhouse, staying up in the late hours of the night to continue her studies of magic and mechoids, until the next morning of training threatened on the horizon. In many ways, she preferred minimizing her sleep, as even in the exhaustion from overworking her body, she couldn't keep from revisiting the estate in her dreams.

Some nights, the painful reminders of Theodore's hold on her came without warning, causing her already sore muscles to strain as they seared with the familiar pain. She endured the fits, convincing herself it was a good sign that he remained frustrated. She imagined Theodore in his study, mulling over the situation and using the pain as his only means of getting to her. That suited her fine, so long as he stayed far, far away.

A fresh wave of pain surged through her while she was running through her morning drills. It was unusual for the punishment to strike so early in the day, and the pain was particularly challenging to endure, especially after the outburst from the previous night. Her muscles, still recovering, tensed up, causing her sword to slip from her grip and clatter to the floor. Sinking to one knee, she concentrated on her breathing, waiting for the agony to subside and pondering what could have prompted it.

"Easy now," she heard Harvey say as he knelt beside her, putting a hand on her back.

His hand grew warm, and a tingling sensation spread through the muscles beneath his touch on her back. The sensation spread throughout her body like a wave of sunlight thawing the morning frost, removing the searing sensation instantly. Catching a few more breaths, she gathered herself, watching Harvey shake his head as he spoke. "That son of a bitch has quite the hold on you."

"Really?" she managed to say between breaths. "I hadn't noticed." She pushed herself back up, grabbing the sword that got flung to the side. Avery felt her body giving her no arguments as she walked, even the soreness from training the day before disappeared. Harvey eyed her, waiting for her to say something.

Arching an eyebrow at him, she spoke first, "You're a mage?"

"Really? I hadn't noticed." he mocked. "You need to take a break, kid?" he asked, glaring down at her slightly off balanced footing. She corrected her stance, looking straight forward, not meeting his gaze.

"No, let's go again."

In the evening, Avery had an increasingly difficult time trying to concentrate on the elements around her. The pen she had been trying to move taunted her, remaining stubbornly still. Harris stopped trying to throw it at her long before now. It was becoming clear the professor was exhausting his resources, unable to provide Avery with any further guidance to produce magic.

The lesson ended the same way it always did with the professor walking her out of his lab, trying to keep her in good spirits by repeating his assurance that she would be able to do it with enough time. Avery did not have the heart to tell the professor she doubted she would ever have enough time, knowing that Theodore would not forget about her existence. Harvey did not do much in the way of assuring her of anything. He mentioned she would need to learn how to incorporate magic into her training if she wanted a fighting chance of getting through the worst of her route to the capital. Even Leah gushed over stories of sword wielders who used magic to increase the power of their attacks. Avery had seen this firsthand when Captain Adler had taken out the mechoid in the forest before she arrived in Farewell.

Leaving the professor's lab, Avery set her sights on visiting Leah, hoping to find something to take her mind off the lesson. From her view up on the hill, she could see another guild hall meeting was going to take place that night. Many people were exiting the main building of the research facility, walking down the hill in groups or pairs. When the road flattened out and spilled into the plaza, Avery took notice of Captain Adler who was posted at the front doors of the guild hall. He was alone this time, greeting the members coming in for the event.

According to Leah, the guild meetings were held to discuss any relevant news that came in from overseas or throughout the kingdom. There were often missions endorsed and delegated between the guard and the guild members.

The guard was another subject that fascinated Leah. Although she did not express a desire to be anywhere other than the bookstore, it was clear Leah enjoyed listening and learning about the various ongoings of the guards. She spoke of their encounters with the mechoids that came within the perimeter of the city and their work to help collect materials needed for the research facility. The captain had been the subject of various stories, apparently having stepped into his role at a young age, when Farewell needed a specialized team that could withstand the worst of the field missions.

Standing at his post, the captain turned his gaze over to Avery, as if her presence set off some silent alarm that needed investigating. Their eyes locked with enough time for the captain to shift to a glare, giving Avery all she needed to know she did not care whether he was Farewell's prized champion or a prince for that matter. She ignored him, feeling his stare follow her all the way into the bookstore where the familiar jingle chimed happily above her. The front desk was empty, but a cheerful voice called down to her from above, "I'm up here, Avery."

"You should have seen the way he stared at you!" Leah practically burst out of her chair once Avery reached the top of the stairs and joined her at their normal spot in the window alcove. It was no surprise from the view that Leah caught the entire interaction between the two. Avery pretended not to notice but moved to make sure she was not in view of the window. Leah continued staring out at the plaza, watching the entrance of the guild hall. "I don't think he likes you."

Avery gave a short scoff, finding the thought amusing. "Great, I'm afraid he'll have to brood a little longer, that list is getting to be rather large."

"You okay?" Leah asked, seeing the annoyance plainly on her friend's face.

Avery shrugged and sighed. "Another rough lesson with Harris."

Leah poured tea and attempted the same reassurance as the professor. "I'm sure you'll figure it out, Avery. Besides, if Harris still has hope, so should you."

The two sipped their hot drink in silence, until Avery

set her glass down, slowly shaking her head. "I don't know, Leah. The professor seemed kind of off today too... like his heart really wasn't in it."

Before Leah could respond, the muffled sound of Malcom's voice rang in, coming from outside the shop. They both looked down from the alcove to find Malcom and Harris making their way inside the shop.

"I'm telling you, Mal, something should have happened by now. She's the hardest working pupil I've ever seen. If she hasn't figured it out yet, there may be no hope if I don't take her," The professor spoke quickly with a note of concern that made Avery's heart sink.

"It's too dangerous, Harris, she isn't safe out there." Malcom sounded strained and the chime of the store bell came again. They waited until they watched the two men appear on the stairwell, discovering the girls at the window.

"Ah, Avery! I see you're already here!" Malcom cheerfully unloaded his arms of the various packages he was holding onto the table. "Good, Harris was just telling me how you were coming along with your lessons in magic."

"Progress is frustratingly absent," Avery said plainly, her words coming out a little colder than she intended. Her tone caused Malcom to purse his lips, taking in her dissatisfaction. Harris took the opportunity to step in.

"About that Avery, I've had an idea. I was going to ask you during our lesson today, but I thought I might run it by Malcom first and see his thoughts on it."

"And I don't agree!" Malcom quickly interjected, but Harris continued anyway.

"I know of a mage who I think can shed some light on your condition. I would like to take you to meet her and have her look at your vessel."

Avery considered the idea, turning cautiously to Malcom. "You don't like this idea?"

It was Harris who answered. "The thing is, she lives about three days from here, outside a village called Grimsby. We would have to go outside the protection of the city."

Malcom further expressed his disapproval of the idea, shaking his head. "Avery, I don't want you sticking your neck out more than you have to. I think we should write to her, see if she will come here first."

It was Harris' turn to show the disapproval. "Knowing my mother, she won't like the idea of coming to the city, even in this case."

"Your mother?" Avery asked and Harris nodded, agreeing. "Yes, she's an eccentric woman, but her methods are usually effective."

Malcom continued to shake his head, trying to reason with them. "Even with you there, it will be too dangerous. She's only just started training."

Harris seemed prepared for this, quick to defend the point. "Harvey said she should be fine. She will take his sword with her." The notion surprised Avery, as Harvey did not seem to express any faith in her abilities before now.

"For goddess sake..." Malcom muttered, shaking his head slowly.

Touched by his concern for her, Avery considered the matter, but the opportunity to learn more about her inability to use magic was alluring.

"You really think she can help me?" She aimed a question at the professor, who she caught glancing at his watch.

"If I was a gambling man, I would bet credits on it."

Avery did not know if this enthusiasm made her feel better or if it made the sinking feeling in her grow deeper. Regardless, it was another chance for her to figure out how to use magic, and it was better than trying to make the whiteboard marker move. She faced Malcom who must have seen her make up her mind. He sighed deeply, taking off his glasses to rub at his temples. She tried smiling at him reassuringly. "I appreciate you looking out for me, but I need to do this if I am going to have a chance at making it to Astoria. Besides, I think it will be good field practice for me."

"Well let's hope we can avoid any encounters on our way there," Harris said, looking relieved now that the matter was settled. He walked back toward the stairs. "I expect we will be gone for a couple weeks so we will need to prepare before we leave. I have to make it across the street for the meeting, we can discuss more tomorrow."

The professor hurried off to make his appointment, leaving Avery and Leah to discuss the new development while Malcom attempted to reconcile with the decision.

◆ ◆ ◆

Avery's dreams of the Sinclair estate were interrupted by the sound of raised voices.

"Let the poor thing rest!" Cecelia called out in clear exasperation.

"She needs to get out there, Cecelia," the unmistakable voice responded.

Upon recognition, Avery bolted out of bed and quickly through the door to her room. Barring the way to the hall, Avery found Cecelia in a night gown, her hair falling out of a loose bun. The old woman's eyes were narrowed at the supposed intruder, but she addressed Avery, trying to use a friendlier tone. "No need to get up, dear. Harvey was just leaving."

"You're right," Harvey barked. "Let's go, kid." He motioned to the door, pausing a moment to glare at her. "Where's your sword? Get it and let's go."

"Goddess, have you any idea what time it is, Harvey?" Cecelia shouted at his back, then turned her disapproving gaze onto Avery. "That old bull knows better than to be coming here at this hour. I don't know what's gotten into him."

"What's going on?" Avery asked, watching Harvey leave through the kitchen door.

"You coming?" he yelled over his shoulder, sending Cecelia into another fit of anger after him.

Without waiting further, Avery scrambled to her room to pull on some warmer clothes and grab the old iron sword Harvey demanded she kept with her. Avery made it outside the farmhouse after being stalled another moment longer by Cecelia. The old woman attempted to assure her it was not necessary to listen to Harvey who, according to her, clearly lost his damn mind.

The blanket of night draped over Farewell, which was long before Avery would normally be rising for her morning training. The glow of Harvey's cigar showed where he was leaning on his cane near the road, his own blade strapped to his back. He grunted as she joined him, turning away from the farmhouse as he walked toward the forest.

"Where are we going?" Avery asked, getting into step with him.

"Got some drills I want you to run."

"In the forest?"

He grunted, which she was learning could be an affirmative, but the bite to his bark kept her from trying to confirm the theory.

They continued walking for quite some time, Avery knowing better than to try asking any questions before Harvey found whatever it was he sought after. Warmed up from their hike, Harvey finally stopped, pulling out a glyph. He tapped at the small, lit screen.

"What are we looking for?" Avery asked, watching as Harvey continued messing with the device.

Harvey ignored her question, concentrating on his task.

He did not speak again until he pocketed the glyph once more. The old man eyed Avery, giving her the unapproving scowl. "Mechoids are designed to track down any technology that broadcasts a signal."

"We're fighting Mechoids?"

"No, you are," he said gruffly. "I'm here to make sure you don't die."

"How kind of you," Avery said flatly, her grip tightening on the hilt of the sword.

Harvey grunted, maybe a laugh. "If you're going out with Harris, there are some things you'll need to learn. One of the biggest responsibilities you'll have is keeping watch at night." His eyes scanned the forest. "There's only two of you, which means the watch will be long, and with any luck, it'll be quiet and boring. Mechs can see just as good at night as they can in daylight. You need to spot them before they spot you."

A distant howl cemented the tension that had been settling around them. Harvey remained unmoved as the howling drew closer. Avery scanned the forest line with him, feeling her heart rate increase, her mind on high alert for any movement. Harvey brought his voice down to a whisper. "They are closing in. Keep your mind clear. Don't focus one area too long, let your eyes naturally follow where they are drawn."

She did her best to maintain slow and steady breaths, keeping her eyes moving as she fought off unsavory thoughts of Harvey's new drill. In the distance, floating among the darkness within the trees, pulsing green lights drifted toward them.

"See it?" Harvey asked under his breath.

Avery silently nodded, slowly moving herself into a ready position. The moonlight glimmered off the metallic frame of the beast as it reached inside the small clearing.

A low, warning growl stirred from within it. Only mere moments transpired before it leapt at her, but it was enough time for her to get her blade on one of its front limbs, crippling it. The beast staggered, the remaining front claws ripped into the ground as it tried to stable itself. Undeterred, it lunged at her again, but she sent the blade through it once more, this time striking the core upon its chest.

She stood over the now motionless machine, the severed circuits not able to spark in the powerless state. She let go of the held breath she didn't realize she was keeping, her nerves shaken by the sudden accomplishment. A distant yet familiar sound trickled in her mind, she turned toward the source, realizing how far they ventured outside Farewell. Her eyes scanned the cliffside, hearing the quiet call of the whispering ruins.

"Avery!" Harvey's bark startled her, but the Prowler beside her showed what she should have feared. It pounced on her, missing her head with a claw, its body collided into her. Knocked back, she dug her heels in, trying to stay upright. The mechoid thrashed violently, its jaws fighting against her blade as she forced it back. With a heavy effort, she was able to land a hit against one of its back legs, giving her enough room for a calculated strike through its core, and the mechoid collapsed. Avery pulled her sword out of the beast's chest as she caught another Prowler charging in from the corner of her eye. Pivoting to face it, she braced herself for the attack, but Harvey's sword came down, slicing clean through the head, sending it tumbling at her feet.

"What the hell are you thinking?" Harvey roared. "Where there is one Prowler, there is always more." He sheathed his sword behind him.

"I heard something," she admitted, frustrated with herself for letting the ruins nearly get her killed once again.

The insistent whispering mocked her. "I was trying to figure out where it was coming from."

Harvey grunted, disapproving. "You're lucky these are just Prowlers; a Stalker would have already killed you."

"Yeah," Avery breathed, regaining herself, "lucky sounds about right."

"Stay focused." Harvey glared at her. "Plenty more where those came from." With a sharp gesture, he indicated for her to pivot, and together they resumed scanning the area, bracing for the inevitable onslaught of mechoids.

6

THE OLD WITCH
IN THE WOODS

That night, Harvey kept Avery out until dawn, using the glyph to lure in the hordes of mechoids. The old man hustled her out of the forest, grumbling about the need to leave before a patrol from the town guard showed up and started asking questions. Avery tried to recall how many mechoids she managed to take out while Cecelia tended to the various cuts from where the mechs managed to land their claws. There were at least four packs of the Prowlers that hunted them throughout the night, and despite dealing with most of them herself, Harvey remained reluctant to encourage her on the progress she was making in combat.

The next three days seemed an eternity as Avery anxiously awaited their departure from Farewell. Cecelia eventually took pity on Avery's restless nerves and gave her jobs to do to help around the farmhouse, something the old woman was reluctant to do before. Avery appreciated the change of pace, glad for a chance to repay Cecelia's kindness, even in the smallest of ways.

The day finally arrived to begin their journey outside of Farewell. After a quick check in with Malcom and Leah, Avery left the protective city walls with the professor. They ventured on foot, as Farewell seldom accepted transports

— a result of the church's involvement with the Farewell politics — and it was their best chance at keeping a low profile from the mechoids. Even though she was more physically prepared for the journey, much like the time she spent getting to Farewell, the days of travel were long and exhausting.

An uncomfortable stirring lingered in the back of her mind, like a throbbing ache. She found speaking with Harris to be the best distraction from those pestering thoughts. She welcomed it whenever the professor passed the time by discussing theory on vessels or the history of mechoids.

The night's watch was surprisingly peaceful. The crescent-shaped moon kept her company as she bathed in its light and scanned for signs of danger amongst the tree lines. The green lights of the mechoids did not appear, leaving their nights undisturbed. She even caught a few glimpses of the wildlife taking advantage of the lack of mechoid activity, grazing happily upon the thriving berry bushes.

By the evening of the second day, they came upon Grimsby. It turned out the term village was suitable for the handful of homes that clustered the area. It was a wonder how people survived outside the safety of a city walls with the threat of mechoids lurking in the area. The homes looked worse for wear. Deep scratch marks and broken fences showed the village did not go without its mechoid challenges.

The professor guided them around the outskirts of the city, taking a short pause once they passed it. He held out a palm, conjuring a small shape in a bright yellow mist. Avery watched as the shape morphed, outstretching small transparent wings. The small bird hopped around the professor's palm, looking up at him with interest. In another moment, the bird took flight, soaring out above the rooftops and trees. Harris smiled widely at Avery's stunned expression, her eyes following the bird's path out of sight.

"That's a *whimsper*," he said, and seeing that Avery still did not understand, he elaborated further, "My mother cannot get letters the traditional way for she is quite secluded. So, we use a little magic to get messages to each other. I sent word to let her know we were leaving Grimsby. That way she can expect us by tomorrow evening."

Creating more distance between them and the village, Harris went on to explain more of whimspers, highlighting their usefulness when travelling. He referred to this method of magic as the *Mage's messenger*, which could take on any shape determined by the caster.

Another day of traveling brought the two through denser forests. The route took them past the paved roads she was accustomed to following. Instead, their pace slowed as they were forced to forge some of their path through thick foliage, often finding themselves climbing over boulders or fallen trees. A task that seemed to become more daunting as the night engulfed them.

Undeterred, Harris conjured a small orb of light, a trick he had performed before as a demonstration of his ability with light magic. The small ball acted as their lantern, steadily floating in front to illuminate any rocks or overgrown roots that served as tripping hazards. The bright yellow orb gave a subtle warmth to contrast with the chill that pressed upon them.

Avery began to worry they would not make it to their destination before long, forcing them to camp another night in the dark woods, but Harris relieved her of that discomfort when he broke their long, focused silence.

"Ah, here we are! I promise it's a lot more lovely during the day." The professor indicated ahead of them where a dim light could be seen at a distance, offering a beacon of hope. It was too dark to take the area's details, but as they neared, the front door of a small cottage opened, spilling a light out into the night. The silhouette of a small, old woman was framed in the door, and a cheery voice greeted them.

"Why does it take an emergency for you to come out and visit me?" She stepped down the front porch to embrace her son.

"I assure you, if you lived closer, I would be more frequent company." Harris tried to explain, but his mother was quick to change her attention over to Avery, giving her a once over.

"My, look at those blue orbs of yours! Your father must be a strong mage to compete with your mother." She continued assessing her, wobbling with a bouncing energy that made it hard not to smile. The old woman pressed on, not waiting for Avery to respond, and taking a step back to take all of her in again. "With an aura like yours, it's a wonder Cecelia didn't try to teach you some magic herself. I've heard you've been staying with her." Not knowing how to unpack all that was said, Avery settled for the first thing she could think of, shooting Harris a questioning glance. "Cecelia's a mage?"

With the bright light at the back of her, Avery did not realize until too late that the old woman had taken a hurried step closer to her, snatching one of Avery's arms in her small and wrinkled hands.

"My goodness, Harrison, you weren't kidding..."

Clutching her arm, the old lady mumbled a few words under her breath. Although she came up to the height of Avery's nose, she still leaned in closer to examine the inside of her arm.

"Uh, excuse me, Lady Colleymore," Avery stammered, darting a pleading glance at Harris. "What exactly are you looking for?"

The old lady waved a hand dismissively at her. "Oh hush, we'll get to that!"

After another long look and a few indistinguishable mumbles, she released Avery's arm.

"Let's go in and get you two refreshed…and some tea I think." She nodded her head, agreeing with herself before she turned on her heel and headed back into the small cottage. Avery looked over to the professor who lifted his hands defenselessly in the air before following behind his mother.

The small interior of the cottage made it easy for the furnace in the back corner to keep the entire space at a comfortable temperature. A small kitchen took up the opposite corner, leaving enough room for a double cushioned couch where they shared tea after washing up. The old woman, who insisted on being called Irene, watched Avery fondly from behind her tea glass. "In all my years, I have never seen something like this."

"You mean, someone like me?" Avery asked, resting the tea glass on her lap.

Irene patiently took a sip, nodding. The pangs of doubt slowly started creeping back into Avery's mind. Harris believed his mother could help her, but it was starting to sound like her condition was going to be the first for everyone she encountered. She stared silently into her drink, wondering if she really needed to learn magic to make her way to Astoria. Irene set the tea glass aside on a small table next to her, outstretching a hand toward her. "Let me see your arm again."

Avery set her own glass down and stood up, extending her arm for the old lady to take. Again, the old woman examined her forearm closely, flipping it over to inspect the back.

"Tell me, what were your early years like?"

"My early years?" Avery repeated, trying to understand the old woman's intentions and unsure of how much the professor had already relayed to her. "I was confined to the Sinclair estate."

"Yes, and that man... has he always had *that* control over you?"

The question forced Avery's mind to recall the first time Theodore demonstrated his power. From very early on, she learned which battles, if any, were worth the consequence of a swift and precise punishment. She often found herself on the receiving end of painful lessons. If there was one thing she did have control of in her life, it was making absolute sure Theodore knew she despised him.

She was just over ten when he first used his power over her, establishing a strict boundary she would have to learn to navigate as she got older. She imagined he refrained from using it before because she was always so frail and could hardly be out of bed for very long. But as she got older, she became stronger, more restless. Wanting less to do with her everyday surroundings and desiring to explore the outside world. The expectation was that she was not to step outside the grounds of the estate. Naturally, her curiosity led her beyond the gate walls one day. Avery never understood how he found out, but when she returned from her walk, Theodore summoned her to his study where he was there waiting.

"I hope you enjoyed your stroll." he said, his lips curling into a wicked, yet measured grin. Without touching her, without moving, he stared at her as she dropped to the floor screaming. A rush of pain overwhelmed her. A pain that could not be relieved by any means. Perhaps the pain had only lasted for a few seconds, but it felt like it went on for an eternity. Until it subsided, and he waited patiently for her as she gathered herself off the ground, sobbing as she examined her invisible wounds. The pain that left no marks. In a slow and cold tone, he addressed her. "Let that be a lesson you easily learn."

Shaking the memory out of her head, Avery shrugged, meeting the wide brown eyes of the old woman. "I was very young. As long as I can remember."

"Mother, let's not do this right now." Harris protested as he watched over Avery with tight and worried eyes. "We've come a long way…Let's discuss this when we've had time to rest."

Irene shook her head, giving her son an all-knowing smile. "Harrison, you're tired dear. Go get some rest. I want to talk with Avery."

Harris continued his protest, but his mother shot him a stern look and he forfeited, bidding them goodnight. Irene took time to rekindle the furnace and made a fresh pot of tea for the two of them to share. Avery watched her attentively, trying to gather what she could not discuss in front of her son.

"Avery, I think I can help you to tap into that power of yours."

Avery straightened in her seat, staring at the old woman in disbelief. "You can?"

A faint smile tugged at Irene's lips as she observed Avery's doubt, though her eyes still betrayed her concern. "I believe so, but even I must admit, it may prove to be more dangerous." There was a change in the old woman. The free-flowing energy from before seemed to have vanished, and now she stared at Avery much in the same way Harris did moments before. "I'm worried that if I do, you'll only end up getting yourself into deeper challenges."

Avery frowned, trying to parse out the meaning of her words. "I'm afraid I don't understand."

Irene smiled, bobbing her head slightly. "You see, when I look at your arm, I'm not looking at the strength of the veins that carry your blood, but rather, I'm looking at the veins in your body that is the vessel for magic."

The old woman rose from her seat, reaching out to touch Avery's arm once more. A chilling sensation ran through her as if an electric current had awoken all the nerves in her body.

Avery shuddered and looked down in alarm as thin blue trickles of light formed all throughout her arms. They pulsed, fading out then lighting back up spontaneously, seeming to have a mind of their own. Many of the pulsing lights strayed from their set path, whipping violently at random intervals. Irene held out her own arm and tapped it lightly.

Faint lights appeared, much the same as it did for Avery. However, Irene's pulsed with a yellowish hue, the lights all traveling in the same orderly manner. They did not fade, but rather remained strong, running along in a fluid motion. Not like her own volatile lights, which she had difficulty tracing before they vanished with another taking its place.

"That man took something from you that is preventing your vessel from naturally interacting with the world. You, who should be a very strong mage, cannot feel anything. Your vessel is being contained, and your body cannot handle it." The old woman frowned deeply at the lights. "I'm sure Harris has told you about those who have a natural ability to wield magic. You have the vessel, and a strong one at that, but you've lost what is needed to control it. You are like a body of water with no outlet to release the built-up pressure."

Avery focused intently on the pulsing lights, watching as they danced along her arms. "I still don't understand, the magic is there but my body is rejecting it?"

"Precisely, these cracks in your vessel are the result of your body trying to fight the power that man uses against you. It is desperately trying to protect you."

"How did Theodore get that power?" Avery asked, growing more frustrated by her own lack of understanding. "How did I end up like this?"

"How, I do not know," Irene said plainly. "I can only guess how he acquired the power to do so. It would have been risky. He must have been extremely desperate to take it."

"Take what?" Avery asked sharply, wishing the old woman would understand the urgency of the information and stop giving her cryptic answers.

The old woman looked at Avery through sad eyes. "I believe he found a way to take your soul."

Avery didn't say anything, she only watched the old woman carefully, deciding if she was trying to play some trick on her. "My soul? But is that...is that even possible?"

Of course, she had heard of the concept of a soul, but she thought it more as a figure of speech rather than a real thing, let alone something that could physically be taken away.

"I wish I had answers for you, Avery," Irene said, the resolve in her eyes showed she meant it. "I have only heard of it being possible in legends and folktales." She patted her arm. "That is why I think it wise you go to Astoria. The council of mages has been around for many generations. I believe they will have the answers you need."

"You said you would teach me how to use magic, but it is dangerous?"

The old woman closed her eyes, bobbing her head as she hummed. "Very risky."

"But you will still do it?" Avery pressed her, unable to hide the desperation in her voice.

"Yes, I do not believe it is my place to determine whether you choose to use magic. You have the right to decide that for yourself." She opened her eyes once more, taking Avery in. "However, with caution. You will need to take what you learn very slowly and must not overextend yourself. Otherwise, the damage you do to the vessel can become damaged beyond repair or may bring you greater peril."

Without wasting another moment, Avery shot a determined look at the old woman. "I want you to teach me."

"As long as you understand the stakes, my dear."

Avery let out her held breath, giving a single cold laugh. "From what you say, I really don't think I have much of a choice. Either Theodore will kill me, or I will find a way to be free of this. It doesn't sound like I have a fighting chance without learning how to use magic."

Irene looked favorably upon her, "There is strong blood within you, Avery. I become surer of that the more I hear from you."

Avery did not say anything and instead stared down at the pulsing blue lights beginning to fade away in her arms. "So, you will teach me?"

"No," the old woman said, casually getting up from her seat. Avery jerked her head up to stare at her once more in disbelief. The old woman shook her head, chuckling as she indicated the couch for Avery to sit. Avery slowly transferred seats, watching Irene for any glimmer of what she had planned when she moved in front of her, bringing her eyes down to her level. "This will be uncomfortable."

Avery's heart raced as she stared back into Irene's eyes, the color of amber crystals. Determined to see it through, she took a deep, calming breath. "I'm not worried about it, if you aren't."

Irene gingerly placed a small, wrinkled hand just below

her neck, above where her heart pounded viciously.

"I've never seen a stronger vessel."

A slight stinging sensation formed where the old woman's hand rested. The thin blue lights fading from her skin returned with a raging vitality. A searing pain in her chest rapidly increased, and she tightly closed her eyes to endure it.

7

THE UNSEEN HUNTER

Across the Arcadian Sea, a man patiently listened to the representative droning on as he tried to defend the council's actions. The representative was a meek specimen, making a valiant attempt not to seem intimidated by the uncomfortable situation. His voice cracked for the third time now, expressing the growing concerns for the way an investigation was being handled in the Pearl District. Earlier in the week, a Prowler was discovered loose in the middle of the city, and it was only one of many headaches that needed the man's attention.

"This is hardly something the Knights need to be involved in." The representative reached into his vest for a document, sliding it across the desk that separated them. The man stayed sitting back in his seat, not removing his eyes from the representative's nervous gaze. Not anticipating the lack of movement, the representative gestured to the letter. "The chancellor sends his own assurances that it will be handled accordingly."

"Representative Dawson." The response came from another man in the room who was standing at attention behind the representative's chair. He was a younger man, a captain with brown hair, cut short, and still lacking the ability to not show his emotions upon his face. His blue eyes narrowed down at the representative, who did not bother to turn when addressed.

Regardless, the captain continued speaking to his back. "I have already explained this to you in my last message. We cannot ignore a mechoid running wild within the city borders. Two civilians were killed, and their families deserve an answer. This meeting is wasting our time."

"Young man," the representative chirped, still not facing him, "the council regrets greatly that this happened, especially so close to its own borders, but having your people there is only making things worse. We cannot operate in such conditions. We will continue to investigate this matter without the assistance of the Knights."

The captain went to retort but stopped as the man behind the desk raised a hand for silence. Exuding a commanding presence, his sharp features were accentuated by his clean-shaven face, and his light-colored hair framed emotionless eyes that bore into the representative with unwavering intensity.

"My son is right, Representative Dawson, this cannot be ignored." His voice was cool and forceful, making the representative shift nervously in his chair. The man leaned forward on the desk, regaining the full attention of the representative, who was looking as if he regretted volunteering to deliver the message on behalf of the council. "I fully expect the cooperation of the council in letting the Knights investigate the matter." The man continued, "They should be able to finish a thorough investigation and vacate the premises immediately. I will not be recalling the Knights I have assigned to the task." He tapped the envelope on his desk without removing his strict eyes from the representative's face. "You can inform the Chancellor I will be in touch very soon."

The representative stood up and bowed slightly,

addressing him dryly, "Thank you for your time, your grace."

Silently, the representative moved out of the office, and the two men waited long enough to know he had left the manor. The man took the time to study his son's face. The captain had been away for a majority of the week following up on the leads gathered over the last few months. He would never show the exhaustion from the relentless challenges that kept showing their ugly heads. "Everett, did you find anything definite?"

The young man shook his head, his brows furrowed, tension radiating from his posture. "No sir, Talisen and El are there now."

The man looked out the window, taking in how late it must have been. "I want a full report once they get back. We are running out of time." He returned his gaze to his son, who stared fixated upon the letter on the desk.

"They know we are making inquiries. The Queen will not be pleased." Everett frowned, contemplating the weight of the statement.

The man shook his head slightly. "That is for me to deal with. It can't be helped now that they know. We can only make sure that our time has not been wasted, and that we have something that justifies us showing so much of our hand."

He understood his son's assumption but did not himself feel concerned with the Queen. After all, she was the one who urged him to stir the pot. This week was more than enough to show that their concerns were valid. Although, he did regret that they were not able to be there sooner and perhaps save the two lives. From watching the glare Everett was giving the letter, he knew his son must have felt similar.

"Go get some rest, report back any news tomorrow." The man waved to his son.

Everett rose from his chair, bidding his father a

goodnight and making his way to the door at the other side of the room.

Reaching for the letter on his desk, the man froze as a shattering coldness swept through him, as if stabbed by a blade made purely of ice. The chill sent his whole body on alert, every nerve of his being on a sharp edge. A flutter of a thought flashed through his mind, quickly fading away like a memory he could not quite place. Rising from his chair, he listened intently for anything that would have caused such a powerful reaction.

Across the room, Everett was stone-like, with his hand instinctively clutching his sword, ready to draw it at any sign of the source.

"Did you feel it?" the captain called over his shoulder, not looking back at his father.

He did not respond, and they waited silently while the feeling continued to stir within them. When enough time went by to prove their effort fruitless, Everett finally turned to face his father, slowly easing his hand off the hilt of his sword. The sensation simmered into the background until it became nothing more than a light tug at their vessels.

"What was that?" Everett asked, knowing it was a pointless question.

The man tried to make sense of it as well, but placing the occurrence became harder with every passing moment. "Strong, whatever it was."

This did not ease Everett's concerns, and he brought up a hand to rub the back of his neck, trying to parse out the stirring in his body. "It felt...familiar." The captain searched his father for some form of confirmation.

The man lowered himself back into the chair, thinking the matter over. Realizing he would get no further, he aimed a firm nod at his son. "Keep an eye out. I don't know what this means but I don't want to take any chances."

Not looking comforted in the slightest, Everett returned the nod and left the study, leaving his father alone to think.

The man sat motionless for some time as he fought with his mind to retrieve the vision he had glimpsed for that brief moment. The feeling seemed to have imprinted itself in his mind, yet he could not willingly pull it into view. With a deep breath, he grabbed the Chancellor's letter, deciding he could not put it off any longer. There was still much to do, and it was only made more difficult to concentrate as he kept seeing a pair of blue eyes whenever he closed his own.

◆ ◆ ◆

Avery opened her eyes, finding herself lying on the couch within the small cottage. It took some time for her to recall where she was. Her mind was preoccupied with thoughts of the vivid dream where men in a study searched for some unseen disturbance, and she watched as an invisible spectator. With every passing moment, the dream faded, and her attention was pulled back to the warm cottage. She sat up, feeling the weight of her body strain from the sudden movement. Next to her, a startled Harris rose from where he sat across from her.

"Avery! Thank the goddess you're awake." He put a hand on her shoulder, trying to gently push her back. "Now don't overdo it! I thought I was going to have to tell Harvey and Malcom my mother nearly killed you."

Avery did not budge, pushing his hand away from her shoulder. "I'm fine. What happened?"

"Well, you tell me!" He huffed, exasperated. "I left you to talk with my mother and next I find you out cold. She insisted you were fine, but it's been two days!"

Avery gawked at the professor. "Two days?"

"And I expected at least a week!" Irene practically sung out, appearing from the kitchen with a tray of what looked to be soup and bread. She smiled warmly at Avery, absolutely sure of herself. "A strong vessel indeed!"

According to Harris, this was nothing to celebrate, and he argued with his mother while Avery's head continued to spin, struggling to remember what happened after Irene agreed to help her.

"Absolutely insane, Mother," Harris mumbled, realizing he was not making any ground arguing. He gave up and kept a watchful eye on Avery. "How do you feel?"

Mentally, Avery checked through her body looking for any anomalies. She still felt quite dazed and found it hard to concentrate. Her body seemed to be picking up on the slightest changes, overloading her senses. The overwhelming feeling only increased in intensity as Irene moved closer to her. There was a faint throbbing she felt that did not come from any aching muscles. It was a pulsing sensation, like a flame, growing brighter or dimming as it reacted to the world around it.

"I think I'm alright," she managed, fighting the persistent daze.

Irene motioned to the tray, "Eat up and get your bearings. Come find me in the garden when you do." She left, the bouncing energy flowing with her.

With the fog lifting from her head, Avery stepped outside the small cottage only after polishing off the soup and taking time to freshen up from the long rest. For a moment, she was stunned, finding Harris did not exaggerate upon their arrival as she took in the garden that surrounded his mother's home. In the light, the cottage was engulfed in vibrant colors, making it nearly impossible not to take in the beauty of the garden beds, filled with a variety of flowers and other plants Avery could not identify by sight.

The warmth of the sunlight hit her skin as she found the old woman snipping off sections of herbs, placing them in a small basket that was already almost full. The throbbing she felt became more intense again, causing a shiver to trickle down her spine.

"Ah," Irene murmured, catching Avery's hesitation when she stopped in her advance toward the old woman. "You can feel it now."

"What is it?" she asked, nearly breathless again.

"There is a living energy all around us. The essence of what is and what can be, a constant dance to a rhythm that guides the world around us. Our vessels harmonize with its flow. It is what we call a mage aura." Irene turned back to the herbs, resuming her task with the leaves. Avery tried to concentrate on the feeling, registering how the pulsing centered around the old woman.

"Does that mean what you did worked?"

Irene did not answer immediately, continuing to work away at the plant. She put down the trimmings and stood up to stretch, a hand bracing at her lower back.

"Come, let's go for a walk."

Avery trailed behind Irene as she walked out of the garden into the adjacent forest. For some time, they travelled in silence, and it was a toss-up on whether it was a path known to the old woman or if she was leading them on a whim. They stopped once Irene found a fallen tree, which she decided was a good spot to rest. Irene settled herself on it, smiling favorably upon Avery.

"Your soul responded well to the call, but you are still not whole."

Irene's eyes closed, and Avery awkwardly waited for her to continue, but when Irene remained silent, meditating upon the makeshift seat, she prodded her for more.

"You mean, only a part of it has returned?"

The old woman acknowledged her with a few bouncing nods and a "Mhmm."

Avery felt a small pinch in her chest,

causing her to raise a hand to it.

"Yes, your vessel is still broken," Irene said softly, her brown eyes once more watching her. "It struggles to cope."

Avery frowned at this, beginning to feel as though all her efforts were in vain. "Then...I still cannot do magic?"

Irene raised an eyebrow. "You are quick to assume the worst."

A pang of annoyance shifted through Avery's mind as the old woman smiled at her. Restraining herself, she answered honestly, "I haven't exactly been given a reason to expect otherwise."

Irene seemed unfazed by the comment, her grin widening with a hint of excitement. "Shall we find out if you can use magic?"

Avery paused, slightly anxious from the old woman's sudden mischievous ploy. "Just tell me what I need to do."

Irene snickered softly. "There is no value in that."

Avery stared blankly at her, certain the old lady was enjoying the mind games she was playing.

When Irene seemed to be content in her seat, she let out a satisfied sigh. "I'm told Harvey speaks highly of your growing skills with a sword."

The notion caught Avery off guard, the surprise showing plain on her face. "I didn't realize Harvey spoke highly of anything."

Irene chuckled, again nodding in agreement. "We shall see if you can learn to wield magic as quickly as you learned to wield a sword."

The old woman brought her hand out and snapped her boney fingers. A wave of force washed over Avery, the pressure pushing her down. She hit the ground hard, her hands barely getting out in front of her to avoid her head sharing the same fate of what would surely be bruised knees. Feeling slightly nauseous, she scrambled to her feet, finding both Irene and the tree no longer in front of her, or anywhere within her vision for that matter. The result of a quick scan showed only that she was still somewhere within the forest. Where or how far away from the cottage remained an unknown.

"Irene?" Avery called out, a rush of adrenaline wiring her senses. Listening carefully, she forced herself to stop the vulgar thoughts of the old woman and instead focused on where she would go next.

Maneuvering through dense thickets, she cautiously followed the sound of light pattering amongst the brush ahead of her. She peered around a wide tree and froze. In the distance, a sleek, metallic figure loomed over the mangled remains of an animal that was indiscernible amidst the carnage. Her stomach turned uncomfortably at the bloody scene. The beast was not a Prowler, although it shared the general four-legged shape. However, this mechoid housed flexible panels embedded throughout its frame that could blend seamlessly with its surroundings, making it hard to spot amidst the foliage. The distinguishing feature was what made the Stalker so deadly. A mechoid capable of delivering swift strikes without ever being detected.

Grateful the mechoid remained occupied and unaware of her presence, Avery did her best to silently retreat, hoping to put as much distance between her and the beast before it grew bored of its prey. A sudden thunderous crackling sounded from above her, barely giving her enough of a warning to dodge out from under a collapsing branch. A haunting silence swept through the forest, shattering any hope she had at a soundless escape. She watched as the nearby bushes began to move before she took off in a full sprint in the opposite direction. From behind her, the heavy foot falls of the hunter trailed after her, and even in her panic she knew the mechoid would eventually overtake her. She took a sharp turn, hoping to buy herself enough time to find the beast before it struck.

The forest around her sat quiet, aside from her heavy breathing. Her eyes quickly scanned through the trees, searching for any sign of her pursuer. A faint glimmer caught her attention, a subtle shift in the way the leaves on a bush jostled as if bothered by the wind. Her hands instinctively shot up to defend herself from the steel jaws of the beast as it lunged for her. She could not prevent the metal from cutting into her hands as she tried to pry its head away from reaching her throat. Pain erupted from her chest before a blinding light appeared. Released from the crushing weight of the mechoid, Avery scrambled to her feet, her vision blurred. Through the haze, she glimpsed the Stalker, its sleek form poised for another attack yet staggered by the unseen force that had repelled it.

It too seemed dazed, parts of the mechoid's camouflaged paneling flickered an array of chaotic colors or remained dark where it cracked from whatever blasted it. Frantically, she searched around, looking for where Irene must have been hiding, but the Stalker pounced again, forcing her to focus on getting out from under the persistent threat. Again, her arms instinctively came up to defend herself, this time she watched as the bright white light emerged from her hands, producing a small wall to shield herself from the attack. The mechoid slammed into the barrier, its metallic frame recoiling from the impact and collided with the unyielding trunk of a nearby tree. The mechoid convulsed violently, liquids ruptured from the seams of the metallic frame. The mechanical beast stumbled toward her, struggling with each step to stay upright until it collapsed in a heap before her. The hum of its power core dwindled to a feeble whisper, until it lay quiet and motionless. Avery watched it, ensuring it stayed down long after it fell. She looked down at her shaking hands that stung, seeing the various places where the Stalker tore through her skin.

"How fascinating!" a voice called from behind her.

Avery whipped around to face the old woman, watching in a stunned silence as Irene investigated the scene.

"One must expect the unexpected," Irene muttered as she leaned over the fallen mechoid, "but I must say you continue to surprise this old lady."

Avery wiped her bleeding hands on her pants in an effort to get them to stop stinging. She sent narrowed eyes toward Irene, realizing it was no coincidence that the branch mysteriously broke off the tree earlier. "One would think you were trying to kill me."

The old woman laughed, shaking her head as she reached for Avery's hands. "You are of a bloodline that's hard to kill." Reaching out, Irene traced the cuts on Avery's hands, a warmth spreading as the wounds disappeared behind Irene's gentle touch. "Even with only a fraction of your soul, you manage to wield much power," she continued, lightly patting her shoulder to commend the job well done.

Avery flexed her hands, finding the divine magic healed the remnants of the mechoid fight entirely. Irene's words circled her mind as the small stinging in her chest reminded her of the magic used to defeat the beast. Even now she could still feel the subtle energy the magic left behind. Avery held her hand open, doing her best to reproduce the feeling. A small trickle of light built upon itself and gleamed brightly in her palm. She stared at the light, transfixed, until it slowly faded away.

"It's certainly curious," Irene's voice came again, her eyes twinkling with a knowing look. Avery felt her own lips tug into a small, genuine smile. A fresh wave of hope began to thaw through the doubt she had collected over the many moons.

It was welcomed progress.

8
LIGHTBRINGER

When they returned to the cottage, Harris met them in the garden, surveying the two for any sign of good news. Avery buzzed with a proud grin, eager to fill him in, but Irene held a palm out to her son. "Moonlight, but she can give the details later. You must go."

"Go?" Avery asked, seeing Harris shared the same startled question.

Irene nodded. "You will not be the only one to know that you've been reconnected with part of your soul. You are better off in the city, where you can continue to train with Harvey and Harris."

The explanation seemed to be enough for the professor. He immediately abandoned the idea of arguing and resumed his concerning gaze upon Avery. "Very well, we can start making our way back tonight."

"No," the old woman commanded again. "Avery cannot control her powers. It's best you get back sooner, where Cecelia can keep an eye on her."

"Mother, that'll be quite the toll on you."

"Harrison, don't argue. Go and grab your things."

The urgency in her tone washed away all the relief Avery felt, replaced with the familiar sense of dread that came with her thoughts of Theodore. "You think Theodore will know I can use magic?" she asked Irene, unable to hide the anxiety in her voice.

Irene reached over and patted her arm. "Regardless of how little has returned, it will make an impact on the whole." She did not give Avery time to parse out her meaning. Lowering her voice, she said, "Remember Avery, you must take care not to overdo it."

Harris reappeared from the cottage door, holding both of their packs. Avery took hers, not wanting to leave. Irene already provided her with many answers, although most only came with more questions. She was positive the old woman knew more than she was willing to share with her, but she needed more time to ask the right questions. However, Avery was not afforded the opportunity to object to the abrupt departure. Harris hugged his mother goodbye, joining Avery where she stood.

"I'll visit before winter," he promised his mother, putting a hand on Avery's shoulder.

"I will hold you to that." Irene scolded her son, then transferred the brown eyes onto her. "Goodbye, Avery. I'm sure our paths will intertwine again." She raised up her hand and snapped her fingers once more. A chill flashed through her body, and her stomach turned nauseous as the world around her spun.

The professor's hand braced Avery's shoulder, preventing her from tumbling forward. Wet droplets hit her bare skin, and the sound of muffled barking filled the air by the time her vision cleared. A few moments passed before she realized they no longer stood outside the small cottage and were standing in the rain just outside of a farmhouse.

Removing his hand from her shoulder, the professor adjusted his glasses, "Sorry, Avery! I probably should have warned you. That must have been your first time traveling by warp."

"Surprisingly, no," Avery muttered, getting her bearings. The door to the farmhouse opened and Scout came bounding out to greet them.

"Back so soon?" Cecelia called to them, peering out from inside the back door that led into her kitchen.

Inside and seated at the table with tea and muffins made fresh that morning, Avery went over her encounter with the mechoid. Harris was not thrilled to learn exactly how his mother managed to get her to use magic. There was the notable pulsing from Cecelia as she sat across the table from Avery, an aura that felt much like Irene's. The pull was more prominent than what she felt from Harris, but it drifted off into the background, as if it was trying not to disturb her.

"Moonlight?" Cecelia repeated the same question which harassed Avery's mind. Both aimed the question at Harris.

"What does that mean, professor?"

"My mother believes you have an affinity for moonlight. Do you recall reading about affinities in our lessons?"

With the late hours of studying finally paying off, Avery recited her knowledge, "Yes, some mages have stronger relationships with certain elements. The variety of elements a mage can channel does not make them stronger, but rather it is the strength of those relationships that determines the strength of the mage."

"Exactly; which means there will be some mages with connections that others do not possess." He held out a palm and a yellow ball of light appeared, floating above his fingertips. "See how when I channel light, it is bright and emits a yellowish hue? You can feel the warmth radiating from it." He dissolved the orb and motioned to Avery. "Now you try. Remember just let your body naturally produce the result, don't force it."

Avery held out a hand, concentrating the flow of power through her into a ball like she managed for Irene. Eventually, a smaller, much less stable orb formed and hovered above her hand. The tips of her fingers became cold, and the bright light bounced unpredictability around, making it harder for her to focus.

"Very good, Avery!" Harris beamed, delighted to see it. "Notice how your light does not emit any color? Feel how it is cold? It seems your body reacts more instinctively with the moonlight."

Avery stared at her orb until she finally let it dissolve. "How did Irene help me use magic?"

"My mother has an affinity for the celestial magics and is much more in tune with the bonds that our vessels create. She lives in seclusion because of these fragile connections. As for how she managed to aid you, my guess is she helped your vessel reach out to your soul, and it answered the call."

Cecelia pursed her lips, shaking her head slightly. "That was mighty risky, even for Irene." She looked over Avery with worried eyes.

Harris took a long drink from his glass. "I agree, but I wasn't there to object. It seems to have worked out for the best." He checked his watch, rising from his chair. "Well Avery, it seems we will have much more to cover in our lessons now. You should take it easy for the rest of the day. We can pick this up again tomorrow."

Avery spent the rest of that evening pouring back through the various books on affinities, finding very little that covered the moonlight variety. From *The Dawn of Mages,* she read of the concepts the professor spoke of, expanding upon the theory that mages were more proficient when surrounded by the elements they wished to control. The book offered to explain why so many skilled mages were determined by their environment, a theory that Harris did not support during several of his lectures. The professor insisted there was no way to know the true limitations of any mage. There were researchers that argued the environment a mage grew up in would contribute to the elements they have an affinity with. However, it was purely trial and error that helped guide a mage on what they could or could not do. The different domains of magic each had their own challenges, although some were generally known to be more complicated. Fire, as it turned out, was one of the more difficult of the core magics to learn. Harris explained it was because fire was volatile by nature.

Light magic, however, seemed to revolve around sunlight, and the books contained only a brief mention of the colder void that was moonlight, nor was there any mention of a magic capable of capturing souls or the kind of magic Theodore used to so effectively punish Avery whenever he deemed it necessary. The thought fed further into her restlessness, and she struggled to sleep, eager to start incorporating magic into her training.

Harvey's narrowed eyes met her the next morning when she showed up at her usual time to train. "Back already … and you have that overconfident look in you again." He closed the ledger he was glaring at before she arrived and gave her a once over. "So, she must have helped you."

Ignoring his comment, Avery made her way into the bar, sitting down across from him. "Yes, and then sent me right back. She said it was better for me to train here with you and Professor Colleymore."

He pulled the lit cigar out of his mouth and tapped the ashes off the end. Slowly, his eyes shifted down to her arms, staring at them long enough to raise an eyebrow. "Alright," he grunted, "you better fill me in."

He half listened to her recount using magic during

the encounter with the Stalker. A noise escaped him, and he busied himself behind the counter. Upon reaching the tavern, she was rather excited to share with Harvey that she managed to take out the Stalker, but her enthusiasm was curbed as his grunting only became more unpleasant the more she went on.

"That was sloppy!" he barked. "You need to discipline yourself and not get distracted so easily. That mistake could have been your last."

Avery met him with silence, knowing he was right. Any progress she thought she made evaporated with each shake of his head. Harvey surveyed her, creating an awkward pause when neither could break the tension. With a sigh, he reached under the counter, pulling out a package. It thudded heavily as he tossed it on top of the counter in front of her. The object was long and poorly wrapped in wrinkled paper, tied together tightly with string. Avery's eyes lifted from the packaged up to Harvey. "What's this?"

He pushed it toward her lazily. "I want you to start training with this instead of my old iron sword." He walked away from the bar top, making his way to the back door. "Open it and we will start going through the day's drills." He called over his shoulder as he disappeared into the courtyard. "Make it quick!"

Jaune, who was busy with the morning menu, peeked his head out from behind the kitchen doors. His eyes lit up when he saw Avery, and he gestured for her to open the parcel. Pulling it closer to her, she started unwinding the knot. A fine leather sheath spilled out from the wrapping, revealing the hilt of a sword. She lifted it up, already feeling the weightlessness of it compared to the one she trained with. Slowly, she drew the sword from the sheath, the light illuminating the freshly polished blade. A deep blue hue was forged into the blade, resembling the same color of her eyes, which she saw in the reflection. Jaune made an approving sound, before tending to whatever he was cooking that filled the tavern with a mouthwatering smell.

Clutching the sheathed weapon, she met the old man out in the courtyard. Harvey was busy setting up the training equipment, avoiding her gaze. When he continued to refuse to acknowledge her, she called to his back. "This is a beautiful sword."

Harvey only grunted, pulling the training dummy out from the shed. With the target in its proper place, he finally turned to Avery, motioning for her to get moving.

"It's not doing you any good sheathed; pull it out and let's give it a good run."

Avery obeyed and proceeded to work through the morning drills. The difference the sword made was already noticeable. The lighter weight meant her movements were swifter, and she could recover more easily. Harvey even supplied a few satisfied grunts that improved Avery's mood significantly.

When the morning training was over, Avery cleaned off the sword and admired it one last time before returning it back into the protective sheath. She placed it back on the counter in front of Harvey who scowled down at it. "Do you not like it?"

The return of the cold tone caught Avery by surprise. "I love it," she stumbled over her words trying to explain, "...It's much lighter, and I have a better handle on it."

Harvey pushed it back across the counter toward her, shaking his head. "Then keep it with you. It suits you better than my old one." He walked away from her toward the end of the bar where he cleaned the beer taps.

Avery put a hand on the sword, shooting a questioning glance at him.

"You want me to keep it?"

"From now on, I don't want you to go anywhere without it! Take care of it, and it will take care of you." His tone was gruff, but something told Avery he was pleased to see she admired the sword.

Jaune brought out the usual overfilled breakfast platter, giving her the most approving nod he could manage. Avery felt her face get warm as she worked on fixing the strap of the sheath to fit around her. Before exiting the Big Hen, she took notice of how right the sword felt there on her back, as if it had been made for her.

♦♦♦

A secluded life from other mages was a tad more understandable now that Avery could feel the constant pushes and pulls of other mage auras. The sensation caused her already strong aversion to crowds to become much more prominent. Through the next few weeks, Avery continued her previous routine, although this time, her progress was expedited from her heightened awareness of the world around her. Logan, the ex-sailor, found it hard to keep up with Avery's learning curve, a satisfaction she felt the taste of for a fleeting moment before Harvey stepped in to spar with her. The old man ensured she would not be feeling overconfident any time soon. Most of their spars ended with her on the ground, or with his sword inches away from demonstrating just how deadly her mistakes were.

During one of their morning spars, Avery successfully blocked an oncoming blow from the old man. He grunted his praise, pausing briefly to allow both to catch their breath. A faint pulsing alerted her to an unknown presence, and her body snapped into an alarmed state. She whipped around to face the source, finding her attention was pulled beyond the courtyard and up to the lookout point on the hill. A man was leaning on the railing, unmistakably staring down at them in the courtyard. Even from the distance, she could feel the subtle stirring his aura brought.

Annoyed at her sudden distraction, Harvey sent the flat part of his sword at the back of her leg, checking her balance. The force was enough to send her to the ground. Tumbling, she recovered, returning her attention to Harvey's drawn sword in front of her. The old man was glaring, not bothering to look behind him.

"Ignore him. Don't leave yourself open like that!"

She rubbed her leg where the sword made the impact, returning the glare. "How long has he been there?"

Instead of answering, Harvey engaged her blade, forcing her to concentrate again. She chanced another look when she managed to land another staggering blow on Harvey, but the captain had already moved on.

Nearly a week after that, Avery crossed paths with the captain again, discovering how truly overwhelming his aura was. After restless nights where Avery's dreams were haunted by the Sinclair estate or flooded with the sounds of the whispers that beckoned her into the ruins, she found herself up and out of the farmhouse much earlier. She usually spent the time burning off the excess energy, jogging around the skirt of town between the Farewell walls and surrounding forest. On occasion, she found herself venturing deeper into the forest, finding solace in her thoughts and isolation from everything. Equipped with her new sword, Lightbringer – a name her and Leah came up with after Harvey insisted it was a tradition to name a blade but offered no further elaboration – Avery no longer feared encountering mechoids. In fact, she welcomed the rare opportunity to test her blade against the Prowlers that wandered too close to the city.

A small pack of Prowlers intercepted her on the route back to Farewell, and she managed to take out the mechoids, although not unscathed, and she knew she would have a hell of a time trying to explain to Harvey how she managed to gain the several cuts and bruises when she showed up for training. As she walked back through the forest, she found Harvey would be the least of her worries, when the captain and two other guards appeared over the hill, immediately catching sight of her. She swore, cursing her luck for encountering their patrol, and knew it would look even more suspicious if she suddenly tried to dodge them. Instead, she chose to face them head on, and hoped the remains of the dispatched mechoids were out of sight.

The mere contact with his aura was enough to make her regret not trying to avoid the encounter. The force of it collided against her like a wave smashing into a cliffside in a bad storm. It took every ounce of willpower she had not to react to the overstimulation and continue her path as though she could not feel the power radiating from him.

The captain was as she remembered, especially with his green eyes glaring down at her. The two other guards trailed slightly behind him. One was a lean female with brown hair cut at her shoulders; the other was a taller man with dark curly hair that seemed to have a mind of its own. Neither of their silver eyes shared the captain's glare, offering Avery a polite morning greeting as they neared closer. She doubted if either of the two guards were mages, although she could not be certain with the captain's aura demanding so much of the space.

"Awfully early to be out on a stroll," the captain said, his tone was neither malicious nor friendly.

"And yet, here you are," she replied, perfectly friendly.

He ignored her comment, his eyes tracing the gashes on her arms. "You're bleeding, is there a problem?"

"No," she said, not technically a lie, "not anymore."

She kept the casual pace of her stride, expecting the

guard to stop her. He didn't. Instead, he motioned to the others, "Let's keep moving."

The captain continued scanning the forest, ignoring her when he passed by her. His aura tugged fiercely at her vessel, a deep pulsing that sent a shiver down her spine. The sensation followed her until she made it a good distance away, back toward Farewell.

◆ ◆ ◆

"That must be how other mages feels about you, Avery," Leah suggested when Avery recalled the encounter later that day. She endured an extra-long training session with Harvey which seemed to be the old man's way of scolding her for taking the risk out in the forest.

Leah practically spilled out of her chair when Avery mentioned her chance encounter with the guard captain, attempting to squeeze her out of any details.

"I heard Professor Colleymore talking to Malcom about your aura," she continued "Apparently, it is extremely potent."

Avery closed the book she was struggling to focus on, the proposed possibility not a comforting one. "It's unsettling if that's the case. I don't need others to know I'm a mage." She looked out the window, glaring at the guild hall. "I wish Captain Broody would stop running into me, I can't shake the feeling he is just waiting for an opportunity to throw me out of town."

Leah smiled uncontrollably, gazing out the window dreamily.

"I think the captain just takes his job very seriously, and it doesn't help that he probably thought you were a scavenger. They are always making trouble for the guild."

Annoyed at her friend's admiration for the captain, she opened the book again, ready to avoid the conversation if it continued to center around him, but Leah slightly pivoted topics. "Mindy told me the other day that things were getting pretty heated at the last guild meeting. Apparently, there was a lot of disagreement on what work needs to be done, and there has been an increase in mechoids around Farewell. The Guild Master is pushing to revisit a plan for getting a team out to recover some parts needed for the research facility, but the church was against it."

"Why are they against it?"

"Technology once brought the world to ruin; they are weary to bring it back. Humanity was given a second chance by the gods, utilizing something they forbode is an awful way to repay them."

Seeing Avery's quizzical expression, Leah chuckled. "I hear a lot about it from Mindy. She's the protegee of the High Priestess here in Farewell. I'll have to introduce you sometime. She is good friends with Captain Adler."

A slight scoff escaped Avery. "That's alright. The last thing I desire is to get into his inner circle. Harvey is right, I just need to keep my head down."

Leah agreed, not pressing the subject, allowing Avery to return to her research.

With part of her connection to her soul restored, the lessons with Harris were accelerating at an alarming rate. She could channel the basic magics, and through trial and error, they worked day after day to find where her current limitations were. Light magic came naturally, and she learned how to conjure shields of powerful beams of light that could be used to protect her in an encounter, although Harris relied on Harvey to teach her how to utilize the offensive side of magic.

By the time the beginning of summer rolled around, Avery was able to consistently summon most of the core magics, with fire being the least reliable for her to create. Though, the ability to use magic came at a steep price.

Theodore's painful hold on her brought on another level of intensity. Whenever he dealt his punishment, her vessel attempted to combat the pain with a barrier, straining her already exhausted body from the long day of training. Although the barrier provided some relief from the pain, she did her best to focus on suppressing the magic, following Irene's caution on overstraining her vessel. It made for many hard nights, which she imagined was exactly what Theodore hoped for.

On a particularly hot morning, Avery awoke from a pathetic amount of sleep after an outburst from Theodore kept her up. Shortly into her morning run, Avery looped around the perimeter of Farewell, sticking close to the wall as requested by Malcom and demanded by Harvey. Rounding a corner, she slowed her pace catching sight of Captain Adler at the archway into town. He was with only one other guard, from the looks of it, the same woman who she encountered with him previously. Neither of them took any notice of her, and she used the opportunity to reverse her course, determined to avoid any more inquiries from the captain if she could help it. In doing so, she veered off the path, making the exception to venture deeper into the forest again.

Lost in her thoughts, it was not clear to her at what point she started to hear the whispering invade her mind. As if she had been drawn toward it, she emerged from the canopy of the forest, finding herself in front of the cliffside ruins. A deep part of her yearned to find the source of beckoning. She wanted to know why the haunting sounds filled her dreams or why it seemed like she was always being pulled toward the hidden facility. The hum of whispers continued, telling her there was only one way to find out.

9
THE RESTRICTED RUINS

Avery's mind raced through the justifications for each step she took closer to the entrance of the forgotten ruins. A clean scope around the perimeter satisfied her concern for mechoids lurking nearby. Cautiously, she peered into the small gap between the two steel plates that barred the entrance into the structure. The darkness proved the effort a useless one, prompting Avery to create a small orb of light in the palm of her hand. With the wave of her hand, she guided the orb through the gap, sending it deeper into the darkness. The light bounced off the walls showing a barren room.

Finding no sign of danger, she gave one of the steel plates a good shake, testing its durability. A corner of the plate wiggled slightly. The bolt that held it in place was decaying from rust. Before she could change her mind, she aimed a hand at the spot and fired a focused burst, knocking the bolt off completely. The steel plate teetered, and it took removing another bolt before she was able to slide the plate over to create a big enough gap for her to squeeze through.

The stirred-up dust scratched Avery's throat as she ducked under the door. She pulled out Lightbringer, providing her some comfort as she adjusted to the darkness around her. She summoned another orb of light, illuminating her path as she took cautious steps forward. An eerie stillness suffocated the air. The temperature dropped rapidly the further she traveled within. Much like the walls, the room sat barren, as if any object was forcibly removed from near the entrance.

The whispering was louder now, echoing the nonsensical words more excitedly the further she travelled. She traversed a hallway, peering inside doorways that led to similarly empty rooms. The corridor ended abruptly, the wall at the end donning enlarged block writing of the old way, which she translated – AUTHORIZED PERSONNEL ONLY.

Curious, she reexamined the wall, seeing no indication of an entrance. As she moved closer to investigate, a loud sound rippled through the air. The noise reminded her of pressurized steam being released, and it came from somewhere within the walls. The wall, or more accurately, a part of the wall, slid to the side, creating a doorway for her to step through.

The narrow passage opened to a formidable room where Avery needed to field a few more lights. A soft buzz sounded, and she froze as light emitted above her. An industrial sized light switched on, followed by another, then another until the final panel turned on and the ceiling beamed down upon the vast space.

Despite the passage of time, the facility seemed frozen in a moment of pristine preservation. Aisles lined with sleek metallic panels, their surfaces gleaming under the soft glow of the overhead lights. Advanced machinery hummed quietly in the background, their intricate mechanisms a testament to the technological prowess of the facility's creators.

Unlike the rustic charm of Farewell, the interior of the ruins exuded an air of innovation and sophistication that was both awe-inspiring and unsettling. Avery could not help but feel a sense of unease as she navigated the labyrinthine setup. The unfamiliar technology and uncanny sterile surroundings left her feeling out of place. Even Theodore Sinclair would have been impressed by what would surely be considered priceless relics of the first era.

Everywhere she looked, she saw evidence of the facility's advanced capabilities. Monitors and control panels adorned the walls, displaying complex data and intricate schematics that would take years to fully translate. Strange devices and apparatuses lined the shelves, their purpose and function a mystery to her.

An eerie stillness hung in the air, as if the very walls themselves were holding their breath, waiting for something to happen. Avery could not shake the feeling she was being watched, as if unseen eyes were following her every move from the shadows.

The whispers persisted, their elusive voices echoing through the chamber. Avery's gaze gravitated to the back wall, where a red and white sign hung on a door, adorned with ancient script warning against entry.

Standing before the sign, she hesitated, the hiss of the wall cutting into the silence as another door materialized before her, obedient to some unseen command. Feeling a mix of trepidation and intrigue, she stepped through the doorway, the whispers urging her forward. The room beyond was dimly lit, illuminated only by faint streaks of light filtering through the door. Avery summoned additional orbs of light, casting their glow across the space as she cautiously explored.

The room was smaller than the one before, dominated by towering consoles filled with enigmatic devices from the ancient past. Monitors lined the walls, their screens dark and silent, devoid of any signs of life. In the center of the room, atop a low platform, rested a curved blade that tapered to a sharp point, resembling the shape of a crescent moon. Its surface, adorned with intricate patterns and etchings, hinted at well-made origins. The sword was hooked up to a myriad of cables, as if it were being meticulously analyzed and probed by the mysterious technology of the old ways.

Avery approached the platform, her senses on high alert as the whispers grew louder, their words barely audible above her own heartbeat. A strange pulse seemed to emanate from the sword, drawing her to it, her curiosity overpowering her apprehension. As Avery reached out to touch the blade, a sudden hush fell over the room. Startled by the abrupt shift, she instinctively withdrew her hand, a tingling sensation lingering in its wake. The whispers were no more, yet, a curious fascination drew her back to the blade, compelling her to reach out once more.

This time, as her fingertips made contact with the cool metal, a strange energy coursed through her, sending shivers down her spine. The silence enveloped her, punctuated only by the faint hum of the machinery from the other room. Avery listened, acutely aware of the pulsing rhythm emanating from the blade. With each touch, the connection between Avery and the sword deepened, an inexplicable bond forming between them. Breathless with wonder, she hesitated only briefly before grasping the hilt firmly in her hand, a surge of determination coursing through her veins as she lifted the blade from its tangled cable nest.

Her footsteps reverberated through the empty chamber as she conducted a final sweep, her eyes scanning every corner. It was a treasure trove for scavengers, a veritable goldmine of parts and artifacts that could fetch a fortune. Avery paused, her senses alerting her to an unfamiliar tapping resonating in the air. With caution, she gingerly placed the crescent sword aside on a nearby platform before reaching for her own blade, the tapping growing louder with each passing moment.

As the noise abruptly ceased, Avery remained still, straining to detect any movement. The silence stretched on, punctuated only by the unsettling feeling of being watched. Hastily summoning another orb of light to illuminate the room, she was taken aback when the glow revealed the metallic form of a mechoid.

Its sleek metallic form gleamed under the dim light of the orb. Instead of the usual beast shape, complement of appendages, this mechanical monstrosity boasted six sinuous tentacle-like arms, each ending in razor-sharp claws that glinted menacingly in the faint illumination. Its movements were fluid and precise, the tentacles weaving and undulating with a predatory grace as it hovered toward her, never touching the ground.

Avery swung Lightbringer at the advancing mechoid, the clash of metal ringing out in the stillness of the chamber. The mechanical assailant, undeterred, launched itself at her, forcing Avery to dodge and parry its multi-strike. Each blow exchanged between them echoed through the facility, the mechoid hurling debris at Avery with deadly accuracy while she fought to keep it at bay. She analyzed the mechoid, searching for any indication of where its core resided. She severed one of its arms, revealing the faint red glow of a power core nestled between where all its appendages converged. The beast retaliated by wrenching her own sword from her grasp and ensnaring her in its cold embrace.

Gritting her teeth against the searing pain, Avery summoned every ounce of her strength to unleash a powerful blast, sending the mechoid reeling in agony. Seizing the opportunity, she picked up her blade and drove it into the exposed core, the mechoid convulsing before falling silent.

Breathless and battered, Avery retrieved her sword and the crescent blade, fighting to catch her breath as she made her way across the room, ready to escape the abandoned facility before any more of those mechoids showed up. As she reached the door, a whirring rumbled behind her, and she turned just as the fallen mechoid emitted a piercing noise, filling the chamber with an ear-splitting ring that brought Avery to her knees.

The deafening sound gave no indication it would stop. Avery struggled to reach out a hand in front of her, channeling magic. A pain came from her chest, and she watched as the blade of the crescent sword emanate the magic that she attempted to cast. A blinding light emerged, and the next moment, she was sent flying backward into the hard wall behind her.

Avery awoke in a haze to find herself met with the piercing gaze of familiar yellow eyes. Contempt radiated from the narrowed stare, sending a shiver down her spine. Somehow, she found herself standing in the middle of a desolate road, pressed against a small transport vehicle partially lodged in a ditch.

"Theo, he will come find you," a voice intoned from behind her, but she couldn't muster the strength to turn and face it. Frozen in place, her entire body tensed as the figure approached. Theodore loomed before her, his black hair swept back, his face fuller than she remembered, devoid of the dark circles that usually haunted his eyes.

"I gave you a choice, Amelia, and you chose poorly. I warned you there would be consequences." His voice cut through the air like ice, his anger palpable. Avery's heart raced as she struggled to comprehend how she ended up back on the road and how Theodore had managed to track her down. Yet, his intense gaze was not fixed on her, but on someone behind her—a woman with long brown hair and defiant violet eyes.

Turning away from Theodore, Avery watched in silence as the two engaged in a heated exchange, oblivious to her presence. Theodore advanced menacingly, his hands outstretched in a gesture of finality. "I'm done being reasonable. You've hidden behind him for too long. You knew I would find you," he accused, his voice dripping with malice.

In response, Amelia extended a warning hand, her voice resolute. "You're delusional if you think any of this is reasonable."

"If you hadn't been so foolish to believe he loved you, none of this would have happened. Now, he'll use your children just as he's used you. You're a disgrace to your blessing." Theodore's words cut through the tension, his tone dripping with disdain. As he spoke, a powerful energy began to swirl around them. Avery could feel the source came from Amelia, channeling magic.

"Leave my family out of this, Theo," she pleaded, her outstretched hand trembling with raw emotion.

Ignoring her plea, Theodore pressed in closer, his voice lowered. "You know nothing of the venomous blood that runs through them. Their bloodshed will be on your hands."

The atmosphere darkened, and Amelia's eyes glowed with a violet light. "You will not touch them!" she declared, unleashing a blast of power toward Theodore.

In a swift motion, Theodore raised his hand to block the attack, the light in Amelia's eyes dimming momentarily. Seizing the opportunity, he grabbed her outstretched arm, channeling his own magic to restrain her.

"You made your choice, Amelia. You knew there would be consequences," he hissed, tightening his grip. "You and your daughter will return to Tracos with me, where you'll remain until I decide what to do with you."

Amelia did not struggle, but her gaze flickered back to the overturned transport. "He'll find out, Theodore. You underestimate the power they wield."

"You're still too naïve to see the bigger picture." Theodore's voice cut through the tension, filled with superiority and anger. With a swift motion, he summoned an unfamiliar magic and struck it into Amelia's chest. She cried out in pain, staggering backward, as the power seemed to envelop her.

A sudden crack echoed through the air, startling even Theodore. He took a step back, his expression shifting to one of alarm as he assessed Amelia's condition. Frantically, he attempted another form of magic, but when she showed no response, his desperation grew.

With trembling hands, he released her wrist, muttering to himself in frustration. As if snapping out of a trance, Theodore abruptly turned his attention to Avery, who tensed under his gaze. But he passed by her, his focus elsewhere, and approached the overturned transport. With a silent intensity, he opened it and retrieved a bundle of blankets, cradling it with disdain evident on his face.

Compelled by intrigue, Avery moved closer, her eyes falling on the sleeping child with bright blonde hair. Theodore stood there for what felt like an eternity, contemplating the situation, before turning his glare back to Amelia, his expression filled with disgust and resentment.

"Jarek!" he demanded, and in a moment, Jarek appeared from nowhere, seeming to have warped on command. Avery wouldn't recognize him if she hadn't heard Theodore call for him. He was scrawnier and still had most of his hair. He bowed deeply to Theodore, taking in the wreckage.

"My lord?" he asked nervously, his eyes catching where Amelia remained lifeless. His master ignored his questioning glance, addressing him directly.

"I want you to make it look like a mechoid attack. Do so quickly, the fallout may have been overheard nearby." Theodore's attention went back to the small child that stirred uncomfortably in his arms.

Jarek stared at it wide-eyed. "M-my lord, Is that-?"

"Yes…Avery. The youngest." Theodore's lips curled with a hint of satisfaction. "We may still gain something from Amelia's betrayal."

10
COMMUNITY SERVICE

The steady drum of a heartbeat played in her ear as she drifted in and out of consciousness. She became aware she was being carried, the rhythmic motion stirring her senses. Opening her eyes, she found herself still surrounded in darkness, save for a faint blue light casting shadows over the man carrying her. His green eyes glanced down at her intermittently in a mixture of concern and impatience. Resting her head against the warmth of the shoulder supporting her, Avery attempted to piece together her fragmented memories. The man's arms tightened around her when she tried to move.

"Easy now, you've taken quite a blow. We're almost out." His icy tone cut through the darkness, his face briefly illuminated again by the fading blue light. He muttered something else, but Avery struggled to stay conscious, surrendering to the comforting embrace and allowing herself to drift once more.

When she opened her eyes again, she found herself propped up against the rough wall of the cliffside, her head throbbing in echoes of her mother's voice.

"Captain, she is coming around," a voice beside her announced, belonging to a woman adorned in the light armor of the guard, her brown hair cropped short. Avery's body tensed as she attempted to rise, a surge of resistance coursing through her.

"Whoa, careful! You're really hurt. You need to wait until we can get someone out here to help you." The woman reached out a hand to help stabilize her.

Leaning against the sturdy stone wall for stability, Avery surveyed her surroundings, her gaze drawn to the once formidable entrance to the ruins, now reduced to rubble and charred remains. She started registering the overwhelming presence of someone approaching when the towering figure of Captain Adler emerged from the shattered remnants, seething with barely contained fury. His gaze locked onto Avery with unwavering intensity as he strode purposefully toward her. Lightbringer's hilt protruded over his shoulder, safely nestled in its sheath, while his own sword remained at his side. In his free hand, he tightly grasped the crescent-shaped blade salvaged from the ruins.

As Captain Adler drew nearer, the fog in Avery's mind began to dissipate, replaced by the overwhelming presence of his aura. "Reya, leave her to me. Inform James we've located the source," he commanded, his attention fixed solely on Avery. With a quick acknowledgment, the guard hastened back toward town.

The resounding crash of the crescent sword hitting the ground snapped Avery's focus back to the captain, who regarded her with a piercing gaze. "You're in a hell of a lot of trouble. Mechoids from all over have been drawn to this place. We had to kill six of them just to get here. Whatever you did in there set them off. "

She stood her ground, maintaining a facade of calmness. "I didn't know—"

"Bullshit," he interjected sharply, closing the distance between them. "This isn't your first time trespassing here."

Avery raised her hands slowly, sensing the danger in his eyes. Her mind raced, images of her mother flashing through her thoughts as she struggled to piece together what had happened. The captain's skepticism only heightened as she hesitated, carefully choosing her words. "There was a mechoid in those ruins. It triggered an alarm when I destroyed it. I couldn't—"

"So, what's your excuse this time? Get lost again?" He glared down at her. The howling of a Prowler sounded in the distance. Avery returned the glare up at him, knowing he had a point. There was no valid reason for her to trespass the area again, and it was clear he was not going to accept any argument supplied to him.

"Nothing I say will justify what has been done. If what you say is true, then we can't waste time arguing. We need to address the mechoids." She attempted to move forward, but he blocked her path with outstretched arm, forcing her to retreat until her back met the cold stone wall. His glare deepened, brimming with distrust. "Listen, Blue eyes. The only place you're headed is a holding cell. You've caused enough trouble as it is."

Avery locked eyes with the captain, her thoughts racing through her limited options. Evading him was out of the question, yet the idea of willingly surrendering to a cell was equally unappealing. His aura reminded her, with overwhelming intensity, that she was not ready for a fight, despite the magic stirring uncontrollably within her.

For a fleeting moment, her gaze flickered to the crescent sword lying at her feet, its blade shimmering with an energy that mirrored her own restlessness. Sensing her hesitation, the captain's hand grazed over the hilt of his own sword. "You can't be that reckless," he muttered, a faint trace of amusement in his voice. Avery's heart quickened, a sharp pinch in her chest warning her against the dangerous impulse.

"That's enough." The unmistakable bark forced the two to shift their attention to where Harvey stood at the edge of the forest. The old man's sights were set on Avery, giving her a once over. "Can you walk?" There was a coldness in his voice that sent a chill down her spine. She gave him a small nod in response, and he inclined his head back, motioning for her to move, "Let's go." He turned his back to them, starting to walk away.

Stunned, Avery hesitated, casting a wary glance back at the captain. As she moved to follow Harvey, the captain's hand shot out once more, his gaze fixed firmly on her. "I can't let her go, General. The council will want answers," he called over his shoulder, unwavering.

"I'll deal with the council later," the old man called behind as he continued on, "Let her go."

A tense standoff ensued between Avery and the captain, their gazes locked in a silent battle. Slowly, he lowered his hand, his jaw clenched tight as Avery took a step forward, determined to seize the opportunity. Without waiting for the captain to reconsider, she swiftly left the ruins, feeling his eyes tracking her until she caught up with Harvey. Together, they walked in silence back to the city, the pace brisk despite the old man's limp.

Farewell was on high alert, evident in the bustling activity of guards and guild members scattered throughout the city. They hurried in every direction, likely conducting patrols and reinforcing security measures. Meanwhile, the remaining residents sought refuge indoors, leaving the streets and plazas eerily deserted. Approaching the arch entryway that led into the city, they encountered a stationed guard who recognized Harvey and attempted to halt their progress. With a grunt, Harvey brushed past the guard, his determined stride leaving no room for argument, and

Avery followed closely behind.

They entered the Big Hen to find the tavern empty, save for Jaune, who emerged from the kitchen at the sound of the door opening. One glance at Harvey's expression sent Jaune scurrying back into the safety of the kitchen, deepening Avery's sinking feeling. Harvey made his way behind the bar, retrieving a bottle of whiskey and pouring himself a glass before settling onto a stool, his glare fixed on Avery once more. With a slow sip, he lowered his glass just enough to speak.

"Talk," he demanded.

Avery stood before him, knowing there was no adequate explanation for her recent actions. "I'm sorry," she began, but Harvey's indifferent response halted her.

"I don't care," he replied, his voice colder than she had ever heard. "Why were you in the ruins?"

Avery hesitated, struggling to find the right words. "There was something—" she started, but caught herself, realizing it would not suffice.

"Well?" Harvey's impatience was palpable.

"I've been hearing something calling out to me since I arrived in Farewell," she confessed quickly, shifting as Harvey's gaze bore into her. Seizing the opportunity, she explained the strange whispers, recounting her journey into the old ruins before Harvey's frustration escalated.

"So, let me get this straight, Avery," Harvey interjected, his tone incredulous. "You start hearing something or someone calling for you deep in the forest, and despite everything you know about Theodore... after all you've been through, you follow it?" Avery kept her gaze fixed on the floor, prompting Harvey to swear loudly before returning to his whiskey.

"What caused all the noise then?" Harvey demanded.

"A mechoid attacked me. But it was unlike any you

described. It had unnatural arms and sounded an alarm when I took it out," Avery explained, meeting his scrutinizing gaze. She wondered if she looked as battered as she felt. Her right arm throbbed, dried blood staining her skin where the mechoid had pierced through the skin. Bruises blossomed on her arms where the steel tentacles had struck, and a dull ache settled in her chest. As her stress ebbed, her headache intensified. Harvey remained silent for a while, studying her behind his fury.

Finishing his drink, he rose from the stool and retrieved his walking stick. "You look like hell, kid. Get patched up and don't leave Cecilia's until I come for you," he instructed, gesturing at the exit. Avery nodded, following Harvey out of the Big Hen. She parted ways with him, heading toward the farm while he made his way to the guild hall.

Avery arrived at the farmhouse to find Cecelia waiting anxiously on the porch chair, her expression shifting from worry to relief upon seeing her. Without a word, Cecelia fetched a medical kit and set to work on Avery's wounds. With practiced hands, she tended to the worst injuries, applying a soothing heat with the warm touch of her hand to alleviate the pain. Avery watched as the deep cuts healed under Cecelia's touch, leaving no trace behind. The smaller wounds were carefully bandaged and treated with ointments.

Once Cecelia was satisfied with her work, she urged Avery to eat something, but she declined and retreated to her room for the remainder of the day. The all-too-familiar sense of dread lingered, rendering sleep impossible.

Every time she closed her eyes, haunting images of her mother flooded her mind. Theodore's voice crept in, a constant reminder of his deceit—how he fabricated the accident that robbed Avery of her mother and trapped her in his grasp. Anger simmered within her, directed not only at Theodore but also at herself for believing his lies. Harvey's warnings echoed in her mind, a bitter reminder of her own foolishness in venturing into the ruins.

Regret gnawed at her, knowing that her actions had endangered others and made her a target in the town's eyes. The weight of her mistakes pressed heavily on her shoulders, leaving her feeling powerless and empty-handed despite the risks she had taken.

As morning broke, Avery sat on the porch, the weight of the situation settling heavily upon her. Absentmindedly, she stroked Scout's fur, finding solace in the dog's presence.

Cecelia joined her, offering a warm cup of tea. "This isn't the first trouble Farewell has seen, nor will it be the last, dear," the old woman said softly, lowering herself down to sit beside Avery. Although grateful, Avery found she couldn't return the smile, setting the glass aside as she muttered quietly, "I've never seen Harvey so angry."

"Is that what you're worried about? The amount of trouble that one has stirred up for this town far outweighs anything you can do." Cecelia chuckled. "…Not that you should take that as a challenge." Seeing this did not improve Avery's mood she continued, "No, I think that old bull has taken a liking to you, Avery, and he's not good at that sort of thing."

Alarmed by the suggestion, Avery turned to take in Cecelia's words. The old woman bobbed her head playfully. "Besides it seems you took quite a beating already. If he keeps on hounding you, I will make sure to remind him some of the trouble he caused me all these years."

"Don't act like you weren't part of that trouble, Cecelia," Harvey's voice cut through the air as he joined them on the porch. Scout greeted him with exuberance, bounding around him in joyful circles as he made his way over to Avery and Cecelia. Lightbringer was tucked under his arm, and he tossed it to Avery once he reached the porch steps.

"Part of it?" Cecelia gasped, feigning offense. "You damn near dragged me into it every time things got too hot for you."

Harvey just grunted in response, shaking his head at her.

"Did you speak to the council?" Avery asked, not really knowing if she prepared for the answer. Harvey was puffing at a cigar already. "Yup, one hell of a show. Most Mechoids they've seen gather in one place outside of the dead zones, but they never get out of town much anyway."

"Was anyone hurt, Harvey?" Cecelia asked softly, placing a comforting arm on Avery's shoulder.

"Nothing they can't recover from," Harvey reassured them, his gaze momentarily lingering on Avery. "You got lucky, Avery," he added, his tone stern.

"So, I'm not in trouble?" she asked, not feeling like she had won any prizes.

"Well, I didn't say you were out of the woods." He readjusted his cigar, reaching down to pat Scout who was looking hurt from being ignored. "Rhyker was bent out of shape, saying he caught you there before and warned you about the area. They tried to get down my throat for training you, but there aren't any rules that say you have to have a license to learn to fight. Harris was there and discussed some things privately with James and Sylvie, which probably helped take the heat off you for a bit. It's all just politics."

Avery felt another wave of guilt, knowing that Harris was also pulled into the mess. "So, what's going to happen?" she asked.

The old man grunted, reaching into his pocket for a leather fold. He pulled out a small card. "Well, I struck up a little deal with them, and it seemed like the waters are settled now." He held it out to her. Avery set her sword down and walked up to take the card, reading it. "Avery Carter – Farewell Guild License." She read it again. "A guild license? But, why?"

"I told you I struck a deal with the council. They won't put anything against you so long as you do a little community service." He tapped the end of his cigar off. "You'll report to Rhyker tomorrow."

"Captain Adler?" she asked, and Harvey's piercing stare was enough to confirm it. "I don't understand," she continued. "He gave me the impression he wanted me to rot in a cell. Why would he want me to work for the guild?"

Harvey shook his head. "He didn't. He was dead against it and made that real clear in the meeting. He had half a mind to come find you and put you on arrest, especially since I pulled you from the scene." The corner of Harvey's mouth twitched up, threatening a smile. "But James insisted that we focus on why the mechoids were behaving like this and gained the backing of the church. Rhyker had no choice but to accept the proposal. He eventually agreed but only on the condition that he would be in charge of your community service to make sure you don't cause the town any more trouble."

Avery picked up Lightbringer, her eyes still fixed on the license. It was odd to see her name next to Harvey's. The old man waited, his gaze steady and unamused. Avery could not think of an alternative, and she knew Harvey and Harris were both already sticking their necks out for her. "Alright," she nodded, slipping the card in her pocket. "I'll report to the guild hall first thing in the morning."

"No," Harvey interjected coldly. "You'll come train with me first. You can head over there when I'm done with you." With that, he grabbed his walking stick and nodded to Cecelia before striding away.

♦ ♦ ♦

Later that evening, Avery found herself sitting across from Leah who stared at her in disbelief. "You have to do *what?*"

Leah and Malcom came down to the farmhouse to check on her after finding out through Professor Colleymore that she had been the reason for the lockdown.

"It could have been worse, Avery." Malcom shook his head. The author shared Harvey's disappointment, but he expressed more relief when seeing she was mostly unharmed. "Thank the goddess the captain found you, or who knows what could have happened."

Although she knew Malcom meant well, Avery hated to think that the captain saved her *again*. She had to give Leah a stern look to prevent her from discussing it.

"I can't believe they just *gave* you a guild license!" Leah had been admiring the card since Avery showed it to her. "Avery Carter," she read off the name, grinning widely. "You know it kind of suits you."

Avery attempted to lift the corners of her mouth, but the weight of the last two days still hung heavily on her, making it difficult to fully mask her unease. "I really hope the professor isn't in too much trouble," she confessed her worry, hoping to pivot topics. "I didn't realize he could get in trouble for teaching me magic."

Malcom sighed, considering the issue. "Well, it's not that he is in trouble for teaching you magic. I think they were more upset that there was a powerful mage in town, and they didn't know about it. In Harris' position, he is supposed to help keep the council informed on any developments that may impact the town, and well, I guess you qualify."

Leah moved her glass to cover her mouth, finding it hard to suppress a giggle. "I wonder what the captain is going to have you do? So much for trying to stay out of trouble!"

Avery rolled her eyes at the thought. "Honestly, I'm more worried about my morning training with Harvey." She looked at her sword that sat in the corner of the room, knowing the coming day would be very long.

11
THE BLITZ TEAM

If the reinforced lessons the next morning was not enough to solidify Harvey's frustrations with her, the soreness she would feel in the coming days would do it. Harvey was relentless when he sparred with her, trying to catch her by surprise with different techniques. Any success he gained in landing a strike was quickly followed by barking corrections at her. Avery took each direction without complaint, despite her body still aching from her previous encounter with the strange mechoid. Several of the smaller cuts along her arms stung from her sweat. Yet, the looming appointment with the guild hall meant they would have to finish earlier, and Harvey was not going to waste any time.

There was only a brief pause to eat the breakfast Jaune prepared for her. The chef did not voice any concern over the previous day's events, but his worried eyes occasionally lingered on her when he passed by the kitchen doors. Avery stalled there in the tavern for as long as she could, until the glares from Harvey became too much to endure. Accepting her fate, she ducked out of the tavern, the knots in her stomach reminding her how uneasy she felt about it.

As Avery stepped into Pioneer Plaza, the stillness of the early hour enveloped her, casting a serene quiet over the usually bustling square. The neighboring bookstore, its windows dark, stood silent, as she walked past it and around the pioneer statue which stood as a sentinel to the awakening town. Across the plaza, the imposing facade of the guild hall loomed, its tall wooden doors adorned with intricate carvings and vibrant maroon and silver banners that fluttered in the faint breeze.

Approaching the entrance, Avery took in the grandeur of the hall. The polished wooden doors stood tall, inviting yet commanding respect. The sight that greeted her as she pushed the doors open was both welcoming and unanticipated. The spacious foyer resembled more of a mess hall or common room. Tables with sturdy benches were arranged throughout the room, some occupied by guild members enjoying their breakfast and exchanging morning greetings. Freshly brewed coffee mingled with baked goods, the scent wafting through the air, creating a comforting atmosphere.

A sweeping staircase beckoned her attention, leading to an upper floor where she could discern the murmur of voices. Alongside the staircase, a corridor extended, hinting at more passageways and meeting rooms hidden within the guild hall's interior. A sharp pulsing sent her eyes immediately upon Captain Adler, whose mood was unimproved from the day before. He stood next to a table where two others were conversing over breakfast. One was Reya, who accompanied the captain in the ruins. The other was the man with long, curly brown hair who she had seen out on patrol with the captain before.

Their conversation halted as they noticed Captain Adler's gaze fixating on Avery. She struggled to maintain a neutral expression as his sharp eyes assessed her. The captain's attention briefly flickered to the hilt of Lightbringer strapped behind her shoulder before returning to her face.

His expression remained unchanged as she approached him.

"I'm here to report in," she offered politely, struggling to keep her tone amicable.

"Clearly," he said, not hiding his annoyance. He turned to the table and addressed the man who sat watching them. "Milo, I'm putting Blue Eyes with you. Have her help you go over the parts collected and get them to the research facility. I want them to stop asking me about when they are going to be delivered."

Nodding in acknowledgement, Milo rose from his seat, picking up his empty plate as he got out from under the table. Rhyker turned back to face Avery. "If she starts getting any ideas, go ahead and show her the holding cell we've been keeping warm for her." A smirk played at the corner of his mouth when she narrowed her eyes. He stepped toward her so he could lower his voice. "Just play nice, Blue Eyes, and we can all get this over with." He moved past her, taking a side door to leave the room.

Milo navigated around the table and reached out a hand. "Was it Avery? I don't think I can get away with calling you Blue Eyes." He grinned widely, and Avery did her best not to show her surprise from his friendliness as she shook his hand.

"Yeah, Avery's fine."

"Milo Cymas." His dark bushy hair bounced as he moved. "We can head to the workshop in the back."

Avery followed him, noticing a few of the other guards staring curiously at her while she maneuvered around the tables and benches.

"So, are you Harvey's granddaughter or something?" Milo inquired casually as he led them further into the guild hall, heading toward one of the open doors at the end of the corridor.

"Not exactly." She paused, considering how to explain

the relationship. "He's more like a family friend."

Milo seemed content with her response, not probing further as they entered an office, which also served as a storage room. The space was filled with large crates containing various mechoid parts. Avery peered into one of the crates, spotting a clipboard with neatly organized data. "That's quite the haul," she remarked.

"Yeah, it's impressive how quickly we accumulated so much these last few days. With your help, we can get them cleaned, cataloged and sent over to the research facility." Milo picked up one of the crates and moved it to a desk cluttered with tools and trinkets. He radiated a lively energy as he examined a random part pulled from the crate. "When inspecting them, we need to make sure we don't send over anything that isn't usable, or we'll get an earful from Rhyker."

The part he was inspecting apparently was not making the cut, evident by his dismissive toss of it into a nearby bin before moving on to the next item. Intrigued, Avery stepped closer to examine the discarded piece.

"What is it you are looking for?"

"Power Cells, working sensors and other parts that may be used or studied." He held up a power cell that looked to have come from a Prowler. "Some of the people harvesting the parts are careless and bring back broken parts." He raised a dark eyebrow at her. "You've never scraped a mech before?"

Avery shook her head, and Milo let out a confused "Huh." and surveyed her, then the parts in the crates. "Well, then let's get you familiar with the different parts first, then we can worry about teaching you how to spot the good from the bad."

Milo spent the time pulling out as many different parts as he could find to be suitable examples of each, including going over smaller bits that the research facility was not interested in keeping. The parts salvaged were not limited to Prowlers and Stalkers, apparently some of the guards came back with parts from Drones and crawlers. When she asked about them, he excitedly delved deeper into his explanation, showing Avery his own sketch books and journals, which he used to document his work out in the field.

"Crawlers are annoying little pricks." He flipped his journal to a page with a detailed sketch of the mechoid. The sleek metallic frame, reminiscent of a spider's segmented body, was adorned with intricate plating. Housed within it was a central orb-like structure, which Milo pointed to. "These sensors grant the crawler unparalleled situational awareness, allowing it to observe and alert other nearby mechoids. Each of its eight legs are equipped with articulated joints which make for swift and silent movement across different terrain." Milo dug around in a crate until he found one of the sensors, a few legs dangling from his hand, still attached. "In other words, these creeps will spot you, alert other mechoids within a small radius, and then scurry off."

Avery tilted her head thoughtfully. "That does sound rather annoying."

Milo sighed, nodding. "Tell me about it, I can't even tell you how many times we've been delayed out in the field because a couple of these mechs snuck up on us. Their stunners hurt like hell too."

Milo took another look at the sensor, then swore under his breath and tossed it into the bin. Avery chuckled and flipped through a few pages of Milo's journal.

"What about this one?" Avery asked, showing him the page.

"Ah, the CyCorp Conductor." He set down the part he was examining and used a cloth to clean the oils that lingered on his hands so he could point out the parts. "The same maker of the crawlers, much more intense and rarer to find. They hover like a Drone and their appendages are hard to cut through. These Octoids- Rhyker hates when I call them that – seem to have been built to work on and protect the technology of the old ways, but I've never seen a working one myself.

That sketch is from a model they had up at the research center once."

Avery studied the page. "Does it also have an alerting mechanism like the crawler?"
Milo paused a moment to consider it. "I wouldn't be surprised. I haven't been able to get my hands on one of their cores."
"Did they recover anything from the one in the ruins?"
Milo looked at Avery quizzically, then his eyebrows shot up in realization. "Is that what you encountered in there?"
"I think so." Avery nodded.
"Gods," he whispered, "Never would have thought a Conductor would be lurking in there." He grabbed a pen tucked behind his ear, somehow not lost in his curls. "I wonder if that's what drew the attention of the other mechoids."
"That was my thinking. You mentioned the crawlers do something similar."
"Yes, but on a much smaller scale. A crawler can only really draw nearby Prowlers in. What happened at that facility seemed to affect all mechoids within a much wider radius."
"I hit the core of the Conductor but didn't disable it. That's when it started a horrendous noise, and I-" Avery stopped, she could not recall what she did. She remembered the crescent sword illuminating, and a flash, and her mother's eyes.
"Damn, I wish you hadn't destroyed it!" Milo whined,

continuing to jot notes down in his journal. "I mean, I can't really complain. Because of that explosion, I was finally allowed to go inside the ruins to ensure the incident was contained."

"You hadn't been in there before?"

"No, strictly forbidden by the Farewell Council. The technology in there is considered too dangerous, that's why it was sealed off." Milo laughed. "Or at least it was."

Avery let out a small laugh, relieved that Milo continued to be friendly.

Milo sighed. "Alright, let's start cataloging these parts. It will take us some time to get through them all."

By the late afternoon, Avery was cleaning off the parts and sorting them into more organized piles, preparing them for Milo to inspect and catalog the entries. There was a steady rhythm the two managed, and she found herself grateful for the opportunity to inspect the parts up close, outside the heat of battle.

Throughout her first week of community service, Milo had been genuinely pleasant, guiding Avery through the intricacies of mechoid parts. He often launched into long, Leah-like explanations about the uses of various components and the mechoids they originated from. Milo's deep fascination with mechoids was evident, and his enthusiasm made the time pass more quickly.

On a few occasions, Reya joined them for the work, usually in between her patrol shifts. Reya Brealle was second hand to the captain, and according to Milo, she was one of the few who could last in a spar against the captain. With her slender frame and the effortless way she moved, she resembled more of a dancer than a fighter. Yet her quick eyes and sharp wit made it apparent she should not be underestimated. There was no apprehension from Reya after the incident in the ruins, in fact, Reya was incredibly friendly toward Avery, and together with Milo, she shared stories of their time in the field.

They were the only two members of the guard that made up the captain's team, and it had been that way since he took the position nearly five years ago. The guild referred to them as the "Blitz Team", sending them out on field missions that dealt with the more dangerous mechoids or if it required a trip, in or around the dead zones.

Dead zones were something Avery was already familiar with from her time working under Theodore. These areas were once heavily populated cities in the first era that have gone to ruin over the centuries. Now, the cities lie abandoned aside from the hordes of mechoids that roam throughout. Leah and her shared an interest in reading about the dangers within the desolate locations from their favorite author, Grey Highcroft.

Although Milo and Reya spoke often of the captain, Avery did not see much of him, other than when she reported to him upon arriving to the guide hall each morning. If it had not been for the overwhelming waves of his aura tugging at her, she would have been convinced he did not remain in the guild hall while she worked.

The eagerness of the research facility led to many long days of cataloging the remaining mechoid parts in order to be prepared for an upcoming delivery. On the night before the delivery, Avery volunteered to stay later to assist Milo with the last of the parts. Alone in the small office, she delved into one of Milo's field journals detailing a large mechoid encounter from the prior summer. The sketch within depicted a Mezzo Systems Leveler, or "Dozer," formidable giants with heavy armor reminiscent of siege artillery.

Lost in the report, Avery failed to hear the approach of

the man whose icy voice disrupted the silence.

"I specifically recall telling Milo you were not to be left unsupervised," the captain's voice cut through the room.

Avery casually looked up, meeting his disapproving gaze as she brushed off his comment.

"Right," she mused, turning her attention back to Milo's notes, "then I suppose my recklessness must be wearing off on him already."

"What are you still doing here?" His commanding tone irritated her, and she had half a mind to retort with something less than friendly, but she knew it was best to humor him so he could be on his way again. She indicated the small monitor that showed the minor progress the machine made in deconstructing the data they needed.

"Waiting for the last of this data to transfer so we can finish cataloging the parts we are delivering to the research facility tomorrow. Milo went to grab something to eat as it seems we will be here for a few more hours."

The captain apparently couldn't find a reason to pick apart the explanation but that did not change his clear displeasure with her being there. Choosing to stick out the silent war he was waging on her, he moved into the room picking up one of the clipboards that rested against the finished stack of parts, settling himself down to review it. The notion irritated Avery as she knew he was only doing it to show her that he did not intend on letting her remain unsupervised.

After enough time went by without any indication that he would get bored of it and leave, Avery closed the report, unable to concentrate with the weight of his aura pressing in on her.

"I have no intention of disturbing the peace here, if you want to go resume your brooding someplace else."

A smile grew on his lips at his apparent victory in

making her break the silence.

"I think I'm right where I need to be. After all, you haven't given me any reason to expect anything but the contrary."

Avery matched his tone, unbothered by the remark. "It was my understanding I did not owe you any explanation."

Rhyker pushed himself from the table and walked toward her. He stopped just short of where she stood, finding her unwilling to give up any of her own ground to him.

"You know," he started, the sarcasm already dripping in his tone, his eyes hinted at amusement as he continued to survey her. "I wonder how much I would have learned about you had your *Uncle* Harvey not come to cover for you."

Avery dawned the polite smile again and crossed her arms comfortably in front of her.

"If it would have been anything like this attempt at interrogation, then I doubt you would have learned anything new."

The captain didn't buy it and shook his head. "I suppose we will never know. In the meantime, it's my job to make sure you don't cause Farewell any more headaches."

Footsteps came from behind them, and Milo rounded the corner into the room.

"I hope you don't mind ham, Avery. It's all they had left." He chimed brightly but slowly trailed off seeing the two of them there. Rhyker did not bother to turn to face Milo and instead kept his eyes trained on Avery. He spoke aloud, resuming his icy tone.

"Don't let me find her alone again, Milo." Without another word, he turned and made his way out of the room, making sure to transfer his glare to a stunned Milo as he left.

Recovering from the momentary shock, Milo grinned at Avery, attempting to cool the tension. "The council must really be on his case. He's not usually this irritable." Avery did not say anything and accepted the dinner offered. She knew from her discussions with the two that both Milo and Reya were close with Rhyker and everything that came to mind would jeopardize her own blooming friendship with them.

12
THE LUNAR KNIGHTS

The next morning, Avery missed the usual training with Harvey to arrive at the guild hall extra early. The research facility arranged for Milo to use a transport to haul the shipment up the hill. Farewell's aversion to transports meant they needed to get loaded up and moved out of the plaza before the rest of the businesses in the town were set to open.

Although she had traveled by transport a few times in the past, she still found the mechanical vehicle fascinating. The facility's model proved to be even more curious. The exterior was angular and industrial, with reinforced plating and a matte finish in various metallic shades. The mechanical structure emitted a soft hum, indicating its immense power and efficiency. The body was elongated, providing ample space for storage, and featured multiple compartments accessible from both sides and the rear. These compartments were equipped with automated doors, controlled by the driver, who worked for the research facility and helped the morning crew load up the parts.

Unlike the transports she had used before, the facility's cargo hauler did not use the standard all terrain track but instead utilized thick, round wheels. The massive wheels supported the transport, each one intricately designed with durable treads and mechanisms for optimal traction and stability.

Later, during their climb up the hill while following the transport, Milo explained that there were compromises the research facility made with the church. If the facility needed to use the transport, it was restricted to the lowest levels of power and many of its features were disabled. This restriction ensured that the powerful vehicle would not disturb the surrounding environment excessively. Avery was not quite sure how much of what Milo said she understood, but his enthusiasm made it hard to interrupt, and asking questions only sent him further down a tangential path.

Their task brought Avery to a section of the research facility she had only glimpsed from the outside. As they entered through wide double doors, Avery found herself in a spacious lobby that resembled a museum. The high ceiling and polished floors added to the modern feel of the space. Objects that Avery assumed to be relics of the old ways were meticulously displayed in glass cases, each accompanied by a placard detailing its significance.

Milo patiently guided Avery through some of the exhibits, providing additional context for the discoveries. He explained the history and functionality of various artifacts, their importance in the Era of Silence, and how they had been rediscovered. Their impromptu tour was interrupted by a woman who approached them while they were examining a rebuilt Prowler. Milo introduced her as Professor Cynthia Bradac, the overseer of the facility's resource intake.

After the brief introduction, they spent the remainder of the morning unloading the transport and organizing the parts within the facility's back room. The room was a labyrinth of shelves and storage units, filled with categorized mechoid parts and tools. Avery marveled at the efficiency and precision of the storage system. Milo showed her how to correctly catalog each part, ensuring they were in the right place for future use. Professor Bradac occasionally checked in, offering insights and making sure everything was in order.

Professor Bradac occasionally pulled Milo away to discuss an upcoming project that would require many more sensors from the crawlers going forward. The two would be out of the room and out of earshot before Avery could catch much of the discussion. However, she did hear Milo drop Professor Colleymore's name a few times. Eventually, Harris arrived as they were slated to take a break for lunch.

"I thought I felt your aura!" The Professor greeted her. "Do you have a moment? There are some people in my office who would like to meet you."

Avery understood his assumption, as her own vessel told her there were many mages around the research facility. With too many auras in one place, it was hard to differentiate any of them.

Avery looked to Milo for confirmation, and he nodded. "Sure, we were about to eat."

"Perfect," Harris beamed. "Why don't you grab us all some food? We can eat in my office," he asked Milo, who agreed, leaving Avery to walk with Professor Colleymore through the campus.

As they left the main building, the professor made small talk. Their lessons had been on hiatus for the time being. He assured her it was not due to her incident at the ruins but rather his increased responsibilities as the interim representative for the research center. The previous incumbent had been ill for some time and finally decided to resign, leaving Harris without many free evenings.

On their route to his office, Harris steered Avery away from their usual path, opting to go toward the courtyard that made up the center of the campus.

"Before we head into my office, I want to have a quick chat," he explained after Avery shot him a puzzled look. "The people you are about to meet have agreed not to question you about your time in those ruins." He lowered his voice slightly as another pair of faculty members passed by on the other side of the garden. "However, you should know that there is a lot of discussion regarding what happened, and it has put a lot of people on edge." He turned to face her. "I need to know, Avery, did you take anything from the facility?"

"No," she shook her head. "I was attacked by a mechoid. I think it was a Conductor."

"A Conductor? Are you sure?" he asked, his eyes widening.

"Well, Milo showed me a sketch of one similar to it." She searched the professor's face. "Didn't they find the remains of it in the ruins?"

He shook his head. "I went in there myself to assess the situation. There was a lot of damage to the facility, but no remnants of a mechoid."

"There was nothing left of it?"

"No, although we could tell there was some sort of altercation based on some of the scarring at the scene. You appear to have used some powerful magic. Although I am pleased to see how effective your light magic is becoming, there was an awful lot of damage. I'm glad you didn't get badly hurt." He eyed Lightbringer, then her once more. "Where did you find the crescent sword?"

"In a room in the far back. It was hooked up to a bunch of cables and sensors. It looked like it was being studied at some point."

"How did you get in there? How did you restore power to the facility?"

Confused, Avery focused on the question. "Restore power?" she asked. "The place was already powered when I got there. Most of the equipment in there was working."

The professor furrowed his brow in silent concentration. Avery hesitated, her curiosity getting the better of her. "Professor, what did they do with that sword?"

"It's in my lab, being examined. I'm currently appealing the church's request to have it melted down." He looked thoughtful again. "You say it was connected to the equipment there?"

Avery nodded. "I removed it. That must have been what set off the mechoid."

The professor stood silent, staring at the ground until the shuffling of footsteps showed another small group of people entering the courtyard. He indicated for Avery to continue along the path.

"We are fortunate that Captain Adler can attest to the fact you didn't bring anything else out of the ruins, so the investigation should keep them clear of you."

"Investigation?" Avery asked. "Why? Was there something else missing?"

"Yes and no." His voice got lower once more as they entered the building. "That sword wasn't in there when I helped reseal it nearly five years ago, and the data on the consoles seem to have wiped themselves clean. That facility should have never powered back on. The church is calling it a blessing and asking that the facility be destroyed before anyone else can get hurt." The professor sounded slightly annoyed. "But I've already said too much." He sighed as they neared the office. "We shouldn't discuss it further. As I said, the council is concerned, and I suspect we will see more movement because of this. Only, I'm not certain what direction we will move in."

A heavy pit formed in her stomach, sinking lower with

every word the professor said. "Professor, it was never my intention to make things difficult."

"These things happen. It was only a matter of time before we would be questioned why you were here. I only hope they will continue to listen to Harvey."

They arrived in front of the professor's office, and Avery could feel the pulse of two mages from within the room. The professor gave her a reassuring smile before opening the door and ushering her inside.

Inside his office, the two mages were seated at the table in discussion. They both set their eyes on Avery once she was guided through the door by the professor.

"I stumbled upon Avery assisting Professor Bradac with the delivery. I thought it might be appropriate to introduce her with both of you present." Professor Colleymore motioned to the two. "Avery, this is High Priestess Sylvie Dalmorie and the Farewell Guild Master James Norris."

Both stood up from the table to meet her across the room. The Guild Master was the first to reach her and shake her hand. Much like the first time she had seen him, the Guild Master was in a suit that dawned the maroon sashes on his chest. His dark brown eyes complimented his darker skin, and a bright energy seemed to radiate from his smile.

"Ah, finally seeing you with my own eyes. I've heard so very much about you." His voice carried far, and the ease of his friendliness told Avery it was effective at addressing a crowd.

Behind him, the High Priestess greeted Avery with a warm nod before extending her hand. Up close, Avery noticed the intricate embroidery adorning the long black robes she wore. Her dark hair was loosely pinned up, framing light hazel eyes that shone with quiet authority. The aura emanating from the High Priestess was powerful, effortlessly overshadowing that of the Guild Master. "Yes," her soft voice contrasted the Guild Master's. "I have already heard great things about you, Miss Avery."

Sylvie's smile turned into a look of concern, and she tilted her head slightly. "However, I must say I am disturbed over the recent events that have taken place. It seems you inadvertently put yourself and others in danger. I hope you will tread more carefully in the future." She spoke with a slight accent that made each word sound silky.

Avery bowed her head slightly, knowing the topic could not be avoided. "Yes, I understand, and I'm very grateful for the opportunity to work with the guild in an effort to repair some of the damaged caused."

The High Priestess offered another warm smile, and it felt as though the entire room lightened in her presence. Avery felt awkward, standing silently, engaging in the dreaded small talk. A knock came from the office door. They all turned to see Milo enter, his hands full of lunch trays. Avery moved to help him, but the professor beat her to it.

The Guild Master seized the opportunity to satisfy his curiosity, probing Avery for more information. "It's quite rare to hear that Harvey has taken on a pupil. How'd you manage that?"

Feeling more prepared for the inquiry, Avery leaned on the earlier explanation she shared with Milo. "Harvey is a family friend and is doing it as a favor for me."

"Ah, training to become a knight, are we?" He seemed to grow more animated, his enthusiasm evident. "I wanted to work alongside the Duke myself when I was your age, but I ended up falling in love with Farewell and couldn't bear to leave it."

The High Priestess let out a small chuckle, waving a hand as if to dismiss the notion. "It is an amusing thought," she said. "You are too levelheaded for that work. With how things are run in the capital, it's a wonder we ever manage to keep the peace."

Seeing Avery's interest, she continued, her tone more serious, "Duke Vanguard is far too impulsive for my taste, but I cannot deny he has helped Arcadia maintain peace throughout his tenure. Far more than his predecessor."

Avery listened intently, absorbing the perspectives offered by both the Guild Master and the High Priestess. The Vanguard name was familiar to Avery as Theodore kept a close eye on his involvement within the Arcadian politics. It was often the duke and his knights whom Theodore referred to when discussing the dangerous game he played for the Traconian empire.

The duke held one of the highest positions among those Theodore hated, and Avery learned it was best to avoid discussion of the Vanguards altogether, else find Theodore in a bad mood. It seemed the duke's reputation for being cold and ruthless were not limited to the whisperings heard outside of the Arcadian borders.

"I've heard you're a hard worker, Avery," the Guild Master said, snapping Avery out of her thoughts. "I'm glad we could turn the situation to our advantage." Though he still wore a wide smile, Avery had a feeling the praise wasn't coming from Captain Adler.

"Thank you, sir." She forced a polite expression, and as the awkward silence stretched on, she shifted her gaze to Harris. To Avery's relief, Harris seemed to understand her plea for help and took the opportunity to steer the conversation. "Yes, well, we should really get to our lunch." He addressed both the Guild Master and the High Priestess, who seemed to understand they were not invited to stay for lunch. "I shall see you both tonight?"

The comment seemed to remind the Guild Master of something, and he checked the large clock on the wall. "Oh yes, we best get going. I need to get a few things together before tonight." He checked to see that the High Priestess was ready to leave before returning his attention to Avery. "It was a pleasure to meet you, Miss Avery. I'm sure I will be seeing much more of you."

The grin he gave her made her feel like future small talk was inevitable, and she silently hoped it would be a while before she would have to converse with the two again. It felt unnatural for them to be so warm toward her, considering the damage she'd caused the town.

The two departed the office, and Avery spent the remainder of the lunch retelling of her adventure in the ruins with the octoid, only leaving out the bits about hearing the sword whisper to her and the vision she experienced after she was hit by the recoil of her magic. The crescent shaped blade sat under a display case in the corner of the professor's office. Although the whispering seemed to no longer pester her, a strong beckoning drew her focus to the blade, and she had to resist the urge to follow it once more.

After lunch, Milo and Avery resumed their work, processing the remaining parts from the delivery well into the afternoon. Walking back to the guild hall, Milo paused to peer over the edge of the walkway, his eyes scanning the bustling Pioneer Plaza below.

"There's another guild meeting tonight," Milo mentioned, breaking the comfortable silence. "The council will be moving forward with plans to conduct more research, and they will be endorsing a field mission out to the dead zone."

"The dead zone?" Avery echoed, her curiosity piqued. "Why do they want to go out to a dead zone?"

"The guild and research facility have been eager to do some research out there. There's a lot more to learn about the mechoids and where they are coming from."

"And the church has always been against that," Avery

finished.

"Exactly," Milo agreed. "They think they've been lenient with the research that has already been done, but they believe that further research would only lead to more weapons rather than answers."

They continued walking down the long, winding road, Avery's mind racing to process all that had been said that day. Her thoughts were soon interrupted by Milo's next question.

"So, you're looking to join the Lunar Knights?"

Surprised by the directness of the question, Avery took a moment to respond. "Oh, yes, something like that."

"Best of luck to you, that's one tough gig," Milo said, his tone genuine rather than condescending. "You have to be the best of the best to join their ranks. I mean, even Rhyker didn't make the cut."

"Really?" Avery asked, her interest raised by the revelation the captain was not as perfect as he had seemed.

"Yeah, and he is by far one of the best swordsmen around."

Avery suppressed a groan, recalling a similar conversation with Leah. "That's what I keep hearing," she muttered under her breath, hoping to steer the conversation away from the captain as they continued their descent down the hill.

13
THE MEETING OF
THE MINDS

As they approached Pioneer Plaza, they observed the normal hustle of guild members and guards filing into the guild hall. Rhyker stood in his customary spot by the door, nodding to people as they passed by. Noticing the captain's oncoming glare, Avery took it as her cue to say goodbye to Milo and started making her way across the street to visit Leah.

The sound of an unpleasant grunt came moments before a hand caught her shoulder and forced her to turn back around. "Where are you going?" Harvey removed his hand and continued walking past her, toward the guild hall. "Let's go, kid."

She quickly followed behind, getting into step with him. "Why are we going to the guild meeting?"

He ignored her and proceeded to lead them into the guild hall. Avery kept at a close distance behind him, unable to avoid the captain's gaze as they traversed through the door. She tensed, anticipating his quick resistance to her accompanying Harvey. The two shared the threatening look of distrust, but he made no effort to prevent her from entering.

Harvey led Avery to the second level of the guild hall, a place she had only seen once before during Milo's tour on her first day of community service. The wide space was designed to accommodate a large audience, with rows of benches arranged in a semi-circle around a raised platform. The platform, bathed in soft, amber lighting, had three solitary chairs prominently positioned, each draped with the Farewell colors of silver and maroon. The room buzzed with the murmurs of conversation as more people filtered in, taking their seats on the benches.

Guiding her through the throng, Harvey steered past a large wooden podium at the front of the stage, where a woman in a modest but elegant black dress was adjusting a stack of papers. As they moved closer to the back of the room, Avery noticed a table set off to the side, covered with refreshments—pitchers of water, trays of biscuits, and fruit—provided to ensure the attendees could sustain themselves through what might be a lengthy meeting.

Finding seats among the audience, Harvey settled in, and Avery followed suit. Ignoring Avery's questioning stares, the old man reached into his pocket and pulled out a cigar. He paused for a moment before returning it to his pocket.

In an effort to avoid glaring at Harvey, Avery continued to survey the scene, observing as the High Priestess and Guild Master arrived from an office door at one end of the room. Both found their way into two of the chairs on stage. The Guild Master's eyes swept across the room, his expression brightening when his gaze settled momentarily on Harvey and Avery. High Priestess Sylvie's eyes followed suit, but instead of a smile, a subtle arch of her brow revealed her surprise upon spotting the two of them seated among the crowd.

Again, Avery looked to Harvey for some semblance of reason for their presence, but Harvey remained neutral to it all, not giving a glimmer of concern. The Guild Master and

High Priestess engaged in light conversation on stage while the audience continued to gather, and Avery wondered briefly if Captain Adler was to occupy the third and final chair. However, the question was quickly answered when Professor Colleymore made his way to the front of the room and took the seat.

Most of the chairs in the room were occupied by the time the meeting began. Avery caught the stares of a few people who quickly averted their eyes, rushing into hurried whispers among their neighbors. The High Priestess stood up, taking up the podium as the crowd simmered down to listen.

"Thank you everyone for joining us again for our meeting of the minds." She welcomed the audience. "We have a lot to cover this week, so let us begin."

The lights above the general audience dimmed slightly, creating a more central focus across the stage as the High Priestess continued, "For the first update tonight, it is with great sadness I am announcing that Trenton Bushnell has officially resigned his position as Director of the Farewell Research Facility. I am happy to report he was in good spirits these last few weeks, but despite his steady recovery, he wishes to pivot his time and energy to focus on his loved ones. There is a plan to honor his time and dedication to both the Research Facility and the betterment of Farewell during our Harvest festival this year, and I think we all know Trenton will not cease in his constant involvement in our community." She paused to wave a hand graciously toward Professor Colleymore. "In the interim of determining a new director, Professor Colleymore has agreed to continue to be our acting director and assist the facility in this time of transition." She offered the professor a courteous bow before turning back to the audience. "Now, I'm sure many of you are anxious to get into the more pressing matters from recent events. Let us hear from the Guild Master."

The Guild Master stood up and thanked the High Priestess as she regained her seat. Avery's attention was pulled toward the far side of the room where the captain eventually made his way into the meeting. He was leaning up against the wall, listening as the Guild Master commanded the stage.

"As you all know, this last week has had its own challenges. Although we were caught by surprise, the guard and the addition of our trained reinforcements were able to respond quickly enough without any fatal casualties. The same cannot be said on the mechoids' side." The Guild Master paused, allowing for a few laughs to break the tension throughout the room. "It has reminded us there is still much we do not know about them, and this incident has reinforced our views that it's necessary to do more research." He stood aside to motion to the other two sitting behind him. "Collectively, the three of us agreed it's time to endorse the effort of tracking the mechoids."

Harvey swore under his breath, loud enough he caught another raised eyebrow from the High Priestess. The Guild Master only smiled empathically, addressing the restless crowd. "This will be our first opportunity to be proactive rather than reactive. Captain Adler has agreed to lead these missions with his team. I am hoping there are others out there who can *volunteer* their time to the cause." The Guild Master's eyes landed on Avery and then on Harvey. "Especially after the damage done this week, we welcome *all* the help we can get."

Avery did not have to look at Harvey to guess what the Guild Master was implying.

"I assure you," the Guild Master continued, "that the council is prepared to delegate whatever resources needed to provide our community with a means to better predict and prepare for similar incidents in the future." He moved a few papers around on the podium, "Now, let's review some more of the upcoming plans for improving our community."

Avery found it difficult to concentrate on the community projects the Guild Master listed off. Her mind circled back through the proposed solution to the mechoid incident. She recalled Milo mentioning a trip to the dead zone was inevitable, and she did not think this field mission was a coincidence. She wondered how she would be expected to help since Rhyker's team would be gone. Did that mean she would not finish out her community service time until they returned?

It seemed Avery was not the only one losing focus as the meeting continued. She found Rhyker staring intently at a spot on the floor, not paying attention to anything that was said. By the way he was glaring at the ground, as if expecting it to ignite on the spot, she gathered he was similarly processing the information. Rhyker lifted his gaze from the ground up to Avery, and she quickly reverted her attention back to the stage.

The High Priestess was at the podium once more, explaining the church finished reviewing the planned town improvements for Pioneer Square, and they were ready to approve the changes. The younger woman wearing the black dress that matched the High Priestess, stepped forward from where she had been standing on the other side of the room. She walked with a subtle grace that made her seem weightless. Long brown hair was tucked behind her ears, and her smile could thaw any frozen heart. She reached the panel, handing out a document for the three chair seats to sign. With her task done, she stepped away from the stage and glided over to join Rhyker, who greeted her with an easy grin.

The stirring from the audience pulled Avery's attention away from the pair as there seemed to be an uncomfortable stirring when the High Priestess continued to address a list of concerns submitted by the Farewell residents. The report included an increase in the number of mechoid sightings, which upon investigation, were dismissed as the town being overly cautious and on edge from the incident in the week prior. The High Priestess closed the meeting by encouraging the community to continue to report any further sightings. Realizing the meeting was adjourned, Avery went to stand, relieved that they could step away from the crowd, but Harvey grabbed her arm, "Hold on kid, we ain't finished. Sit tight."

As instructed, Avery resumed her seat and watched the others file out of the room and down the stairs. Many people lingered to speak with the members of the panel, but eventually the room emptied until very few attending members remained. Rhyker walked with the young woman toward the stairs but stopped, looking back to see Harvey and Avery were still seated. He shared a few words with the woman who nodded her understanding and started her way down the stairs, alone.

Harvey stood from his chair and motioned for Avery to do the same, turning her attention to the Guild Master as he approached them.

"It was a pleasure to see you in another meeting, Harvey. Thank you for accepting my invitation!" The Guild Master reached out to shake Harvey's hand and then shifted the energetic gaze to Avery. "It's amazing how busy a retired man can get, even for an old friend."

Harvey grunted, "You know I wouldn't be here if you hadn't been so convincing." He shook the Guild Master's hand, then politely nodded to the High Priestess who left her chair to join them. She offered a smile, but Avery noticed the cautious glint in her eyes as she watched them closely.

"I figured there had to be a reason you joined us, General." Her suspicious glance was transferred over to the Guild Master. "What is the occasion, James?"

The Guild Master brought his hands together and let his wide smile work the room.

"I was hoping that he would agree to let Miss Avery accompany Captain Adler and his team on the retrieval mission."

Rhyker, who silently joined them, appeared to have been anticipating this and stepped in, "Sir, this was not what we discussed. I can't risk taking a civilian into a field mission like that."

The Guild Master was not deterred and only continued smiling, "She is not completely a civilian anymore, Captain. We have granted her guild rights."

A flash of annoyance showed on Rhyker's face, and he protested through a tight jaw. "Right, for the duration of her community service. A field mission is not an appropriate way to serve that time."

James favored the captain with a mischievous grin. "With the right candidate it could be."

Avery looked to Harvey, hoping for some guidance. He was studying the Guild Master, listening to him and the captain argue.

"What are we talking here, James? What are they after?"

"A Dozer, we need a few of their cores in order to finish a prototype that Harris' team has been working on."

The information caused Harvey to swear under his breath and look at Avery, who felt the other's stares join in. She did not understand why they wanted to send her out on the mission or why Harvey actually seemed to be considering the matter.

"Sir," Rhyker interjected again. "I cannot, in good conscious, take an untrained and *reckless* civilian out there. My team will have enough to worry about as it is."

The Guild Master shrugged slightly. "Professor Colleymore has mentioned she is well adept to the task. I think it would be a valuable use of her time here with us."

Both Avery and Harvey eyed Harris who shrugged sheepishly at the comment. The Guild Master turned back to Harvey. "You've been training her Harvey, is she up to the task?"

Avery was beginning to feel like they were ignoring how she was in the room with them. Harvey did not take his eyes off James. "Sure, she can handle it. But I can't peg why you'd want her to go. Seems like you should be able to come up with someone more experienced than her."

The Guild Master's grin grew wide again. "Unfortunately, as it stands, I cannot, and I think we have been offered a great opportunity to work with the cards dealt to us."

"If I may?" The High Priestess raised a hand gracefully out to gain the men's attention. "I think we are forgetting to ask Avery if she is comfortable with going on this mission to begin with," she interjected, turning all eyes on Avery.

Feeling the weight of their stares, Avery exchanged another glance with Harvey, but the old man only inclined his shoulders as if giving her a choice either way.

Briefly in her contemplation, she wondered if she would have been less inclined to agree had the captain's intense gaze not been there, practically daring her to test his patience. Coming to her decision, she addressed the Guild Master, making it a point to ignore Rhyker.

"I understand I owe a debt to the Farewell's people. I'm willing to contribute my time however the council sees fit."

The Guild Master beamed at her, clasping his hands loudly. "Excellent!" He turned to his co-chairs, considering the matter settled. "Shall we begin our debrief so we can get home before the night is over?"

The others agreed and turned to file into an office nearby. Rhyker quickly followed after the Guild Master, attempting to pull him aside.

Harvey picked up his walking stick he rested on a nearby chair and made his way to leave. "I need a drink," he grunted, not bothering to stop and address Avery's drilling glare.

She followed a few paces behind him as they made their way down the stairs. A shout came from above her as she went to clear the last of the steps.

"Hold it there, Blue Eyes."

She stopped and turned to find Rhyker descending the steps after her. His jaw was shut tight, and his nostrils flared slightly as he reached the bottom of the steps, where she was waiting for him. Avery heard the front doors to the hall shut, telling her Harvey left her there to deal with the captain.

Without a word, the captain motioned for her to follow, navigating her through a door that led into a side yard. The night sky reminded Avery how long she sat through the meeting. Two large lights illuminated the various training equipment scattered throughout the yard of the guild hall, apparently the training grounds for the Farewell guard. Several targets were scattered around the fence post, showing telltale signs of age and overuse. They passed through the center of the yard where a large clearing had been made. The ground in the area was bare aside from occasional dark marks where it looked like it had been burned. The captain did not stop until they reached the middle of the large flat clearing.

"Draw your blade," he commanded, pulling out his own sword.

She stared at him incredulously, taking a cautious step backward. "Excuse me?"

He playfully grinned, but his words came out cool with a sharp edge that told her he fully intended on seeing it through. "Spar with me. Show me you won't just be dead weight if you go out there."

Even in his seriousness, there was a hint of a taunt that dug at her. Avery slowly reached a hand behind her shoulder and gripped the hilt of her sword, refusing to let him believe she was at all frightened.

"Is this really necessary?" she asked, but by the time her sword was out in front of her, he was dashing at her with a speed that sent her spinning.

Despite the sudden advance, Avery managed to block his attack, and their swords clashed loudly as they collided. Rhyker wasted no time, pushing off the blade to follow it up with another strike. In quick succession, he delivered his strikes, giving her no time to think. She could only react with each blow that came in, realizing with every hit that Rhyker was much faster, and packed a devastating power behind his advance.

Avery felt herself growing frustrated as he gave her no room for error, tightening each of their movements as they traded back and forth. Finally in her focus, she found enough of a gap in one of his attacks and managed to execute a parry that forced him to go on the defensive and protect himself from her own attacks. Taking the opportunity, she gained her ground back and could see the captain forcing the quick adjustments. However, the opportunity did not last, and he countered with a blow that staggered her, sending her sword flying out of her hand. He followed his blade through until it reached dangerously close to her neck. Avery froze as he towered over her, not willing to test the sharpness of the blade that threatened her skin, staring daggers into the captain's narrowed eyes.

Rhyker searched her, as if trying to make up his mind. Avery forced calm and steady breaths, frustrated and suppressing the increasing urge to use magic. Neither of them moved for an uncomfortably long period of time, until he finally lowered his sword.

"You're reckless, you had the advantage, and you wasted it."

"Thanks," she scoffed, "I'll keep that in mind the next time I'm forced to spar with a lunatic." Avery's own voice matched the chilling tone he gave her. She found where Lightbringer had fallen and picked it up.

Ryker put his sword away at his side and eyed her, unimpressed, crossing his arms over his chest. "Am I supposed to take you seriously?"

She returned Lightbringer to its sheath, feeling her already increased pulse rise. "It's funny, I was wondering the same about you." She gave the captain an equally annoyed glance. "I'm not here to impress you, *Captain*. I didn't realize I would be volunteered for your team."

Unmoved by her boldness, he let out a hollow laugh, his eyes reading into her as she glared up at him. "You'll have to do a lot more than wave around that pretty sword of yours to be put on my team. This isn't an invitation."

She raised an eyebrow, trying to determine if he was annoyed or more amused with her now. "Great, then we shouldn't have a problem. I'm just here to play nice and get this over with, remember?"

He stepped up to her, tilting his head down so she could fully take in a surprisingly playful smile, "Alright Blue Eyes, if you are coming out in the field with us, then one thing has to be extremely clear. I don't need you endangering yourself or my team because you fail to follow the instructions given to you. If you disobey a direct order, I will send you packing, and James' little experiment will be over."

Avery met his gaze unyielding and holding her ground. She brought two fingers up to her forehead flicking them in a lazy salute. "Yes, Captain." She smiled innocently.

Not amused, he brushed past her, barely avoiding her shoulder as he did. "Report in at the usual time tomorrow. We will be leaving in a few days and there is a lot of work to do." He did not bother waiting for her to answer and made his way back inside the guild hall, leaving her alone in the empty training yard.

Avery took the cue and left, retreating to the Big Hen where she found Harvey sitting behind the bar working on a glass of whiskey as promised. Sinking into the seat across from him she let out a frustrated sigh.

She threw him a glare. "Thanks for the heads up on that one."

Harvey grunted and took another sip. His eyes swept over her as if to check if any damage had been done. "Rhyker rough you up?"

"He tried to," she said, letting out a frustrated sigh, "but I managed. I'm afraid this situation won't improve our chances of being friends."

Harvey let out a real laugh and leaned over the bar top. "Between you and me kid, I think he's just sore."

"What do you mean?"

"Rhyker has been trying to get me to work with him since I can remember. Seemed to think I was some kind of guru." He rolled his eyes as if annoyed at the very thought of it.

Avery's eyes widened in genuine surprise. "Why didn't you ever teach him?"

Harvey set down his glass loudly. "Does nobody in this goddamn town know what the word retired means?"

Avery raised an eyebrow at him, his outrage helped crack

a smile on her face. Harvey shook his head. "Besides, he didn't need any help."

She surveyed the old man again, another thought coming back to her. "High Priestess Sylvie called you 'General'. You've never told me where you learned to fight like you do."

Harvey took the whiskey glass and emptied it before he brought the glass back down to the counter with a loud clank. "And I don't plan on telling you now."

Annoyed, she rolled her eyes, settling herself on the next line of questioning. "Fine, then why am I being asked to go with Rhyker's team?"

He pulled out a cigar and began to go through the routine of lighting it. "I'm not sure, and I don't like it. But I trust James to an extent."

"You don't think it's too risky to go?"

The old man shook his head assuredly. "No, despite Rhyker's whining, I know that kid can handle himself and the people he takes along. Plus, I think some more field experience would do you some good." He narrowed his eyes at her and pointed the cigar at her accusingly. "You're getting overconfident again. Going out there will give you a taste of what you need to know."

At the comment, Avery wondered what Harvey would have said had he witnessed the spar with Rhyker, but she decided he would have yelled at her for dropping her sword again.

"Right, well, I'll do my best not to end up getting killed."

"And don't go pissing off Rhyker either," he barked at her, "although I don't know if you can really help yourself on that front." He favored her with a rare smile and refilled his whiskey glass.

14
A FAMILIAR BARRIER

"Really Avery, this doesn't seem right!" Leah protested, mortified to hear the news that Avery would be accompanying the captain's team to the dead zone. "I mean really, how could they take you with them? It's terribly dangerous!"

Avery shuffled the stack of books she held in her hands, assisting Leah with putting away some of the new books that arrived in the latest delivery. She addressed her friend with a slight grin. "And here I thought you would be ecstatic that I would be stuck with Captain Brooding. I can learn about all his favorite things for you."

Leah shot a disapproving look over her shoulder. "You aren't taking this seriously."

"I am!" Avery laughed. "...But I trust Harvey's judgement. Besides, he's right, I need more experience."

That sentiment was proven earlier that morning during her training. Logan, her usual sparring partner, had not shown up, which meant that Harvey ensured any of the confidence she had gained in her growing skills was quickly shattered and replaced by his barking corrections at her. Although infuriating, she knew Harvey's assessment was right. With her magic developing, Avery struggled to keep it contained in moments when her body would instinctually defend itself. A missed block with her sword often resulted in the strike being blocked by a shield of light, repelling both her and Harvey backward, followed by his vocal disapproval for her lack of control.

"Exactly," Leah practically shouted, setting down her stack of books onto the table in a huff, "It's as Malcom said. It's awfully early to be throwing you into the dead zones."

The author was equally displeased to hear of the council's request and decision, leaving the bookshop shortly after hearing Avery's recap, apparently with the idea of finding Harris to give him a piece of his mind.

"I mean you barely made it out of those ruins." Leah continued, "Who knows what you'll be up against out there?"

It was Avery's turn to shoot Leah a glare. "Your confidence in me is *so* reassuring."

"Oh, stop that!" Leah glared back. "You know what I mean, Avery. You're talking about going into a death trap that most guards spend years training just to go *near*."

"Which I'll have to do anyway if I'm going to get to the capital," Avery interjected, "and besides, Rhyker had the opportunity to stop me from going when we sparred. I don't think he would let me go if he didn't think I could hold my own out there."

Leah froze, watching Avery with wide eyes. "You *what?*"

Avery fought to withhold a grin, having saved that bit in case she needed something to distract her friend from worrying about the upcoming field assignment. The tactic worked like a charm, completely shifting the tone of the discussion. Avery was forced to recall the events of the encounter several times, only saved from repeating it again when they heard the jingle of the store bell sound, finding Malcom returned.

"By the Goddess," the author muttered, flustered as he found a seat and fanned his face with a hand. "They are positively set on letting you go."

"I appreciate your concern." Avery tried not to sound annoyed, hoping the topic would not encourage Leah to return to her rant. "But as I mentioned before, I am willing to go." Malcom pursed his lips, clearly not happy with the prospect.

Wanting to avoid any further dwelling on the topic, Avery set down the handful of books, addressing him. "I was wondering, Mal," she started, appealing to his soft side. "I've heard of great things about my mother's ability to use magic, but no one has mentioned if she had any special affinity."

"Oh, yes." The author released his tight jaw, his mood visibly shifting. "Amelia excelled in her use of counter magics. She would have been an excellent dueler had she had any interest."

"Counter magics?" Leah asked, handing Malcom a glass of water to combat the heat of the hot day.

"The use of a counter magic is to nullify the effects of another," Avery stated. "Typically used to create barriers to protect the caster or completely stop a magic from forming."

Seeing the surprise on Leah and Malcom's faces, Avery clarified, "I read about it in a book. Although, I don't understand. How does one have an affinity for that?"

Malcom contemplated, slightly shrugging his shoulders. "Harris is probably a better resource to ask, but I believe it had to do with her ability to detect what type of magic another mage was casting before it had a chance to form, giving her the advantage."

"Perhaps that explains why my body violently tries to protect me against Theodore's outbursts," Avery suggested, regretting having mentioned it after glimpsing the horrified look on their faces. The topic of her *curse* still being an uncomfortable one for them.

"Speaking of," Malcom eased into the conversation. "How are you handling those now? I haven't heard mention of them for some time now."

"They still come, although much fewer and farther between each one. The last was the morning I went into those ruins."

In truth, Avery tried not to think about it, knowing there was no telling what it meant. There was an unsettling feeling that always lingered whenever she tried to guess at what game Theodore was playing. The others stared at her with fearful eyes, and she avoided them, looking out the windows of the bookshop to see the setting sun.

"Well, I should head back to Cecelia's. I'll make sure to let you both know when I return," she promised. Offering them both a reassuring nod, she slipped out of the bookstore and made her way toward the farmhouse.

◆ ◆ ◆

The two days leading up to their set departure date was spent preparing the equipment and familiarizing themselves with their objective. Avery assisted Milo with creating travel packs that contained rations and other supplies, while also leaving enough space for them to carry back any salvaged parts. Thanks to the summer heat, they only needed to pack bed rolls and a few light tarps in case they chanced the rain. They would rely on making a fire if the temperature dropped enough to warrant it, and traveling with the captain ensured that would not be any issue.

Their packs were piled in the corner of Milo's workshop where they gathered for a quick briefing the night before they were set to leave. Milo gingerly took a polishing cloth over the surface of a cylindrical contraption while Avery helped configure the glyph he would use to document their finding.

Their destination was referred to as the Solstice City dead zone. "Or more accurately, to the perimeter of the dead zone," Milo clarified. "We shouldn't need to travel too far inside to find enough suitable Dozers to harvest."

Reya and the captain joined them in the workshop, adding two more heavy packs to the pile. The last few days proved that Rhyker could no longer avoid Avery while she worked with his team. He rarely spoke to her, only offering the occasional direction when needed. Following Harvey's advice, she tried to stay out of his way, doing her best to ignore his aura's vicious tugging.

Reya kneeled beside one of the added packs, flipping the fold over so she could examine the contents. "The hooks are locked and loaded," she elaborated, seeing Avery's curious stare, "We use them to anchor down the bigger mechs when we can."

Rhyker nodded, eyeing the device Milo held. "I got approval for you to bring the sling, but you know how it goes, keep it put away until we get out of town."

Milo let out an audible cheer as he made himself busy, securing away the contraption in a case that seemed specifically designed to fit his prized device.

"Sling?" Avery asked eyeing the contents of the box suspiciously. Milo shook his head excitedly. "Don't you worry, I'll show you later," he assured her in a hushed tone

Reya perched herself on a nearby crate, crossing her arms comfortably as she watched Milo rifle through one of the packed bags again. "So, what's the plan? We go in, grab the cores and come back?"

"Uh-huh," Milo chirped. "That's the first phase of the project. Professor Bradac has enough crawler sensors, so her team will work on developing the beacon links while we are gone. They are hoping to have a few ready for us to install by the time we return." He haphazardly stuffed the contents back into the bag that would surely need to be repacked once more. "The grid should be functional by Fall."

"What is the purpose of this grid?" Avery asked, handing Milo the glyph back.

"It will work as an early warning system for Farewell. Each of the beacons will be placed at intervals in the surrounding area, set to send a signal back to the control console being built in the research facility." It was impossible to misinterpret his joy on the topic as his enthusiasm spilt over in rapid, excited speech. "Which means anytime a mechoid gets within range of the beacons, we will know where they are and where they are coming from."

Rhyker nodded, making a point to hold eye contact with Avery. "That way, if someone decides to bring hordes of mechoids to our borders again, we will be able to respond quicker."

Avery held her tongue, unable to think of anything to say that would not rile the captain.

"Anyway," Milo continued, stirring the conversation away from controversial topics, "recovering these cores will jumpstart the rest of the project. So, we can expect our return to be highly anticipated."

"We best get an early start tomorrow then," Rhyker added, surveying the stack of equipment for a final appraisal. "We will meet here in the morning and head out before dawn."

The others agreed and left the guild hall, scattering their separate ways in the plaza. After checking in with Cecelia, Avery retreated to her room in the farmhouse.

Admittedly, her nerves were touched with the anxiety of the field assignment, and she was restless as she tried to sleep. Theodore remained dangerously absent in delivering his usual punishment, leaving her night undisturbed.

Though, she was never so lucky as to escape him entirely. Her dreams were still haunted with visions of her mother's death and his wicked yellow eyes upon the realization of what he had done to Amelia. Unable to quiet her agitated mind, she could only remind herself of her purpose and hope that she would continue to have time to get stronger.

15
S.L.N.G

The next morning, Avery arrived at the guild hall before any of the others, and to her surprise it took very little convincing of the night guard to let her into the hall. The early hour found the hall void of any life, aside from the singular guard at his post, awaiting the morning relief to come. Finding Milo's workshop locked, Avery settled herself on a bench in the common room and pulled out Lightbringer, utilizing the extra time to clean her blade.

The wave of Rhyker's aura swept in as the captain crossed the threshold into the common area, nodding to the guard as he made his way further inside. His eyes scanned over her, but he said nothing as he deposited his pack on the table where she worked. They sat in an uncomfortable silence while they waited. She suppressed the shivers she felt from the captain's aura and hoped that the prolonged exposure to him for the duration of the field assignment would dull out the feeling.

The silence was interrupted when Milo's relentless energy tore into the room. "Morning Avery! You ready for some field action?" he asked, handing her some toast he was carrying. His cheerful tone was refreshing versus the icy shoulder she was growing accustomed to from Rhyker.

"I suppose I have to be." She accepted the buttered

toast, thanking him as he buzzed around the table. He practically danced as he made his way down the hall to unlock the workshop.

"Don't let him fool you," Reya's voice chimed in suddenly from behind Avery. The guard's quiet footsteps often made it easy for her to approach undetected. "He's not a morning person." She slid onto the bench next to Avery, her eyes traveling to where Lightbringer was resting on the table. "Where did you get that?"

A proud smile momentarily swept across Avery's face. "Harvey gave it to me after complaining that I was being too sloppy with another sword."

"Can I see it?" she asked, Avery nodded handing it over for Reya to inspect. She turned the blade over in her hands a few times. "Do you know where it was forged?"

Avery shook her head. "I never asked Harvey where he got it."

"It's well balanced." Reya handed the sword back. "Reminds me of the blades my grandfather used to make. He has a special forge he built himself and uses magic to craft his swords."

Milo returned to the group, one of the packs slung over his shoulder and holding out more toast to the two of them. The captain swooped in, nabbing a piece as he rejoined them. He surveyed his team, taking extra care to avoid Avery's eye. "Alright, let's get moving."

Together, the group exited Farewell, with packs and equipment disbursed among them. They traversed both by paved road and by less traveled paths among the forest where they were forced into single file marching order. Reya and Rhyker took turns leading the group, occasionally forcing fallen branches and other overgrown foliage out of their path. The group often slowed their pace when coming upon shredded remains of forest animals or unnatural disruption to the surrounding forest, indicators that there may be mechoids roaming nearby. Reya scouted ahead while the others kept a distance, awaiting any confirmation of a sighting.

Their first day of travel passed uneventfully. Mechoid signs only led to finding the cybernetic beasts had long since moved on. As dusk approached, Milo prepared to shut off the glyph, and the group found a suitable place to camp. They laid out their bedrolls just as the sun was setting. Rhyker effortlessly started a fire, and the group gathered around it, eating and resting while they conversed until establishing the watch order and turning in for the night.

The second day was equally uneventful. The mechoids were strangely absent on the journey forward. The night was set to be much of the same, she finished her shift overlooking the surrounding camp, almost positive that the captain refused to actually sleep during her allocated watch. Milo relieved her of the post, and at some point, she managed to fall asleep. In her dreams, she was in the leather chair of Theodore's study, staring into the yellow eyes that could see right through her. A jolt of pain woke her up, and it did not take her long to realize that Theodore must have had a sudden burst of anger that needed to be directed *somewhere*.

Avery managed the pain quietly, doing her best to avoid waking the others who slept by the fire nearby. To her relief, the seizing pain did not go on long; her body released the vicious hold just as sweat began to dampen her brow. Feeling the need to stretch out her sore muscles, she pushed herself up to a sitting position, startled to find the captain was silently kneeled beside her.

Worried green eyes looked over her. "You okay there, Blue Eyes?" His voice was barely above a whisper with none of the usual icy edge. Avery felt her face burn, and she shook her head, wondering how long he had been there watching her.

"Just a bad dream." She pushed herself up to stand, her muscles rioting as she moved.

He rose with her, unconvinced, the sharpness in his tone returning entirely. "Must have been one hell of a dream."

Avery did not say anything and walked out of the camp, desperate to get some fresh air untainted by Rhyker. The stinging set in throughout her body as she found a large tree trunk to lean against, trying to ignore the feeling that the captain was still keeping an eye on her. It was some time she spent there, quietly staring through the trees into the night sky, until finally the soreness in her body subsided to an occasional ache.

By the time she convinced herself to return to the camp, the captain repositioned himself a little way up the hill that overlooked the camp. The vantage point made it easy to monitor the surrounding area.

"I'm beginning to think you don't ever sleep," he quietly called to her when she joined him.

Avery ignored his comment, adjusting the strap that held Lightbringer on her back.

"I can take the last of the watch if you want to rest."

He shook his head, not making any effort to move. "You should try to get some more rest. I don't need you slacking tomorrow because you didn't sleep."

"I'll be fine." She propped herself against a nearby tree and stared out at the rapidly fleeting night.

"Right," he muttered quietly, his tone suggesting his doubt, "we will want to get going soon anyway."

A silence came between them as they both stared into the night. The time traveling with the captain helped her become more familiar with his rhythm and his stoic mannerisms.

Reluctantly, it was not hard to see what made the captain so intriguing to Leah and her obsessive friends. Aside from his sharp features, he carried himself with purpose, his quick instincts and ingenuity kept his team alive over the years. Their short spar together was more than enough to show Avery the others were not exaggerating about his skills with a sword.

Another, more unsettling thought occurred to her as she imagined how strong the Lunar Knights must be if the captain's skills were not up to their standards. Avery turned to take Rhyker in, causing his green eyes to shift onto her. She held his gaze, her mind searching for a way to break out of the unnerving tension.

"From the sounds of it, your team does this often," she started, trying not to sound the least bit combative. "Have you been out to this particular dead zone before?"

He showed his surprise that she had broken the silence with the slightest raise of his brow. "A few times." He shrugged. "It's not often we get sent out there. I can't say I am glad to be going back, but it's a good change of pace from the day-to-day work."

Finding his casual tone refreshing, she pressed on. "How long have you been a captain?"

"About five or six years now; it all starts to blur. I started pretty young when James was in need of someone to lead a team, and I fit the picture." He fully turned his head to face her, the amused expression returning. "I've now given you two for free, do I get to ask a question now?"

She found herself giving him a single short laugh. "I figured there would be a catch since this is the most you've said to me all trip." She leaned back on the tree and shrugged her shoulders. "Depends on what you want to know."

Rhyker watched her in his contemplation, but after a few moments, he shook his head. "I'll bank the question for now." He stood up and stretched out. "You can owe me one later."

She cocked an eyebrow up at him as he went to pass by her. "I didn't realize I would be loaning it to you."

He laughed, pausing as he crossed in front of her. "Sometimes we get more than we bargained for." He gave her a satisfied smirk when he watched her expression settle on a glare, walking off in the direction of the camp. Unable to think of a suitable response, she watched him start his patrol around their camp, annoyed at herself for letting him get to her.

◆ ◆ ◆

The next morning, Avery did her best to show no signs of slowing down despite the nearly sleepless night. Milo, as warned by Reya, disliked getting up so early and grumbled about their departure. He joked with Rhyker, who seemed *perfectly* capable of having normal conversations with his team.

Her own association with both Milo and Reya seemed to be growing with every passing day. Both had no opposition to conversing with her while they walked. In fact, they encouraged it as they prodded Avery for more details about herself. They were growing accustomed to her providing vague responses or avoiding the subject all together, but they did not seem to hold it against her.

On the other hand, although she and Rhyker managed somewhat of a civil conversation the night before, there was an understanding between the two of them where direct conversation was kept to a minimum. The situation suited Avery just fine, as she had the sneaking suspicion he was trying to get under her skin whenever they did manage to talk.

As another afternoon rolled over, Reya returned from scouting ahead at a trot, signaling to the group to stop. "We have a flock of Drones up ahead. Five of them at my count but there could be others lurking around."

The report was directed at Rhyker, the first real sighting of the mechoids since they left Farewell. The term Drone was used as a nickname for any of the bird-like mechoids that patrolled the skies. Milo's sketch books were filled with depictions of the mechanical menaces, which showcased the variety of different models their team had come across over the years.

Reya led them to the peak of a hill where they could see down into a field of tall grass. From a distance, one could have mistaken the scene for a flock of vultures congregating around the carcass of a larger animal. The light reflected off the dark metallic wings as they shuffled around, giving away their artificial engineering.

"There isn't enough cover in that field," Milo observed, "We will stick out if we go through it, they will spot us as soon as we reach the clearing. Unless you want to backtrack to avoid them, we are going to need to take them on." There was an eagerness as he eyed Rhyker for direction.

The captain also seemed to pick up on this, raising a skeptical eyebrow at him.

"Do they have anything we need?" Rhyker asked. "Or is this a field test?"

Milo grinned. "Their sensors are always useful, especially with there being so many. We have a higher chance of success." He eyed the captain with a hint of disapproval. "That is *if* you leave us with any salvageable parts."

"So don't go for the head, that's manageable." Rhyker agreed and began his descent toward the mechoids. "Reya, you're with me. Blue Eyes, stick with Milo." He called over his shoulder. Milo hastily dropped his pack down, unstrapping the thick black case he was carrying.

"What's that?" Avery asked, watching as he pulled out the cylindrical contraption.

"This beauty is the prototype I've been working on." Milo beamed, "the S-L-N-G," he spelled out. "It uses Spectral beams of amplified Light to Nullify mechoids with a lock on Guidance system." He rattled off, barely giving Avery enough time to process the concept. "I built it using the stunner from a crawler. By adjusting the amount of concentrated light, it can be used to stun or pierce through the mechoids." He took a power cell out of his bag that looked to come from a Prowler. "Unfortunately, the stronger the blast, the faster I go through these." He popped the power cell into the side of the SLNG, grinning widely at Avery. "It's a good thing I brought extras!"

"How does it work?" Avery asked, watching down the hill as Rhyker and Reya made their way into the grassy field. Milo was right, the Drones caught sight of the group as soon as the two entered the field. Two of the Drones immediately took to the sky, demonstrating the large wingspan. The Drones that remained maintained a watchful eye on the approaching threat.

Milo held his prototype up, aiming the open end in the direction of where the mechoids began to circle around his fellow team members. Milo peered through a small lens mounted to the top of the device. The SLNG started to hum, a small volatile spark of light ignited and began to form there. The light was gaining in size with every trickling moment that passed. The humming intensified into its crescendo, where the intense beam of light was suddenly released from its charge, ripping through the air and piercing through the body of one of the flying mechs. The Drone dropped from sky, plummeting down into the field.

"Like that!" Milo's face lit up in a permanent smile as he admired his work.

The other stationary Drones took flight, joining the remaining mechoid while Milo charged up another attack. The SLNG activated once more, striking another Drone out of the sky. In unison, the remaining three mechoids dove downwards, their long steel beaks tore through the air like blades, targeting Rhyker and Reya. Even from the distance, Avery sensed the surge of magic coursing through her veins as a tingling heat spread through her body. Her pulse quickened, her senses sharpening as she watched Rhyker focus, his eyes locked on the approaching mechoids. The air around them vibrated as he summoned a shimmering red shield. The Drones were nearly upon them, and she felt the intensity of the magic deepen, the shield solidifying just in time. The mechoids crashed into it with a deafening impact, their steel shells fracturing and shattering against the barrier's energy.

The humming of the SLNG sounded again, and Avery found Milo aiming it at another incoming flock of Drones at the other edge of the forest. The subsequent attack hit the first of the Drones, causing it to collide with another, taking both down. Two more remained and continued heading toward the captain. Alerted to the additional mechoids, Rhyker turned to face them, his sword at the ready, igniting in flames as he sent the blade through the steel body of the nearest one. The blow sent the mechoid hurtling back from the force of flames that the other machine could not avoid, meeting the same fate as the others.

"I mean really," Milo stared exasperated, holding up the remains of one of the Drones once they descended the hill to regroup. "Did you even try to avoid their heads?"

Rhyker peered over the scene, picking up the charred

remains of the mechoid. It was missing a wing, the word "RANGER" barely visible along the side. The captain detached the head, tossing it to Milo as he grinned childishly. "Saved that one."

Milo swore loudly but laughed as he extracted the sensors. Avery dug in to help, sorting through the remaining mechs. Out of the nine, they were able to produce two working sensors before continuing their set path.

◆ ◆ ◆

"How are we supposed to test out the new girl if all we are coming across are Drones?" Milo whined jokingly after Reya rejoined the group to report the continued absence of mechoids. The setting sun warned them it was time to set up camp, and the group was ready to rest their overworked feet. To her surprise, Rhyker chuckled at Milo's complaint, casting a quick grin her way. "Don't go picking a fight for her, Milo. The last thing I need is for her to start glowing again."

Milo and Reya exchanged a puzzled side glance, then looked to Avery for clarification. She returned the same confused expression, much to the amusement of Rhyker who declined to elaborate when Milo tried to press him.

During her watch later that night, her mind was fixated on the magic Rhyker had used to eliminate the Drones. Other than producing a few shields to block attacks, she had not learned how to start utilizing magic on the offensive side of things. It was difficult to think of anything else other than blocking attacks when sparring and even if she could find an opening, it was a whole other struggle to concentrate on both using magic and the sword. Milo's demonstration with the SLNG gave her the impression that perhaps she could learn to manipulate her own ability to channel light into a powerful strike. She would have to ask Harvey when she returned if he could show her how, and with any luck, she would have an easier time learning to control the magic over time.

A faint blink of a light caught Avery's attention, and she abandoned her thoughts to study the source. Her vantage point gave her a fairly open view of the prairie surrounding them. From within the tree line, Avery could see several Prowlers dodging in and out of the brush, their metallic shells catching the light from the full moon. At first glance, it appeared that the beasts were running in a loop around the trees where they hunted, but then Avery realized she was not seeing the same beasts but rather many of them traveling together in a line. Avery counted them again to be sure, but they were moving so rapidly that she couldn't keep track.

Two red lights emitted from the tree line, another Prowler stepping out into the moonlight, but traveling in a different direction from the others. It slowly moved toward their camp, stopping in the middle of the clearing. It waited there, and Avery got the sense it was staring directly at her. It was an odd mech, besides the red lights, there was something off about it, but Avery could not quite put her finger on what it was, nor did she understand why it seemed to be frozen, watching her.

The rest of the pack of Prowlers moved on without it, continuing their hunt further up toward the cliffs and disappearing from sight. They were still dangerously close, and Avery stood up from her post, determined to take action. She made her way down the hill to intercept the red-eyed mech, but halted, her mind at odds with her body. While she could take on the mechoid without assistance, she could already imagine the earful she would get from the captain if he were to discover she was leaving her post and investigating a disturbance without alerting him.

She groaned, backtracking in the captain's direction

despite her aversion to dealing with his insistence that she be left out of combat where possible. She only managed to get only get within a few feet of the captain before he lifted his head in alert, sitting up to take in her approach.

"A large group of Prowlers are hunting not far from here," she said quickly, not bothering to keep her voice lowered. "I've counted at least seven."

Rhyker narrowed his eyes, but he was not glaring at her, rather he looked confused as he took in the information. He stood up, grabbing his sword from where it was set out beside him.

"What's the matter?" Milo mumbled, turning over in his sleep. He lifted his head up, seeing the two of them standing, their blades pulled out as they did another survey of the area.

"Everyone be on alert," Rhyker commanded, which was enough to get Reya and Milo up and moving.

Leading Rhyker to where she had left her post, Avery pointed down the prairie where she spotted the mechoids gathering. They silently scanned the area, watching for any signs of movement. The deep uncertainty pestered her, her anxiety growing with every moment that passed without a sign of the cybernetic beasts. Time passed by in an agonizingly quiet concentration. Avery regretted going to the captain so soon after spotting the creatures. She should have waited to see which direction they were moving. It was hard to understand how they managed to get out of view so quickly.

Rhyker's deep sigh came after no more signs of the disturbance. He shook his head slightly and turned to her. "Get some rest, Blue Eyes. I'll take the rest of the watch." He got the Reya and Milo's attention, waving them back to camp.

Not moving from where she stood, she aimed a glare

at the captain. "I don't need to rest. I know what I saw."

The captain searched her, she could not get a read on whether or not he believed her. After neither broke the eye contact, he gave a slight shake of his head and sheathed his sword. Annoyed, she tightened her grip on Lightbringer, keeping her eyes narrowed at him. "The last thing I desire is to deal with your brooding."

"They must have gone back into the forest," Milo interjected, rejoining the two, which finally managed to get the pair of them to break off their glares. "Probably picked up a strong signal somewhere-" He started to explain but was interrupted by Reya's shout.

"Captain!" she called out, the sound of her sword striking into metal rang in the air. They all took off in her direction, finding Reya as she pulled her sword out of a Prowler's chest. Three more Prowlers descended upon her and many more of the beasts flanked their group on all sides. A howling echoed around them, and she felt the magic stirring right before Rhyker sent a barrier, protecting Reya from two of mechs that surrounded her.

The humming of the SLNG came from beside her as Milo aimed for one of the mechoids closing the distance between them. The beam of light soared through the air, barely hitting the mechoid in the front shoulder. Milo cursed loudly, blaming the short distance for the missed shot.

Unfazed by the hit, the Prowler leaped at him only to find Avery's sword tearing through the exposed side, severing enough of the machine to render it useless. Finding it unable to get up, she exchanged a reassuring nod with Milo and quickly moved on to the next mechoid pursuing them.

Fully engrossed in the encounter, she took on each of the Prowlers, countering the claws and jaws that relentlessly tried to tear apart her skin. Two Prowlers flanked her, and she barely had time to register the sound of the SLNG unloading a shot, hitting one of the mechoids square in the chest. The impact did not pierce through the steel of the mechoid's frame. Instead, the Prowler seized up, stunned by the blast. Avery took the opportunity to sink her sword into its power cell and used a foot to quickly kick off the beast to free her sword, driving the blade into the side of other nearby Prowler.

"Not bad for the new girl," Reya called from behind her. Avery turned around to find Milo and Reya smiling, all of them catching their breath as they searched around for anymore. Avery felt her already hot face flush and she braced herself. Milo clapped a hand on her shoulder.

"That was excellent!" He beamed. "Although, do me a favor and watch the sensors. Don't be a Rhyker and just melt through them. It makes my job so much harder."

Avery laughed, still trying to catch her breath. She went to turn, nearly colliding with Rhyker who joined the group.

"Alright, this isn't show and tell." His words were sharp, and his eyes seemed uneasy as they traced the tree line. "There is no use in us trying to stay here. Let's quickly salvage what we can and get moving."

"There should be one more," Avery said, giving the captain a puzzled look. A cold sinking feeling erupted in the depths of her gut, her eyes frantically searching around the surrounding area. "I counted at least seven. One had red eyes."

Milo did his own sweep of the area. "Its night vision must be malfunctioning. With a pack of Prowlers that size, I'm not surprised that a few would be defective."

"All the more reason to get moving," Rhyker added. "We don't want to be around if more were alerted to this area."

Milo and Reya nodded, taking their orders, quickly

moving to get their camp packed up. Avery kept her eyes on the surrounding area, finding it harder to dismiss the strange mechoid's presence. Her eyes found the captain watching her, but when she did not feel compelled to say anything he shook his head, his slight smirk making an appearance. "Are you expecting some sort of praise?"

Avery narrowed her eyes at him, feeling her irritation level rise again. "Not from you."

She left him there, finding Milo to aid in harvesting mechoid parts.

◆ ◆ ◆

Regardless of their early start, the group did not rest again until the moon nearly made its full rotation into the next night. Exhausted, Avery managed to get a decent bit of rest before she once again found herself on the night watch. Rhyker's voice came well before she expected to be relieved from her post. She had been lost in thought, admiring the full moon when the captain made his approach.

"I can take it from here, Blue Eyes. I can't sleep. Might as well let you rest."

She looked up at him, seeing his attempt at a civil interaction. The few days in the forest were starting to show in a shadowed beard. Avery pulled the hood of her cloak down and eyed him with one brow raised.

"I'm beginning to think you just don't trust me to keep watch."

He let out a soft chuckle and sat down beside her. "If last night showed me anything, it's that those eyes of yours will find trouble." He stared up at the moon and eased back into a more relaxed position. "I can't shake this bad feeling. I've made this trip quite a few times, I can't say I've ever seen a pack of Prowlers working like that. It may explain why we've only run into a few Drones."

The pulsing of his aura made her uncomfortably aware

of how close he was. She tried to ignore it, focusing on his voiced concerns. "You think they are evolving?"

"I don't know, but that encounter tells me they are getting smarter."

"There was something different about them." She tried recalling the strange Prowler that she spotted amongst the pack. "I travelled a great distance to Farewell without encountering any mechoids. Not until I ran into you and that Prowler in those ruins."

It had been a surprise to both herself and Rhyker that she had shared that information. He sat upright and tilted his head to get a better look at her, clearly turning the information over in his mind. Avery averted his gaze and stared back out at the night, wishing she had not said anything.

It didn't take long for him to break the silence, the questions shining in his eyes. "How is it you made it this far in life for that to be your first mechoid encounter?"

She couldn't have honestly admitted the question surprised her. Between how she had reacted to the mechoid when they first met and her prolonged discussions on mechoids with Milo, she assumed it was only a matter of time before someone would question how little knowledge she had of the creatures. Keeping her gaze fixed on the moon, a faint smile tugged at her lips

"Is that how you want to use your one question?"

He chuckled. "I should have known better than to expect a straight answer from you." The captain paused to throw his head back in fake wonder. "Let me guess..." he prattled on as if it was some game, "you come from some noble family overseas and to nobody's surprise, managed to get yourself into some trouble. Now you must prove yourself by going to Uncle Harvey for some sword lessons?"

The thought amused her, and she reluctantly let out a

small laugh. "That's it, how'd you guess?" She rolled her eyes, and without looking at him, she stood up to make her way back to camp. "Let me know if you need a break from the watch." She quietly called over her shoulder, not waiting for his response as she left him there, pulling her cloak tighter around her.

She convinced herself she was glad to have stepped away. The conversation could not have ended up anywhere good, and she was not about to tell her life story to a man who'd had nothing but a chip on his shoulder since the moment they locked eyes.

16
THE PERIMETER

The captain continued to push them onward, and the following day presented several more encounters with mechoids, mostly small packs of Prowlers intercepting their path toward the dead zone. Despite Avery's adept handling of the mechoids, the captain's opinion of her abilities remained unchanged. He instructed her to stay beside Milo while he and Reya dealt with the mechanical beasts. Avery had to bite her tongue at his commands, often hearing Harvey's voice in the back of her mind, warning her not to rile the captain.

By evening, they reached the peak of a butte, revealing the haunting silhouettes of rectangular structures towering in the distance. "Yeah, that's the dead zone," Milo confirmed after catching Avery squinting down at the view. The dead zone stretched out before them, a sprawling abandoned city swallowed by time and decay. Colossal buildings jutted into the darkening sky, their once-glass windows shattered, and skeletal frameworks exposed. Weeds and twisted vines crawled up the sides of dilapidated buildings, reclaiming the man-made environment with an eerie sense of quiet dominance. Crumbling bridges and overpasses arched over deserted streets, casting long, ghostly shadows. The air was thick with desolation, and the setting sun cast a haunting glow on the ruins, accentuating the city's forlorn beauty.

Milo used a hand to point toward their target. "See the area there between the two barriers? That's the perimeter. Runs all the way around the place. The old cities used them as stop gates. Even if the mechoids made it through the first wall, there was another barrier they would have to get through, giving the city enough time to get reinforcements out and engage some of their bigger weapons."

As Avery's eyes followed Milo's direction, she saw the perimeter—a vast expanse stretching around the core of the dead zone. The outer barrier was a haphazard mix of crumbling concrete walls and rusted metal fences, remnants of hurried construction meant to protect those who could not afford the security of the inner city. The structures within this buffer zone were smaller, more modest than the towering ruins at the heart. Decrepit housing and makeshift shanties stood alongside abandoned markets and factories, their facades marred by time and overgrown with wild vegetation.

Her eyes traced along the gap, a sick sense stirring within her stomach. "Seems advantageous for those that lived within the center," she muttered.

"Unless the mechoids come from within the city," Rhyker added, motioning the team to keep moving forward.

"Why would mechoids be inside the city walls?" Avery asked, directing the question at Milo.

He shrugged his shoulders. "Larger cities of the old ways used underground tunnels for some of their transportation. There is a theory that mechoids were able to breach their way in through those tunnels. Others believed their creators intentionally unleashed the mechs on the cities. Of course, there is also the theory the mechoids were watching and learning, waiting until magic was stripped from the world before they attacked."

Reya groaned, picking up her pace to create distance between them. "Please don't get him started on this, he will be yapping about it all night."

Milo threw a hand in the air, indignant. "I'm just saying it's a theory. It's not my fault we can't get close enough to get answers."

Avery laughed, listening to the two bicker. A memory resurfaced, and Avery looked to Milo. "I thought the Lunar Knights were conducting research in the different dead zones around Arcadia. Duke Vanguard specifically has knights assigned to each of the major dead zones within the territory to facilitate that."

Rhyker shot Avery a curious glance over his shoulder, causing her to wonder if she was becoming careless with her questions.

"Even so," Milo offered, "the knights still face casualties in the dead zones. The sheer amount of mechoids can overpower even the strongest of their ranks. The danger only increases the further you traverse into the city."

She nodded in understanding, her mind shifting through the handful of times she heard Theodore discussing the ongoing struggle Tracos faced when dealing with the Arcadians and these dead zones.

While there were many hot spots within Tracos deemed to be dead zones, the Traconian empire always seemed to be fixated on gaining access to those within Arcadia or the other neighboring kingdoms. The Traconian emperor frequently enlisted Lord Sinclair to secure access to the dead zones, leading to numerous clashes between their forces and the Lunar Knights. Avery had heard countless tales of the bloodshed that ensued in these efforts to uncover the secrets of the dead zones.

Avery pushed the thoughts of Tracos out of her mind. "It's no surprise then that the church is hesitant to approve your field missions. It's incredibly risky to be sending people in," she added.

"Having seconds thoughts, Blue Eyes?" Rhyker asked, a smirk playing along the corner of his lips. "We could always leave you here and pick you back up on the way out."

Avery shrugged her shoulders indifferently. "Is that a direct order, Captain?"

The captain rolled his eyes, turning away to resume his lead on the trail.

"If only it were that easy."

◆ ◆ ◆

They did not reach the first steel wall until the last bit of evening light threatened to vanish. The barrier stretched as far down as Avery could see both ways. Time rendered the wall useless as several spots along the barrier crumpled from whatever had once torn through it. Various trees and other foliage grew through exposed areas. Evidence of scavengers showed in the holes with rusted circuits where lights once helped illuminate the surrounding areas.

Finding an adequate entry point, they each emerged on the other side of the wall by quietly squeezing through one of the cracks. The inner perimeter housed buildings dwarfed in comparison to those that towered in the distance beyond the perimeter. Even so, most were multi-level, and in various states of ruin. Avery followed closely behind the others as they navigated through the jungle of buildings, doing their best not to attract the attention of the mechoids that could be heard howling somewhere off in the distance.

The sun disappeared behind the crumbling structures, rendering it hard to make out details. Avery scanned over the remaining rows of windows across from where they halted their progress toward the next barrier. The captain sent Reya to scout ahead while he and Milo discussed their options for vantage points and the ideal place to set up camp for the night.

A distant pulse on her aura sent Avery into alert. She stopped and waited, feeling another rumble vibrate beneath her feet. She whipped her head toward the source of the sound, recognizing it as the direction Reya had taken.

"I feel it, too," Rhyker's voice sounded from beside her, and he motioned for them to follow. "We need to move."

The captain led the way, traversing between the buildings with Avery and Milo following close behind. Rhyker held a hand out, halting their progress as Reya came from around the corner of the adjacent building. After a quick scan through the alleyways, she signaled for them to join her. The group kicked it up to a trot, following Reya through a gap in a collapsed wall that led them into the protection of an abandoned structure.

"Well, we found our Dozer. It's heading this direction," Reya said in a hushed voice, pointing out the window to the open street. "I haven't seen one like this before. It doesn't have the same markings."

"Alright," the captain addressed his team, "let's put our packs down here and take out the hooks. You two get it locked down. I'll keep its eyes on me." Rhyker turned to face Avery, his eyes narrowing as he watched her unsling her pack and place it beside her.

"Do not engage," he warned, the familiar iciness returning to his voice. "Stay here behind cover."

He dropped his own bag to the side and moved to help Reya prepare the equipment. Similar to the SLNG, the hooks were projectile based, loaded with large, barbed talons, designed to clamp on to its intended target. According to Milo, the launchers were equipped with an automated winch system that, when secured properly, could reel in and or immobilize the target. Milo had cautioned Avery before about avoiding the cables that attached to the hooks. Apparently, Milo had outfitted the devices with some crawler stunners to help neutralize the mechs, and there had been no doubt about accidents in the past, if Rhyker's reinforced glares were any indication.

When Milo had his hook out and ready to go, he gave Rhyker a thumbs up and the three of them slipped out into the street. Avery moved closer to watch out the open side of the wall where a window once was. The shaking in the ground was becoming more prominent, rattling bits of loose stone around with every step the beast moved closer. She watched as Milo and Reya split up, each taking to one side of the street and ducking into cover amongst the ruined buildings. The captain remained in the center of the street, facing toward the danger that lurked nearby.

A low, guttural growl echoed from just beyond the bend in the street. A long, tempered snout, tapering to a sharp point, emerged around the corner. Sharp blue lights scanned the area with an unsettling precision. From its forehead, a pair of curved horns extended backward, adding to its imposing silhouette. The mechoid pressed forward, revealing sharp, ridged plates running down the length of its head and neck, each ridge casting a shadow that emphasized its menacing form.

Milo's sketches had not done justice to the sheer size of the Leveler. Its massive legs supported a formidable frame, each step resonating with power. The body was a fortress of metal, with plates overlapping like scales, designed to withstand heavy assault. Down its spine, sharp ridges continued, adding both armor and a serrated weapon to its already intimidating presence. Its long, flexible tail, similarly armored and ridged, swayed behind it, surely capable of sweeping through obstacles with ease.

Standing in the middle of the street, Rhyker faced the beast. He stepped forward, the long blade of his sword beginning to emit flickers of fire as he slowly waved it, trying to catch the Leveler's attention. The mechanical beast locked onto Rhyker, gradually closing the distance between them. Avery moved away from the window and pressed against the wall, cautiously making her way through the abandoned structures to get a better view of the encounter.

The beast growled, its large horned head hovering just above the ground as it stalked down the street toward Rhyker. Its steel tail flicked anxiously, occasionally tearing away at the concrete structures it collided with. As the captain moved in closer, the Leveler let out a piercing roar, causing glass and other small debris to spill onto Avery from the exposed ceiling above her. The mechanical beast reeled back, preparing to launch at the captain. Milo and Reya suddenly appeared on either side of the mechoid, deploying the hooks onto its thick legs. The hooks, with the barbed teeth, sunk into the mechoid's armor, securing their grip. The creature thrashed violently, attempting to free itself from the hooks. Time being critical, Milo and Reya swiftly attached their cables to already locked down anchor points that utilized sturdy structures in the concrete to secure them.

The Leveler continued its frantic struggle, snapping its jaws at the captain, who deftly parried each attempt with his sword. Using a sudden burst of strength, the Dozer thrashed forward violently, and the cable on Milo's side loosened from the concrete anchor, giving the Leveler enough space to swipe at Rhyker with its freed claw. The captain's arm was just within reach, and he was forced to retreat backward.

Milo scrambled to regain control of his cable as it writhed with each movement of the beast. Diving down, he grasped the cable just as the mechoid shifted its focus onto him. The beast's tail whipped out viciously, but the blade of Lightbringer intercepted the blow meant for Milo. The impact forced the mechoid to brace the ground, its sensors quickly targeting Avery as her blade tore into its tail. The Leveler growled and swiped at her with a massive, pointed claw. She dodged the strike and drove her blade into the overextended claw, slicing through its structure. The mechoid recoiled, attempting to retreat while swinging its heavy tail to fend her off. Rhyker appeared in front of her just in time, his sword severing the tail clean off.

The captain quickly pulled Avery back in the time they gained from the Leveler trying to retreat. "Fall back and stay out of the way!" he yelled at her. The mechoid roared loudly, resetting its sights back on Avery. She shoved the captain's arm off her shoulder, raising her sword at the ready. Rhyker stepped in front of her, forcing her to take a step back. "That's an order!"

Avery glared at him, reluctantly stepping back to give the captain space. She watched as he channeled more magic, hurling fireballs at the beast's head to regain its full attention. Milo seized the opportunity created by Avery's assist to reset the hook. He launched it once more at the beast, anchoring the end to a sturdier chunk of concrete. Milo signaled to Reya, and together, they activated the mechanism within the cable launchers. The devices whirred to life, applying a powerful pulling force that reeled in the beast from either side. The jagged hooks bit into the mechoid's armor, securing their grip as pulsing waves of electricity traveled through the cables, sending stunning jolts coursing through the mechoid. As the cables tightened, the Leveler thrashed, but the relentless tension from the cables shortened the binds until it was rendered immovable.

The beast growled, ceasing its struggle against the stunning force that bound it, and fixed a venomous stare on Rhyker as he stalked toward it, ready to deliver the final blow. A chilling sensation swept over Avery, and a drumming burned in her ears as she watched the Leveler. An overwhelming power emanated from the mechoid, so intense that it sent goosebumps racing across her skin.

She was already moving before she knew what she was going to do. Sprinting toward the creature, Avery rushed to get in front of the captain just as the beast's mouth dropped open. A red light emerged from deep within the creature's jaws. There was no time for warning, no time to get Rhyker out of the way. Standing in front of him, she summoned a shield, hoping it would be enough. She heard Rhyker call out to her just before the blast hit, sending them both flying back from the impact.

A blinding white light receded as Avery fought to open her eyes. She squinted, her vision blurry and stinging as she struggled to comprehend her surroundings.

"You have been warned about asking such questions, Avery." Her heart sank at the sound of his voice. The room she stood in became clearer, revealing the suffocating walls of the familiar study. The yellow-eyed man sat upright in his chair, peering down at her, his hands folded patiently on his desk.

"You know who he is. I have the right to know," Avery heard her own voice, steady but defiant. She was there again, standing in the middle of Theodore's study. The unmistakable intolerance to her outrage was evident in the way his stare burned into her.

"Such trivial matters," his cold voice dripped with boredom. "This defiance is becoming rather irritating."

"I have a right to know who I am," she repeated through clenched teeth. Theodore's stare shifted to amusement, a cruel smile tugging at the corner of his mouth. Avery suddenly dropped to her knees, every muscle in her body tightening in response to the searing pain invading her nerves. This was beyond the point where she would scream, a satisfaction she refused to give Theodore during his sadistic punishments. Avery's compliance was like a drug to Lord Sinclair. There was nothing Theodore prized more than maintaining control over everything and everyone.

"I will not tolerate you raising your voice at me," he warned, and without moving, he released her pain. He waited for her to pick herself back up, shaking as she tried to catch her breath. "You will not utter another word of your father," he said slowly, ensuring she felt the weight of the command. "Is that understood?"

No word needed to be said, the defiance read on her face, betraying her thoughts to Theodore. He let out a soft chuckle and shook his head. Another wave of pain overtook her. She gasped for air, her lungs burning until the pain was once again lifted.

Everything became a blur again as her vision faded, and her eyes once again took in the dark night that surrounded her. "Avery?" a voice called her. The thin silhouette of Reya hovered over her. "Goddess, I thought you might have been killed." Avery slowly sat up, finding herself laying on the hard concrete and not in Lord Sinclair's office. "How'd you even know it was going to do that?" Reya's frantic questions continued. Her silver eyes briefly scanned over Avery again before staring blankly ahead. "I don't think the captain would be here if you hadn't stopped it."

Following the guard's gaze, Avery found where the Leveler remained pinned down by the cables. Sparks erupted from within the giant hole that was now through its head. Aside from the buzzing of the broken mechanical bits, the mechoid was motionless.

"What happened?" Avery asked, becoming aware of a

pain building in her chest.

"Where's Rhyker?"

"I'm here," his voice called from behind them. She tilted her head, feeling her body protest from the sudden movement. Rhyker walked up, clutching his arm, his green eyes assessing the team's condition.

"We all got hit by that blast." Milo appeared, rubbing at the back of his head. "Guess we found out that those mechoids aren't the only ones who can use magic." Milo looked at Avery in a mix of amazement and confusion. "Um, when were you going to tell us you were a mage?"

"It's kind of complicated." she sighed, feeling her head spin as she tried to recall using magic.

"Yeah, talk about complicated, Mr. Dozer over there got a whole face full of complicated." Milo shook his head, looking to his two other teammates for support.

Reya nodded, agreeing, "Seriously Avery, that was something else."

They both looked at her expectantly, and she struggled to find something to say. Her head was still pounding, and her chest felt like it had been badly burned. She assumed they already knew she was a mage, or that Rhyker would have told them.

The captain stepped between them, causing the two to take their stares off Avery. "Alright, were not done yet." He gave the defeated Leveler another glance, then let his eyes search the area. "Reya, scout ahead and make sure this is the only one. They don't typically travel in packs, but we also didn't think they could use magic. It's best we play it safe and look for more. Milo, you're on harvesting duty." He shifted his attention down to Avery who made no effort to get back on her feet. "Blue Eyes and I need to have a little chat about disobeying orders."

His two teammates hesitated, exchanging concerned

glances. Reya, clearly alarmed, was the first to speak. "Rhy, are you serious? She just saved your ass."

"Yeah, you would've been vaporized if she hadn't—" Milo began but was abruptly cut off.

"Did I not just tell you two to get going?" Rhyker's voice carried an icy edge accompanied by the piercing look he directed at them.

"Yes, Captain," they responded in unison, immediately splitting off from the group. Reya gave Avery a supportive nod before disappearing toward the other ruined buildings. She watched as Milo approached the Leveler, by the way his head bobbed erratically, she could tell he was muttering to himself. She stared at the crumpled remains of the mechoid, more startled by their willingness to defend her than whatever it was she did to the mechoid.

"I told you to stay back, Avery." The captain glared down at her. "We both could have been taken out by that blow."

It felt odd for him to call her by her name, somehow making it more irritating than being lectured for saving his life. She returned the glare. "Seems I'm not too great at doing what I'm told."

He hesitated, and although it was brief, Avery had been so accustomed to his quick retorts that it felt out of place for him to pause. After a moment, he laughed, holding out a hand to help her up. "Guess I'm lucky you aren't."

Avery took his extended hand, rising from the concrete despite the ache in her limbs. His grip on her arm tightened as she stood, holding her steady and refusing to let her pull away. He kept her there, at arm's length, and she felt the intensity of his presence as he loomed over her. The forced proximity sent her heart racing, betraying the frustration in her mind. She met his gaze, her eyes full of defiance, but the playful glint in his eyes only deepened the turmoil swirling within her. She felt a confusing mix of irritation and something warmer she couldn't quite name. "Don't make a habit of it. I don't need you thinking you can be even more reckless." He winked, and as he let go, her skin tingled where his hand had been, leaving her feeling more unsettled than she cared to admit. She watched him walk away toward Milo and the Leveler.

The effect of his performance hit her like whiplash. She swore under her breath, feeling her face get hot and combating a strange new feeling that seemed to dull the pain in her chest. Her head spun wildly as she tried to make sense of any of it and after a few moments, she gave up and focused her attention on trying to determine what it was she did to the mechoid that rendered it dead.

She waited for the captain to leave before she checked in with Milo and helped with extracting parts. Milo showed her the power core that miraculously avoided being damaged. According to Milo, the mechoid fired some sort of beam unlike anything he had ever seen or heard of before, and Avery summoned a shield that sent it right back. They took extra care to make sure the core was removed in one piece and salvaged a few other parts Milo deemed worthy enough on which to spend the time.

Reya returned, giving the group an all clear signal in terms of other Levelers, however, warning them of other lurking mechoids. The captain seemed uneasy, and ultimately decided that they were better off establishing a spot to camp outside the perimeter. They would resume their hunt for one more core when they once again had daylight. They found a spot to set up their bedrolls and Milo got busy inspecting each one of the parts collected by the small fire.

"I still can't believe we encountered a mech that can use magic," he muttered, cleaning off some of the oil-like fluid around the core. "The research facility is going to have field day with our report."

Reya tossed the half empty container of her meal aside. "Which reminds me." She stared across the fire at Avery. "You're a mage?"

Milo perked up and threw Avery a hurtful look. "Yeah, when were you going to tell us?"

Avery had kept to herself most of that evening hoping they were not going to pursue the topic. Not that she could blame them for being curious. A small part of her hoped the captain would step in again and derail the conversation, but she could see Rhyker out of the corner of her eye turn his head in her direction, also intent on hearing the answer.

"Yes, I have been learning how to use magic," she said awkwardly, staring into the fire to avoid their gazes. "I assumed you all knew."

"Hold up." Milo pointed the tool he was using at her in his interrogation. "What do you mean by 'have been learning?' For how long?"

Avery's face became warm again. "Well, I suppose a few months. I didn't learn that I was a mage until I came to Farewell."

"What?" Reya and Milo said together in astonishment.

"How does that even happen?" Milo asked, looking to Rhyker for the answer. Avery chanced a glance at the captain, finding him studying her in an intense silence.

Avery gave them a half smile, staring back at the embers of the fire. "Like I said before, it's a little complicated."

Milo went to ask another question, but the arm of Reya nudged him, apparently picking up on the hint Avery was not inclined to go into any details. Instead, Milo went back to cleaning the core, mumbling to himself under his breath. She could still feel Rhyker's eyes fixed on her and after some time she got to her feet and leaned her head back to take in the night's sky.

"It's getting late; shall I take first watch?" she asked, finally meeting Rhyker's stare.

The captain seemed to break out of his thoughts. "No, I'll go ahead and take it. You all need to rest up. I want time to think over the encounter we had with the Leveler. If we're lucky, we can find another one early tomorrow and start making good time getting the cores delivered to the research facility."

Nobody argued with him, each finding their bed rolls and winding down for the night. Avery laid back and stared up at the stars. Her thoughts centered on the aching that throbbed in her chest. She had a bad feeling it was from the impact her shield had made when it collided with the Leveler's beam.

The memory of the conversation she and Theodore had about her father trickled in, and she glared at nothing while it played in her mind. These visions seemed to come whenever she overextended herself. It was reckless, sure, but it had been the right thing to do. Regardless of what Rhyker thought of her, she could not just stand by and let it happen. Though, she still did not understand how she had seen it coming before he did.

The captain's face appeared in her mind, he winked at her. His playful smile beginning to engrave itself in the back of her mind. Irritated, she turned abruptly on her side, knowing it was going to be a very long night.

17

A CURIOUS CONNECTION

Rhyker

Unraveling the useless bandage on his arm, the captain sat perched in a tree, his eyes fixed on the dark night that surrounded his team. His hand mindlessly traced where the claws of the Leveler dug into his arm. His skin remained unscathed, with no hint it had been bleeding a few hours before. The night was mercifully quiet. Their coverage among the thick of the forest provided a sense of relief from the mechoids that hunted endlessly throughout the night.

Restless, his mind picked apart the events that played over again in his mind. The encounter with the Leveler had its issues. Too many things went wrong, and a troubled feeling came when he thought about how the mechoid channeled magic. Reya was right, this Leveler was different. While it held the same general shape, the steel plates that armored it looked newer, and it did not have the familiar marker, AMARIS LEVELER, painted along its back.

Strange as it was, the oversized mechoid was not what had imprinted itself in his thoughts. Something even stranger happened when Avery shielded him from the deadly beam. Perhaps it made more sense now, learning she had only been wielding magic for a short time. Magic can do funny things when it is uncontrolled and untrained.

Somehow, she saw it coming before he did, miraculously channeling a magic of her own to offset it. She must have thrown everything she had into that shield. When the impact from the blast hit, Rhyker experienced a connection with Avery, getting a glimpse into a core memory. He had never been a fan of the clairvoyant magics, and something made him doubt that Avery knew she had done it.

The face of the young blonde girl and her defiant blue eyes came to mind whenever he closed his eyes. She was staring up at a man with yellow eyes who he had never seen before. A man who laughed while she struggled through the pain he imposed on her and had not been satisfied until she stopped resisting.

Rhyker glared into the night, tightening his grip over the handle of his sword. He found himself looking over at Avery, always farthest from the fire, and turned away from the others. The captain had a feeling she was still awake, as he often found her on his watch. For how unpredictable she was, she made up for it in stubborn determination. He had to admit, she did technically save him, but he was still ahead by one on his count.

He quietly chuckled to himself, realizing his thoughts kept centering around the mysterious blonde. She stirred in the distance, and he turned his gaze back in the direction of the dead zone, knowing it was going to be a long night.

◆ ◆ ◆

The others were well rested the next morning, in part due to Rhyker taking on the majority of the night's watch while they slept. Milo and Reya squabbled as they packed up what remained of their bags, arguing over the possibilities of the mechoids evolving over time. Avoiding catching any collateral damage, Avery planted herself against a tree, overlooking the dead zone. She was already packed up, her long blond hair retied to keep it out of her eyes. As usual, she was quiet, always watching and listening until the others were finally ready to make their way to the perimeter once more.

They were not as lucky crossing through the first barrier as the day before. The group found themselves face to face with a pack of Prowlers after a crawler managed to send out an alert before Milo could blast it with the SLNG. The captain also caught a stalker attempting to get the jump on Reya, while she forged ahead in search for more Levelers.

Rhyker's hope they would find a Leveler early on was fulfilled when another crawler caught them entering the bottom floor of a building, which he guessed was some sort of store. The shelves and display cases long abused by time. The crawler was skulking in the corner of the ceiling, taking advantage of a smaller hole in the floor above to escape the blast of fire he hurtled after it. The floor beneath them shook shortly after, signaling that a Leveler would soon arrive. The Dozer burst through one of the walls, finding the floor space emptied. It proceeded to search for them, falling victim to the ambush that awaited it.

Once the Leveler reached the designated spot, Milo and Reya triggered the restraints, getting the mechanical monstrosity stationary long enough for Rhyker to strike it down. It was quick work. The result was what he had come to expect from his team. The Leveler resembled the kind he was accustomed to taking out. The usual markings were engraved on its body along with the wear and tear from roaming the dead zone for who knows how long. Avery returned from her vantage point at the other end of the room, guarding the only other entrance into their trap. Her eyes swept over the scene, only briefly lingering on the captain before moving to assist Milo with the cleanup.

They did not waste time leaving the perimeter, not wanting to risk staying near the dead zone for any longer than necessary. Their trip back already proved to have more mechoid encounters, resulting in their slowed progress toward Farewell. By the end of each night, the exhaustion set into the group, worn down from taking on the unavoidable waves of mechoids throughout the day.

"So," Reya fished for conversation with Rhyker as they patrolled the outskirts of the clearing they had chosen for camp. "The new girl isn't so bad."

Rhyker ignored her, letting his eyes continue to take in their surroundings as they walked.

"She's pretty handy with that sword." The guard pressed on, undeterred. "Doesn't hurt to have the extra set of hands around for some of the work."

The captain remained silent, giving her a warning look as he caught her eye.

She rolled her eyes at him, one of the few who did and could get away with it. "Look, I'm just saying it's been nice to have help. Be a shame to lose such a capable hand because *you* have some problem with her."

Annoyed, he caved on his silence. "Now you're starting to sound like James." He shook his head. "I don't have a problem with her."

"Right," Reya laughed, "I mean she's no Mindy, but you should give her a chance to-"

Rhyker looked over his shoulder at her, keeping his temper in check. "I'm not having this discussion."

She threw her hands in the air, surrendering the point. "Alright, Rhy. I get it." She let out an irritated scoff, picking up her pace to move ahead of him. "Just think on it, alright?"

The two returned to join the others who were setting up camp for what they hoped was the last time before they reached Farewell. Milo was rifling through his bag with the additional salvaged parts found throughout the day scattered around him. He frowned at the bag as he tried to stuff another Prowler core into it. "I don't think they will have anticipated just how much we are bringing back. We are running out of space to carry everything."

Rhyker plopped his bedroll down. "I suspect the council will be sending us out again shortly after we return." He collapsed on the ground with a big sigh and stretched out. Reya offered to take the first watch and situated herself a short way up the hill to watch over them.

Already absorbed in a book, Avery sat across from him reading. A faint white light illuminated her face from a small white orb that hovered between her and the book.

"You think so?" Milo asked, finally getting the strap on his bag to re-latch. "I was wondering if this meant there would be more regular field missions. I hate to say it, but I'm going to miss being cooped up in that backroom."

Rhyker laughed, knowing the complaints would come either way. "Yeah, I think the council is going to milk the Blue Eyes' incident for all they can until the church starts to protest."

Avery lowered her book enough for the blue eyes to peer over the pages. Rhyker grinned widely at her from where he laid back with his hands rested behind his head. She glared at him before raising the book again.

"We need the momentum while we have it," Milo continued. "Gods knows Farewell is way behind the curve in technology."

Rhyker let Milo continue his grumbling, having heard his rambles before. Avery's shuffling in the distance caught his eye, and he watched as she settled more comfortably into the book, which he was sure she had already finished and started over at least once since they have been out in the field. He shifted his gaze onto the night sky, not willing to risk receiving another glare from the mage, as much as he would find it amusing.

The next day, the sun was in full swing as Farewell came into their sights again. The mechoid encounters dwindled significantly as they neared the city. The last few hours of their travel remained completely uninterrupted, allowing them to maintain a steady pace to reach the security of the city walls. The four entered the guild hall, greeted by the enthusiastic Guild Master as they began to unload their bags in Milo's workshop.

"Ah, Farewell's finest have returned!" James cheered. "How did we fair this trip?" he asked, looking over Milo's shoulder as he extracted the two prized cores from the pack.

Rhyker moved to help intercept the nosey Guild Master, hoping to spare Milo from being interrupted. "We got the cores, and some extra parts that have been on the guild's bounty board. I can give you a full report now."

James waited until both the cores were laid out on the table before addressing the captain. "Let's get the cores up to Professor Colleymore, and you can give me a report while your team has a chance to go home and freshen up." He glided over to the table, picking up both cores, handing one to Rhyker for him to carry. "I have some information I want to run past you. We've been a bit busy while you were away."

They started making their way out of the room. The Guild Master stopped to offer Avery a polite bow before continuing toward the exit. James gave Rhyker the wide grin once more. "I'm curious to hear how the mission played out."

"Standard retrieval mission." Rhyker shrugged, knowing what the Guild Master was after. "What's the status of things here?" the captain asked, hoping to steer the conversation away from it.

"The town is still in quite a fuss about the mechoid incident. We've had several more false reports of mechoid sightings. I hope completing this project will help us ease the minds of the people."

The Guild Master waited to elaborate further until they were beyond the guild hall doors, beginning to make their way up the long slope to the research facility. When they were out of earshot of any others, the Guild Master spoke in a quieter tone, instilling an unsettling feeling within the captain's gut.

"It's no secret," the Guild Master started, "that Sylvie and I have never quite seen eye to eye, but I respect her greatly, and I've always done my best to consider her impact when we are working with matters that concern our people."

Rhyker nodded his understanding, but eyed James with concern. "I've never doubted that, sir."

"Good, then I think you'll understand why I'm hesitant to mention this next portion to you, for fear that I am simply being overly cautious." He lowered his voice further. "As you know, the High Priestess is very eager to complete this project." He indicated the core. "She's become extra guarded, and she's prying into guild matters more than usual. It's uncharacteristic of her to be so involved in the status of the other field team."

Rhyker analyzed the Guild Master. "Still no word from them?"

James shook his head. "Unfortunately, no. I've suggested we pause the pursuit of the trackers and put your team on search and rescue, but ultimately it was decided to continue to wait. It wouldn't be the first time that team has gotten held up."

Rhyker pressed the issue. "But you're concerned something more is going on?"

"It could be nothing, but I want to have extra eyes

around in case there is something to it."

"Understood."

"I appreciate it, Captain." The Guild Master let out a deep sigh, then resumed his usual energetic nature. "Now, tell me, how did our newest recruit fair in the field?"

"She's not a recruit," Rhyker warned, but the Guild Master chuckled.

Fighting to keep his expression neutral, the captain took in a deep breath, knowing he would not be able to avoid the discussion further.

18
SHATTERED GLASS
Avery

A very was officially released from the field mission after double checking all the parts she was responsible for carrying were accounted for, and safely stored away in Milo's workshop. Milo and Reya walked her out of the guild hall, discussing plans to start cataloging the remaining parts the next morning. They parted ways for the day, wishing each other a good rest after the long trip.

Scout bounded up the road to meet Avery as she exited the Farewell archway and headed toward the farmhouse. The excited pup circled around her, too energetic to pet properly, weaving in and out of her legs, and darting along the open road as she walked. Cecelia was in the kitchen, likely preparing something for Avery to eat, as the spry woman spotted her through the kitchen window. True to form, Cecelia refused any assistance with cooking and insisted Avery take the time to wash up before dinner was ready.

It was not a hard sell. Avery was more than grateful for the opportunity to bathe herself after being out in the forest for nearly two weeks. The warm water felt like a luxury, washing away the grime and weariness. She sighed in relief, letting the heat soothe her sore muscles. Distracted by her thoughts, she toweled herself down, stopping abruptly as she caught herself in the mirror. Her long blonde hair was sopping wet, dangling on either side of her shoulders.

The color left her face as the startled blue eyes landed above where the towel covered her chest. Faint dark lines covered the center of her chest like shattered glass. The thin marks reached outward, spreading away from the center. She leaned closer to the mirror, trying to get a better look. Her breath caught as if breathing would make it worse.

Her eyes quickly scanned the rest of her body, relieved to find no other trace of the mysterious marks. Avery watched her face slowly regain color as her mind recalled the pain in her chest, the result of using too much magic. This was what Irene warned her about, overexerting her vessel beyond the fragile limits. The damage was starting to surface, and she was no closer to getting it fixed.

She took a deep breath and pulled herself away from the mirror, quickly dressing to rejoin Cecelia for dinner. The old woman took one look at her and stopped stirring the pot on the stove. "Are you alright, dear?"

"Yes," Avery managed, doing her best to play it off as exhaustion. "It was quite the trip." She seated herself at the table, trying to ignore Cecelia's raised eyebrows. The two shared the meal while Avery briefly recalled the experience, attempting to sway the conversation away from Cecelia's worried glances.

"Overall, it was rather productive. I learned a lot from Rhyker's team."

"I'm not surprised." Cecelia said warmly. "I'm glad you ended up getting along with him. I've watched him and his team grow over the years. They're all good kids."

"Rhyker didn't exactly make it easy," Avery muttered.

"It's his job to make sure his team doesn't get in over their head," Cecelia reminded her.

"According to the captain, I'm not considered part of the team. Nor would I want to be." Avery waved the thought away. "I don't understand him, but to his credit, he is a strong mage and an even more skilled swordsman. I can't imagine what the guards of the Lunar Knights must be like if he doesn't even cut it." She was about to add to the thought but stopped when she saw the old woman's frown, and the slow shake of her head.

"That's not true," Cecelia said quietly, picking up the empty plate from the table.

"What do you mean?" Avery twisted in her chair to search Cecelia for an answer.

"What's not true?"

Cecelia paused, ensuring she had Avery's full attention. "It pays to remember we are all battling our own demons."

A pang of guilt hit Avery's stomach, and she fell silent, contemplating the old woman's words. Cecelia got up from the table, letting the time pass so Avery had to stew on the information. The old mage returned to the table once the dishes were washed. She gently placed a hand on Avery's arm.

"Best to forget you heard it, dear. It's not our place to deal judgement or spread theories. Now, you should rest." She patted Avery's shoulder and left the kitchen.

With a full stomach and an even fuller mind, Avery left the farmhouse for a trip to the bookstore, hoping to catch Leah and Malcolm in the late evening. The streetlights flickered on as she made her way up the street, their soft glow pushing back the encroaching darkness. The cool night air nipped at her skin, and the rhythmic click of her boots on the pavement filled the otherwise quiet walk. As she approached Pioneer Plaza, the sound of laughter drifted toward her, bringing warmth to the chilly night.

Avery's gaze fell on a bench outside the guild hall, where Rhyker was deep in conversation with the young woman from the last guild meeting. She no longer wore the black robes but instead donned a pretty grey dress that fluttered gently in the evening breeze. Rhyker, looking freshly showered and clean-shaven, animatedly recounting a story, his arms gesturing wildly. The woman's laughter echoed through the empty plaza, and Avery forced herself to ignore the irritation it stirred within her.

Hoping not to be seen, Avery took the long way around the plaza to reach the bookshop. Inside, Leah's eyes widened with excitement and disbelief as Avery recounted her first encounter with the Leveler. "You *saved* him?" she exclaimed, her voice a mix of awe and astonishment. Both Leah and Malcolm were visibly relieved to see Avery had returned safely. As expected, Leah demanded a full recap of the events, practically bouncing in her seat at any mention of the captain.

"He can't possibly still hate you!" Leah gushed, barely able to stay contained in the chair across from Avery. "What did he say?"

Avery fought to keep her composure, feeling her face flush with heat as she glared down at her tea. "He yelled at me for disobeying orders," she muttered, reaching for another cookie from the table. Every time she replayed the scene in her head, it made less sense to her. Leah, already wearing a dreamy expression, seemed lost in her thoughts about the captain, an impression Avery had no intention of fueling further.

Malcolm's brow furrowed with deep concern as Avery recounted the mechoid encounters. He listened intently, his fingers drumming softly on the armrest of his chair. When Leah finally paused her barrage of questions, Malcolm leaned forward, his anxiety palpable. "And what about signs of Theodore?" he asked, his voice laced with tension.

Avery set her teacup down on the small table beside her, taking a moment to gather her thoughts. "I had one episode on the second night we were out. But there hasn't been much else. I admit, I am growing a little anxious," she confessed, her voice steady despite the worry gnawing at her.

Malcolm pursed his lips, his eyes narrowing as he processed her words. The dreamy expression vanished from Leah's face, replaced by deep concern. She paused, allowing the weight of the situation to sink in, and exchanged worried glances with Malcolm. The room grew quiet, the gravity of Theodore's looming threat hanging heavily in the air.

"I've done some thinking," Avery began, breaking the silence. She straightened her posture, her resolve clear. "I have decided I will head to Astoria once I've finished my community service for the council."

Neither Malcolm nor Leah knew how to respond, both struggling to find the right words as Avery stood firm in her decision. The room was thick with unspoken emotions, the weight of her announcement settling heavily around them.

Malcolm cleared his throat, the sound breaking the silence. Perhaps some part of him was reliving the conversation he once had with Amelia when she decided to leave Farewell.

"You've already come so far in the months since you arrived. If you feel you are ready, we will continue to do all that we can to help," he said, his voice filled with a mix of pride and concern.

Avery found it difficult to meet Leah's eyes, the hurt and worry in them reflecting the close bond they had formed. The somber expressions on their faces struck her deeply, and she mustered a lighter tone, hoping to lift the mood.

"A few more Levelers under my belt, and the trip to Astoria will seem like a walk through the plaza," she joked, though the comment did little to ease their nerves.

Leah's lips twitched into a small smile, her concern

still evident but momentarily softened by Avery's attempt at humor. "I still can't believe you fought those Levelers," Leah said, her voice tinged with admiration and worry. "But you know, Astoria is a different beast altogether."

"Yes," Avery agreed, "but both Harvey and Irene agreed it's where I can find answers."

Another taunted pause overtook them, until Leah visibly stirred in her seat once more, trying to shake away the tears as she shifted topics.

"So tell me again how the Leveler escaped the binds."

Grateful for the out, Avery gladly recalled the details of the encounter once more, spending the remainder of the evening enjoying the company and safety that the bookshop provided.

◆◆◆

The next morning, Avery arrived at the Big Hen and found Harvey at the bar, engrossed in some inventory paperwork. He glanced up as she approached, raising an eyebrow.

"Don't tell me Rhyker already sent you packing," he grumbled, annoyance in his tone.

"No, we got back yesterday afternoon, and I managed to play nice," Avery replied, taking a seat across from him.

Harvey looked at her in surprise. "I'll be damned, there and back in less than two weeks. Did you get what you went for?"

Avery nodded, placing her arms on the bar top in front of her. Harvey's eyes narrowed as he examined her arms. "Let me see that arm," he demanded, holding out his hand.

Avery hesitated for a moment before slowly extending her arm. Harvey flipped it around, inspecting it closely. His gaze traveled up her arm until it met her eyes. "What the hell did you do?"

Avery quickly pulled her arm away. "What do you mean?"

"Do I look like an idiot? I warned you, kid. You need to get a handle on this," he growled, his eyes narrowing in disapproval.

She tucked her arms away, trying to hide her discomfort.

"It was a bit of a complicated situation, Harvey," she explained, trying to make him understand.

"Uh-huh, sure," he muttered, tossing his cigar away and moving around the bar. He seemed lost in thought, mumbling to himself.

"Look," Avery started, her voice urgent as she tried to capture his full attention, "the Dozer we encountered wasn't ordinary. It used magic, channeling some sort of beam at us. I had to react on the spot."

Harvey turned to face her, his brow furrowed. "The mechoid used magic?"

"Yes, it caught the whole team off guard," she affirmed, trying not to sound defensive.

"And you tried to create a shield to protect yourself from it?" he asked, still looking at her skeptically.

Avery sat back in her chair, crossing her arms. "Are you going to tell me it was reckless?"

"Actually," a deep voice interrupted from behind them. Neither of them had noticed the door open, and the Guild Master stood there, smiling warmly, "from what I've been told, it was quite remarkable. Avery doesn't give herself enough credit. Milo mentioned she likely saved the captain from serious harm or worse."

"Is that so?" Harvey resumed his usual unamused tone, raising his eyebrow at her. Avery did not say anything but stood from her chair to face the Guild Master. He gave a slight bow in greeting before lifting his head with a grin directed at Harvey.

"Captain Adler reported Avery assisted his team well. I think we can all take that as a win, considering he protested her joining the mission to begin with."

Harvey grunted and sat on the stool behind the bar. "What brings you here, James?"

The Guild Master looked down at Avery, motioning for her to take the seat she had occupied before he arrived. "I was going to ask that you send Avery my way, but since she is here, I can skip that part."

Avery resumed her seat and pivoted her chair to face him while he continued, "I wanted to give you the option of finishing your community service by running a few more missions with Captain Adler's team. Thanks to the success of your mission, we now have a way to track the mechoids and would like to start getting the equipment out there. The way I see it, you give us your time for a few more missions, and I will ensure all is squared away. What do you think?"

Avery looked to Harvey, hoping to gauge his opinion of the proposal. All he offered her was another grunt as he shrugged slightly. "Up to you, kid."

The Guild Master offered a polite smile, his expression clearly signaling that he was willing to wait patiently for her response. There did not seem to be anything wrong with the offer, and it would mean she could get more hands-on experience with traveling outside of Farewell.

She nodded. "Yes, sir, I can agree to that."

James showered her with enthusiasm. "Excellent. I will inform the captain, and you can report to him for more details. I appreciate you being willing to work with us." He shook Avery's hand and exchanged a few parting words with Harvey before quickly heading out of the tavern, possibly to avoid giving Avery any time to rethink the decision.

When they heard the door shut after him, Harvey turned a raised eyebrow at Avery. She smiled up at him innocently. "Well, it will keep me out of trouble, right?"

He did not buy it and shook his head, returning to

his look of disapproval. "If you don't kill yourself in the process."

Annoyed, Avery stood up and stretched. "What drills are we running today?" she asked, heading for the back door.

Harvey held a stiff arm out, glaring down at her. "Dammit, you need to take a break, Avery. Give yourself the day to rest."

"I don't want to rest. I need to train." She tried to brush his arm off, but the old man grabbed her wrist, his fingers sending faint blue lights skittering across her skin. The lights pulsed, converging at her chest before bouncing back, tracing the invisible cracks etched into her body. "Your body is still recovering from that blow you took."

She yanked her arm away and pulled her cloak around to drape her arms, hiding the lights away. "Then I won't use magic, but I can still wield a sword." She crossed her arms and glared at him. He shook his head, heading for his inventory paperwork again. Avery reached to grab his arm and softened her gaze. "Harvey, Theo has been way too quiet. I don't want to waste time when I don't know how much I have left. I need to be ready for him."

Harvey stared down at her, watching her in silence. Finally, he rolled his eyes and grabbed his sword from under the bar.

"No magic," he barked before heading out the back door into the courtyard. Avery gave a satisfied grin before following him out.

19

A MYSTERIOUS
DISAPPEARANCE

Avery

E arly the next morning, Avery found herself entering the guild hall, feeling the soreness from her training setting in. Logan stopped showing up for the trainings all together, which was fine, because Harvey agreed she needed to start learning how to purposefully utilize magic in combat. That was not something the ex-sailor was equipped to handle.

Much like a bursting pipe, Avery found it hard to stop the magic once she was able to produce it. Often, resulting in dangerous beams of concentrated light running stray or too strong of shields erupting when she sparred. It was also the reason why Jaune was forced to repair the wooden fence surrounding the tavern's courtyard in several places.

Harvey's solution to this was the use of counter magics. He admitted it was among the hardest magics to learn, but the ability to consume or destroy another mage's magical attacks was critical for combat against other mages. Harvey declined to answer any questions she raised about his experience fighting or anything related to his apparent time as a general for that matter.

Whenever Avery channeled too much magic or unleashed an unintentional shield, Harvey absorbed it with the deft use of a hand that seemed to swallow the magic whole. He did not wait for her to recover or hold back his strikes – or his unsavory comments about her performance – the lesson being that it hurt like hell whenever magic was not there to prevent the blow. All of it being another reminder of how much harder she would need to train.

Harvey's sharp corrections rang in her head as she took in the small group of people gathered in the guild hall. Rhyker stood with the Guild Master and some other members of the guild whom she only saw in passing before. They talked in hushed tones, the captain's attention fully on the Guild Master in serious concentration. The Guild Master raised his head, finding Avery walking in and waved in her direction. The others broke their huddle and turned their gazes her way. Avery nodded politely and kept her pace, hoping to avoid any small talk with the Guild Master by seeking refuge in Milo's workshop.

The mechoid enthusiast was already in the room, muttering to himself while a small box buzzed with music in the corner. The crates of parts she had helped organize the day before were now scattered across the tables, making the small space feel even more cramped from whatever method he was using to reorganize the parts.

"Good morning, Milo," Avery called to him.

Holding a smaller crate filled with mechoid sensors, Milo whirled around clearly having difficulty finding a space to put them. Seeing Avery, he sighed heavily, shaking his head, "I lied, I am not going to miss being stuck here."

Avery laughed, joining him in the room. "Didn't like the way I sorted the parts? I thought we had most of this ready to go."

"We did, and we were going to be ready to go by tomorrow, but the research facility brought us a boatload more parts to go through. On top of that, they have some Drone cores they want me to look at up the hill. Rhyker's on my case about getting them what they need so we can get out in the field again." Milo vented, still trying to find a place to put the small crate of objects. While he was less adept with a sword, Milo definitely made up for in his knowledge with the mechoids and the technology they used. It was no surprise the research facility tapped into that knowledge from time to time.

Avery surveyed the parts, trying to gather where he was in the process. "Well, why don't I take over here and finish cataloging the remaining parts? That way you can take a trip up to the research facility, and we can wrap this up tonight."

Milo stopped his hurried search around, his eyes widening as he nodded vigorously. "Yeah, that could work! You already know what you're doing, and I can help you once I get back."

Avery held out her hands to take the crate from him. "It's what I'm here for anyway."

Milo handed off the parts, looking relieved. "I'll let Rhyker know we will be good to go tomorrow. That will save us a huge chunk of time…Oh, speaking of…" Milo interrupted himself, his attention was caught by something behind her. Before she could turn around, the sharp icy tone of the captain rang out from behind her.

"Blue Eyes!"

Avery whipped around to see narrowed green eyes on her. The captain stood in the doorway with his arms folded across his chest. "You know, you're still required to report in with me when you get here."

Avery returned the glare, raising an eyebrow at his demand. "I didn't realize you needed the excuse to glare at me in the morning, captain."

His accusation had not been false. Avery could not find Rhyker the previous morning and rather than wasting time looking for him, she jumped right into the work with Milo.

Nor was she interested in interrupting his meeting with the Guild Master when she arrived earlier. Avery wanted to avoid a conversation with him nearly as much as she wanted to avoid Rhyker.

The captain only seemed slightly annoyed by her remark, apparently growing accustomed to her quick comments. "Unfortunately for both of us, the council still wants me to keep tabs on you," he said coldly. "If I'm stuck playing the part of your chaperon, then you can make it easier by letting me know when you've made it in."

Avery let the comment roll off her, donning a false smile. "Well, then I'll make sure to check in with you in the morning, that way you can start your morning off right." She moved past him, carrying the small crate with her to the backroom with an extra table for her to work. The captain did not bother to stop her, and she heard Milo laugh as she set the crate down.

Even without Milo there to help her, Avery made quick work cataloging the parts. The process was repetitive— cleaning, inspecting, logging, and finally packing each mechoid part—but she found the process to be somewhat cathartic. Especially since it kept her mind occupied and her hands busy. Despite being delayed by having to reorganize them again – thanks to Milo – she finished up the work before Milo had a chance to return from the research facility.

She sat idle for a few moments, contemplating her options. Without knowing how much longer Milo would be, the thought of waiting in the workshop did not appeal to her. She briefly toyed with the idea of leaving and returning later that evening when Milo would for sure be back, but ultimately decided to leave the workshop and head up to the second floor of the guild hall.

Although there was not a guild meeting planned for

another week, the chairs and stage for the event were left out. Many people were scattered throughout the room, some in conversation, some utilizing the folding tables on the chairs to get some work done. She let her eyes scan the room, only a few lifting their heads up to take her in when she entered.

A muffled voice caught her ear. "I cannot spare the captain, he's the only one qualified enough to be that far out in the field." Even in his hushed tone, the Guild Master's voice was easy enough to recognize. "I understand the growing concern, and I have other members looking into Logan's death."

A cold chill swept through Avery's bones, and she abruptly stopped walking further, intent on listening to more.

"There is nothing the captain will be able to do, any trail is weeks old. Whatever mechoid did it is long gone."

"What if it wasn't a mechoid, James?" the stranger's voice spat out in a panic. "It doesn't make sense! Logan wouldn't go down from some mech."

"Unless he was over run, Leif."

"Then what happened to the others?" Their voices were getting louder, moving closer.

"That's why the Knights are getting involved." The Guild Master attempted his calming tone once more. "They've already sent someone to investigate. They are set to arrive even sooner than I anticipated. I assure you, there is nothing more we can do until we hear back from him." James emerged from the open office door, and Avery quickly tried to look busy searching around the hall for someone.

"Ah, Miss Avery! A pleasure to see you," The Guild Master chimed joyously, as if he was not just discussing a man's death moments ago. His companion made no attempt to conceal his anxious expression, his silver eyes showing the familiar alarm when finding her own blue ones. His eyes traveled to the hilt of Lightbringer on her shoulder, and he squeaked in a moment of realization. "Oh, this must be your knight."

James chuckled. "No, although she is training to be one. Working under General Carter no less!"

The man nodded, his stare once again fixated on her eyes. "Ah, apologies, Miss," he muttered, looking anxious once again.

The Guild Master took his cue to introduce the man. "This is Leif Corwin, one of my advisors." Once pleasantries were exchanged, he flashed her a smile. "What brings you up here?"

"I was looking for the captain."

"I believe he is out training some of our reinforcements today." He moved toward a door and waved her over. Avery followed him, finding herself out on a terrace that overlooked the training yard. A wave of sunlight warmed her skin as she took in the flat field where the sparring circle was made. The spot where Rhyker tested her blade before agreeing to take her out on the field mission.

Many onlookers stood around the ring, some anxious and holding simple wooden swords as they watched the current contenders. There in the center, the captain battled against the oncoming attacks from multiple sources. There were three other people in the ring with him, new recruits for the guild, as James proudly explained. Each had a wooden sword and attempted to take the captain on, sometimes in pairs. The captain effortlessly countered each of them, only pausing when all three were momentarily knocked back. He pointed out corrections or made a few example movements before instructing them to try again. Avery watched for a few rounds before the Guild Master swayed impatiently next to her.

Now more than ever, she wanted to leave the guild hall and seek out Harvey to ask about Logan. However, James insisted he would walk with her downstairs. She accepted, hoping to avoid raising any suspicion that she might have overheard their earlier discussion. The Guild Master walked her as far as the door that led outside to the training yard. He wished her a good day before walking onward with Leif trailing awkwardly behind.

Conversing with the captain was already undesirable and doing so with an audience even less so. With only a few moments to consider her approach, she quickly decided what she would say to the captain. It did not take any time at all for the recruits around the edges of the spar to catch sight of her, many nudging at the others to alert them of her presence. By the time all of them had turned their attention away from the training, the group parted, opening her view to the captain. He was blocking an overhead strike and knocked down the trainee that got distracted from the commotion. The other two stopped their assault altogether, nervously looking to the captain for guidance.

The captain did not bother looking at Avery right away, her aura already telling him exactly who it was that disrupted the session. He helped the younger man up, checking that he was good before addressing Avery.

"Did you get lost?" he asked, not even a hint of sweat showing from the exercise.

"Milo went up to assist the research facility," she stated in a simple, pleasant tone.

"That's fine, go ahead and just continue what he was working on. I trust you're not reckless enough to try anything."

"I already finished the work," she said coldly. "I wanted to spare your hurt feelings and check in with you *before* doing anything reckless."

Milo would have laughed at that, but the recruits did not. Instead, they just looked dumbfounded, their eyes threatening to burst from how wide they stretched.

The captain's mouth twitched, hinting at a smile. "Alright," he said, gesturing with a casual wave for her to join him in the circle. "You can help me demonstrate."

The silence from the recruits was excruciating as she hesitated, determining just how much she regretted not leaving earlier.

Rhyker was enjoying her pause, the smirk fully making an appearance as he watched her contemplate. She shrugged. "Just give me a sword, Captain."

Rhyker threw his wooden sword aside and pulled out the metal blade at his hip. "I thought you brought your own?" He snickered. "Unless you'd feel safer if I used a wooden one."

A spark ignited in her chest, her already burning frustration beginning to manifest itself in the magic that begged to seep out. Grabbing the hilt of Lightbringer, she entered the circle. The three recruits scrambled to get out of the way, joining the others as the gap in onlookers closed behind her once more.

She did not bother waiting for him to throw the first strike, knowing she needed every advantage she could get to keep up with him. The moment Lightbringer cleared her shoulder, she dashed at him, his blade meeting her sword in front of them. A collective gasp erupted from the onlookers, and Rhyker had the audacity to full-on grin at her, fueling her frustration further as she pushed off and traded strikes with him back and forth. She erased the thought of the crowd from her mind, completely focusing on her sword and keeping the valve closed on her magic hungry vessel.

They were locked in the spar, neither willing to give up any ground to the other. Her muscles strained, stinging with every heavy block she had to produce in order to stay upright.

Their movements became a blur, each parry and thrust demanding every ounce of her focus and energy. She lost track of time, the relentless rhythm of their matched strikes making it feel as though the duel could continue indefinitely

Until finally she misjudged one of his swings, and the captain noticed too, sliding his blade right past Lightbringer and straight for her neck. She had sense enough to freeze, yielding to the blade the captain so expertly stopped a hair away from killing her, or more likely using an unintentional shield to blast all of them away.

She glared up at the captain. The slight smirk he gave sending her into another internal fit of rage. The heat from the battle caught up to them, both breathing heavy. The captain was close enough for her to see a few beads of sweat on his forehead. A minor victory she would take considering his blade was close enough to pierce her skin if she breathed too hard.

There was a barrage of clapping, both had forgotten entirely about the captivated audience that surrounded them. Rhyker withdrew his blade, giving Avery the space to breathe freely.

"Alright," the captain said, addressing the others to dismiss them. "Let's break for the day."

A few waited around to chat with the captain, many of them continuing their stares on Avery as they collected their things and dispersed toward the guild hall. There was a short time she was alone with the captain while he put away the wooden swords in a storage shed. She contemplated asking him about Logan but changed her mind when she found Milo coming out of the guild hall to join them. He was in a huff, complaining the whole way back to his workshop that he missed seeing the two of them spar.

Since Avery finished the cataloging and Milo appeased the research facility by double checking some of their research, it was decided they would set out the next day to start the first in a series of field missions. They all worked together to pack the necessary equipment and met with the research facility to be briefed on how the new equipment worked. Milo was over the moon, itching to get out and set it up

It was already late by the time Avery arrived back at the farmhouse. Not expecting Cecelia to still be awake, she was surprised to find Scout scratching to get out of the door to greet her, and the old mage seated at the kitchen table with a book and a steaming glass of tea. Her worried eyes brightened as she took Avery in, inviting her to sit down and share the events of the day with her.

Avery obliged, often finding solace in discussing the lessons she learned and gleaming wisdom that only could be acquired through the years of experience as both a mage and as a permanent resident of Farewell. Although, she left out the bit of the discussion she overheard from the Guild Master and, of course, her spar with Rhyker. Not quite sure how she felt about either of the incidents and needing more time to sort it out in her own mind.

The two finished off the warm tea by the time Avery felt ready to retreat to her room. Before she said goodnight, Avery informed her she would be gone again for another stretch of time, the duration not quite yet clear. The old mage wished her luck, urging her to get some rest before the trip.

Avery woke abruptly in the night to Scout's barking. Immediately on alert, Avery grabbed Lightbringer from beside her bed and barreled out of her room. The front door was wide open, and Avery felt the comfort of Cecelia's aura already outside of the house soothed her. Scout still barked as she reached the porch, finding the old mage squinting out into the fields.

"Are you alright?" Avery asked her, her eyes attempting to take in their surroundings for any sign of danger.

"Yes, sorry about that, dear," she said, a slight weariness added to her voice. "I think someone passed by the house and Ol' Scout didn't like 'em."

Scout bounded back, heading straight for Avery. The pup skid to a halt until he was at the base of her legs. He whipped around and hunched down in a growling fit, barking in her defense.

"Alright, easy now, Scout. You scared 'em real good. They're gone!" the old mage tried to soothe the agitated pup.

"You saw someone?" Avery asked.

"No, but I sensed them. Probably the scavenger that's been trying to steal the water heater out in the barn." Cecelia moved to go back in the kitchen. "Come now, dear. It's late!"

Avery followed her inside, finding the glass of tea still on the table, steam clearly rising from it. She flashed Cecelia a curious glance, which the old mage only responded to with the soft shaking of her head and a reassuring smile. "Go back to bed."

When she arrived back in her room, Scout was already curled up at the foot of her bed, apparently with no intention of leaving. After failing to coerce the pup to rejoin Cecelia in the kitchen, Avery settled into bed once more, her mind anxiously conjuring up horrible visions of Theodore showing up to the farmhouse.

She did not go back to sleep.

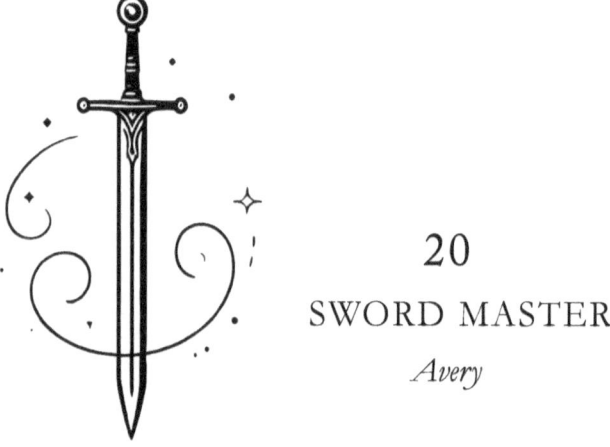

20
SWORD MASTER
Avery

The following weeks blurred together as Avery settled into a new routine. As planned, Rhyker's team, now including Avery – though the captain frequently reminded her she was not a full-fledged member – embarked on missions to deploy signal beacons in the farthest reaches surrounding Farewell.

The signal devices were constructed using parts from several different mechoids. Sensors from crawlers were utilized to scan within a considerable radius, triggering an alert sent through a mesh network of nearby beacons. This network of beacons extended all the way back to Farewell. Each beacon was powered by the core of a Prowler, providing the endless energy required to serve as an early warning system. Avery did not have the chance to see the master controller in the research facility that received all the incoming data, but according to Milo, it was working flawlessly.

For each trip out, they managed to deploy at least five of the devices in predefined locations based on a map and calculations that Professor Colleymore and Milo contrived. When they reached a targeted destination, Milo worked on installing the beacon, often utilizing the bones of giant power poles from the old ways to secure it. Rhyker and

Avery stood on guard while Reya scouted around for other incoming trouble.

Some locations were easier to deploy the devices than others, often depending on their proximity to mechoid hot zones. Milo's process for setting up the devices required using a glyph to sync them, which unfortunately attracted many curious mechoids. As a result, Avery often had her hands full with defeating the oncoming mechs and trying to stay out of the captain's way.

Rhyker was not exactly friendly toward her, but he no longer acted as though Avery was something unpleasant he found on the underside of his boot. He kept his sharp green eyes on her, getting some new satisfaction from pointing out faults in her sword work—to make matters worse, the same ones she heard from Harvey—and they usually came in the form of orders he yelled at her in the heat of mechoid encounters.

On occasion, he sparred with her, mostly to prove a point. The first of these unplanned lessons came after she finished taking out a Prowler that tried to overtake Milo. When they finished their work and were preparing to move onto the next site, Milo thanked her for the assist, but she found the captain shaking his head at her when she turned around. "You're becoming too predictable. You can't keep dashing in like that."

Caught off guard by his tone, she turned back to look at the fallen mechoid. "It got the job done, didn't it?"

"But if you're assailant is smarter than a Prowler, they'll see right through it. You leave yourself critically open to an attack. You need to learn to not project your movements."

"Right, Captain," she mused, her voice dripping with sarcasm. "I'll keep that in mind."

She moved to put her sword away but paused as Rhyker took a step toward her. The metallic sheen of his blade blurred by, and she barely managed to block the incoming sword with her own. He leveraged the pause to swing again at her, following it up with a few strikes before he pulled away, remaining at the ready.

"Try me," he dared, the most infuriating smirk spreading across his face. Reya and Milo stood by, frozen, unable to tear their eyes away from the encounter.

Frustrated, Avery took a few deep breaths before dashing at him, aiming her sword at his side. With ease, Rhyker sidestepped and used his sword to deflect her blade, making it roll off the edge as if it were nothing. With his free hand, he gave her a firm shove in the back, sending her stumbling forward. Avery managed to catch herself before taking a full tumble.

The captain let out an audible laugh, and she turned to see his smug grin taunting her. She tightened her jaw, her face flushing as she struggled to catch her breath. Pushing aside the unsavory thoughts that filled her mind, she focused on the captain's earlier words. Unfortunately, he was right.

Avery moved toward him, stepping forward in her systematic dash. He shook his head, disappointed and preparing for the counter, but she pulled back at the last moment, pulling her sword around to strike at his exposed side. He staggered forward but was quick enough on his feet to recover by pivoting his body, his sword catching her blade before making any contact. She took the opportunity presented by his awkward positioning to cross swords, locking them into place to create a stalemate. His eyes briefly traced the blades of their swords and her positioning before giving a nod.

"Not bad, Blue Eyes. Looks like you *can* take direction."

Annoyed, she pulled back and disengaged, swearing under her breath the unsavory words she saved from before. Sparring with Rhyker was always a trial by fire. His movements were nearly unpredictable yet calculated. Through pure determination, she kept pace with him, even managing to fuel some of her attacks with the light magic she channeled. Harvey had warned her of the dangers of trying this out in the field, but part of her felt like the captain could handle it. The other part of her hoped it might wipe the playful grin off his face, which seemed to be making a regular appearance.

Avery was starting to lose count of the number of field missions she was a part of by the time autumn threatened to take over. For every beacon they set up, the research facility had more ready to be deployed, which kept them out in the field most of the time. Although exhausted, Avery welcomed the experience, because it meant she could more effectively practice what she was learning.

Harvey had already learned of Logan's disappearance and death by the time Avery spoke with him next. The old man didn't have much more to add, except that Logan and his team had been sent out on a routine mission to recover common parts needed for the research facility but never made it back. Avery felt a chill as Harvey mentioned that the rest of Logan's party members had also been found dead, their bodies recovered in scattered locations. Rumors were circulating among the guild that their deaths weren't just the result of mechoid attacks. Whispers of something more sinister had spread through town, fueling an underlying sense of dread among the townspeople.

The town's usual bustle felt tense, with residents moving quickly and avoiding eye contact. The recent increase in guards patrolling the walls only reinforced the sense that something dangerous was lurking just beyond the safety of Farewell. Shop owners shut their doors earlier, and the air was heavy with caution and anxiety.

Harvey, though he never admitted to being concerned, instructed Avery to keep her sword on her at all times—a precaution he hadn't insisted on since he'd given her Lightbringer. His stern tone and cautious eyes told her everything she needed to know: the situation was more serious than he let on. On top of it all, Theodore's painful punishments had become fewer and farther apart, which only heightened Avery's unease. She couldn't shake the feeling that he was scheming something, and she feared she would never be strong enough to face whatever he had planned.

One evening, as if sensing her turmoil, Rhyker presented Avery with another surprise demonstration. He commented on how heavily she was relying on magic to block advances — a problem Harvey was still trying to break her out of. During their spar, the captain found ways to intentionally trigger the instinctual reaction several more times, with no improvement on Avery's part to control it. He reluctantly gave up for the night. It seemed more dangerous the longer they stretched the impromptu spar.

When Avery returned with Rhyker to the small campfire, Milo must have been able to tell she was still frustrated. He tossed one of the packaged sandwiches her way, laughing. "Reya was one of the only people in town who could keep up with Rhyker, but at the speed you're learning, I could see you taking over as captain in a few months."

"Hard pass on that," Avery replied, trying to keep her irritation in check. "I don't think I could handle the research facility and the church breathing down my neck all the time." She flashed an exaggeratedly sweet smile at the captain, adding, "Besides, I wouldn't know where to find the time to practice brooding in the corner during meetings."

Both Milo and Reya laughed at the jest, and Avery

caught Rhyker returning an amused glance.

"Better to be in those meetings than get myself blown up somewhere," he chimed in joining them at the fire. "Of course, captain is pretty ambitious for someone not enlisted in a guard at all." He eyed Avery over the fire. "I happen to know the guy who is in charge of hiring for Farewell doesn't take in strays who can't take orders."

Milo and Reya exchanged worried looks, but Avery did not waiver. "Can't be a problem if I'm not here to prove myself capable of being on his team."

"Right." He set his pack down and grinned, "I hear you've got those blue eyes of yours set higher."

Avery remained silent, refusing to fuel his enjoyment any further. Seeing she did not plan on elaborating, he waved a dismissive hand at her, as if her silence was reason enough to prove his point. "You have a lot more to learn about working on a team before any guard will take you. Let alone the Lunar Knights."

"I'll be sure to ask a *real* Knight the next time I see one." She handed Milo back the sandwich, finding she lost her appetite. "In the meantime, I'll have to finish out these last two field missions before I'll be off your precious team."

She was not sure what compelled her to say it, and partially regretted breaking the news to Milo and Reya in that way. Their faces fell as they absorbed the implication, and they turned to their captain for confirmation. Earlier in the week, the Guild Master had visited the Big Hen to assure Harvey that Avery only had to complete two more field assignments. This meant that after their return to Farewell, she would only have one more mission before she was cleared of her community service duties.

Rhyker watched her from behind the fire, a flicker of irritation crossing his face, perhaps not wanting the others to know just yet. He shrugged. "Until you get yourself into trouble again. Who knows, you might end up in a holding cell next time."

Avery let out a short, hollow laugh. "I doubt it. I'm pretty sure Harvey would kill me first." She walked away from the camp, declaring she would take the first watch. As she settled into her post, she could hear Milo and Reya whispering in hushed argument before they finally called it a night.

When they returned to town, large banners adorned the arches leading into Farewell, their vibrant colors fluttering in the breeze. Festive decorations were being strung up throughout the town, transforming the streets into a lively, colorful scene. Streamers and lanterns hung from buildings, while flower garlands wrapped around lampposts, adding a touch of natural beauty to the celebration. Many people bustled around the guild hall, some carrying more decorations while others transported various pieces of furniture, setting up for what looked to be a grand event.

Despite the festive atmosphere, the team's exhaustion from the successful field mission was evident. After completing the necessary task work, Avery turned in for the night alongside the others. Scout nestled down beside her feet as she settled into bed, and she wondered why the pup refused to sleep elsewhere. Her mind became preoccupied with reviewing the events of the trip, still feeling irritated by her spat with the captain. She forced her mind to think of something else, settling on thoughts of the decorations in town. She made a mental note to ask Leah about the event causing all the excitement in Farewell.

Harvey, as usual, did not show any surprise to see Avery back to training first thing the next morning. He barked his usual disapproval at her performance, throwing corrections at her as needed. "You're getting overconfident again, that block was sloppy."

Avery muttered a remark under her breath, choosing to ignore the jab and focus on her aggressive strike. He deflected it effortlessly, letting her feel the weight of the block. Her arms absorbed the impact, and she did her best to pretend it had not affected her. They traded a few more blows before Harvey pulled away, grumbling about her positioning.

Although he said nothing, Avery could sense the old man's extra tension. She was accustomed to his harsh instruction, but Harvey usually made some snarky comment to take the edge off his bark. When his behavior persisted even after she managed a few good counters, she finally faced him, pulling away from his advance. "Did you lose your favorite cane today, or are you going to tell me why you're so sore with me?"

Harvey did not skip a beat, as if he had been waiting for her to ask, "What's this wild idea you have of leaving once you're done with your community service?"

"What do you mean?" she demanded. "Going to Astoria was your idea, has that not been what I've been training for?"

"What makes you think you can handle yourself out there?"

"I've been doing nothing but train since I've been here. Have I not shown that I can-"

Harvey cut her off with a grunt. "So what is it? You think now that you've got a few mechs notched on your belt that you're prepared for what's out there?"

Avery said nothing, she lost count of the total mechoids she managed to take out in the field, and she was not going to deny she was becoming more confident in her own ability to handle the creatures. He watched her, scratching his beard. "Or is it sparring with Rhyker that's given you some sort of idea that you're ready to take on the world?"

Avery glared at Harvey, a fire steadily growing in her. "Well, I've definitely been managing, haven't I?"

Harvey let out an empty laugh. "Do you really think the captain has been giving you a real fight? He's a sword master, kid! We're only giving you a taste of what's out there. You've still got much to learn before you can take on real combat."

Feeling her face get hot, she felt her grip on her sword tighten. "I didn't realize I had time for you all to be going easy on me."

"And what? You think you can become a sword master in just a few short months of training? Hell, Avery, you can't even control magic. You're not ready to go to the capital."

"And what if Theodore catches up to me?" she asked, her blood beginning to boil. "I think I've done a hell of a lot for myself since I started."

Harvey held up his sword, eyeing her with his jaw tight. "You think you can handle it, fine. Show me."

Slowly, Avery closed the gap between them, raising Lightbringer in preparation for his advance. She struck first, but it only took two quick moves for Harvey to knock the sword from her hand, his blade stopping an inch from her neck. "You're. Not. Ready," he said slowly, each word etching itself into her mind. "Stop arguing and pay attention, or your overconfidence will cost you." Avery glared at him but said nothing, acknowledging that he had proven his point. He lowered his sword, allowing her to pick up Lightbringer before they continued their drills.

Avery left the tavern without saying a word, leaving a confused and hurt Jaune with an untouched breakfast plate. Not wanting to return to the farmhouse yet, she spent several hours walking through the nearby forest, admittedly hoping to find some mechoids to work out her growing frustration. After not finding any—and nearly running into a few patrols, which thankfully did not include the captain—Avery gave up and went to the bookstore, hoping Leah would join her for a walk to help clear her mind.

"Avery, he really cares for you, don't you understand?" Leah said after Avery confided in her about the whole ordeal. Avery had hoped her friend would share her outrage but instead, Leah looked as worried as Jaune. "Maybe he's right; maybe you are getting ahead of yourself."

"That's easy for everyone else to say—they aren't the ones dealing with Theodore's tantrums," Avery muttered. The look Leah gave her told her she had gone too far. Despite how frustrating it was to be told she was not ready, Avery could not stand the concerned expressions everyone shared whenever the subject of her curse came up.

"Anyway, what's with all these decorations around town?" she asked, attempting to change the subject. "It looks like Farewell is getting ready for something big."

The topic had been exactly what Leah needed to forget about her concern. "Oh Avery, I forgot that you wouldn't know anything about it! You'll love it! It's the Harvest festival held every year. It's a week-long celebration where the town welcomes in the autumn season. The point is to celebrate a long and prosperous crop season and ask the goddess Fayne to bless the farmlands." She rambled in typical Leah fashion. "A lot of travelers come through to join the festivities, it's honestly busier here than during the winter solstice."

"Sounds exciting, I should be done with my community service by then. I have my last field mission sometime this week. We are just waiting on more trackers from the research facility."

Leah frowned at the news. "Oh, but Avery when are we going to get you a dress?...and you'll need to learn the

Farewell dance!" Leah took a long breath that was more like a gasp.

"Have you ever danced before?"

Avery raised her hands in the air. "Hold on, dance, dress?" she shook her head. "I don't understand." Avery was not sure she liked where the conversation was going, but Leah was reaching unexplored levels of excited.

"Oh Avery, it's the best part! The masquerade!"

When Avery did not react to the news, Leah nearly lost it. "We can go together! It's a lovely event where everyone dresses up in elegant attire and wears custom-made masks. The tradition comes from the capital, and I can even lend you a book all about it!"

Avery tried not to laugh at Leah's enthusiasm. "I don't know if I'll have time for all this. I have to leave for another field mission any day now."

Leah moved in front of Avery and grabbed her arm, pleading. "Oh, please, Avery, it will be so much fun! I promise I'll find you a dress and get you anything you need."

Avery held her hands up in defeat. "Okay, I'll go with you. Just take a breath, for the goddess's sake."

The development had been enough to keep Leah's mind occupied and far away from thoughts of Avery's curse. The two continued to discuss all Avery's options, and Leah repeatedly reassured her it would not interfere with her work for the guild. The two walked down the slope of the butte, approaching the pioneer statue. Leah's excited rambles persisted until a shout from across the plaza interrupted them.

Milo and Reya were walking around the other side of the pioneer statue and flagged her down. After brief introductions between the two guards and Leah, Milo looked inquiringly at Avery. "We were just going for some drinks, would you two want to join?"

"Sure," Avery agreed, but seeing the captain come around the corner to join them, she stopped, second guessing the decision. "That is... if Leah wants to. We were just heading back to the bookstore."

Leah's eyes lit up at the invitation. "That sounds great! I've heard so much about your field stories, and it would be wonderful to hear them firsthand."

"Oh yeah, and things have only been getting stranger since we found out the mechoids could use magic." Milo beamed, leading the group toward the tavern.

Avery caught Rhyker surveying her, less enthusiastic than her about the sudden company. He attempted to be civil about it, throwing her a quick nod of acknowledgment. In turn, she ignored him, letting him know the feeling was mutual.

Returning to the tavern after the heated discussion with Harvey was the last thing Avery wanted to do, but she knew it was too late to back out once she realized exactly where the group intended to go. Leah's enthusiasm was palpable, and Avery realized this was a perfect opportunity for her friend to escape the confines of the bookstore for a while.

Harvey's eyes landed on her immediately when they arrived, settling into a questioning glare. Avoiding any further eye contact, she joined the others in grabbing one of the longer tables while Reya and Rhyker fetched drinks for the group. Once seated, Avery found it easy enough to enjoy the company, listening quietly while Milo and Reya shared stories with Leah about their time in the field. Rhyker occasionally chimed in, providing details or teasing his team about their various mishaps over the years.

Harvey had taken to pretending the group did not exist whatsoever when Avery glanced up from her nearly untouched drink. In contrast, she often caught Jaune staring at her from over the kitchen doors. Finally giving in to his inquiring gaze, Avery excused herself from the group, taking her drink with her. She moved to the bar top and waved him over. "Alright Jaune, you win. What's your deal?"

"Avery, you haven't eaten all day. You're training too hard to be starving yourself," Jaune said, his voice carrying a silky accent that hinted at his origins from a kingdom far overseas. Despite his tall and stocky build, his manner was by far the gentlest she had ever encountered. His deep-set eyes showed genuine concern, and his broad shoulders relaxed as he leaned on the bar, emphasizing the softness in his tone. Avery could not help but notice the contrast between his imposing physical presence and his caring demeanor, which made his concern for her well-being all the more touching.

Avery offered him a small nod, her expression softening to show she appreciated his concern. "I'll be fine. Besides, between you and Cecelia, it would be near impossible for me to go hungry." Avery's eyes flashed over to Harvey who was at the other end of the bar helping another customer to a drink. Jaune catching her line of sight nodded, lowering his voice.

"You know he cares greatly for you. He is hard on you for that reason."

She stared into her drink again, her mind unable to shake the memory of her exchange with Harvey earlier that morning. She struggled to pinpoint the source of her frustration—was it his harsh assessment of her skills, or the ever-present threat of Theodore looming over her? The uncertainty gnawed at her, making it hard to find clarity amidst the swirl of emotions.

A grunt pulled her from her thoughts as Harvey approached their side of the bar top. Jaune took the hint and retreated to the kitchen, offering Avery a subtle eyeroll before disappearing behind the doors. Harvey picked up her untouched glass, scowling at the contents. Without a word, he replaced it with another glass containing a clear liquid. Avery accepted it, taking a quick sip to confirm it was water.

Finding it much more refreshing, she gave Harvey a soft smile. He responded by rolling his eyes and muttering some choice words under his breath as he walked back toward the other end of the bar top.

"What? You don't drink?" Rhyker's voice asked her from over her shoulder. Avery turned to face him, shrugging slightly. "I find the effects bother me."

The captain moved to stand next to her, putting his empty glass on the bar. The others were still at the table, and from Milo's expressive hands, he was in the middle of another story.

Avery turned back to stare down at her drink, wondering if she should rejoin them.

"You're more quiet than usual today," Rhyker stated bluntly.

Avery looked up at him curiously, finding his tone unusual. "And you're more talkative. It seems a drink makes it much more palatable to talk to me."

Rhyker tilted his head as if to consider it. "I suppose it does increase my tolerance for your cryptic manner." Seeing that she found the comment amusing, he leaned on the bar top, eyeing her curiously. "I don't think you'll make it easy by being plain with me."

Avery laughed, taking another sip from her glass before responding. "Where's the fun in that, Captain?" It was Rhyker's turn to laugh. The unexpected sound sent stares from Milo and Reya, who suddenly seemed very interested in what was happening at the bar top. Rhyker's lips curled into a grin, and he shot Avery a questioning glance.

"What's your plan after finishing-" he started to ask, but another voice cut in.

"Are you gonna order a drink, Captain, or are you going to keep wasting my time?"

Harvey stood behind them at the counter, giving the captain an unimpressed once over. Rhyker stood up straight, agreeing to another drink. The old man handed it to him with an eyebrow raised, watching as Rhyker took it and returned to the table with the others.

Avery caught Harvey's eye, grinning widely at him when he winked at her and returned to cleaning glasses behind the bar.

21
THE HARVEST FESTIVAL

Avery

A very was right to assume she would be sent out again so quickly. The next morning, during her training session with Harvey, their practice was abruptly interrupted. Jaune emerged from the tavern, holding the door open as Rhyker stepped out into the courtyard.

"We're not open yet!" Harvey barked at the captain, his tone gruff and unwelcoming.

Avery straightened from her ready position, watching as the captain crossed the yard to meet them.

"I know," Rhyker replied, his stance unusually formal. "I've come to grab Blue Eyes. We received what we need from the professor and want to head out now so we can be back in time for the festivities next week." It could have been Avery's imagination, but she could swear the captain stood a bit taller and more formal in front of Harvey.

The old man ignored him and turned to Avery. "Alright, kid, I'll see you when you get back," Avery nodded, heading over to the bench to grab her cloak. As she draped it over her shoulders, she heard a grunt from behind her. Turning, she saw Harvey eyeing Rhyker suspiciously. "Well? She knows where it's at, Captain. You don't need to wait around."

Rhyker's expression remained neutral, but a hint of amusement flickered in his eyes. "Right, General, I'll see myself out."

"Quit it with that General crap, kid! I'm retired." Harvey called after him and turned abruptly when he heard Avery let out a small chuckle. Irritated he waved a hand at her. "What are *you* still doing here? Get going!"

She brought up two fingers to her temple and flicked them in a fake salute. "Yes, General!"

Harvey swore loudly behind her as she made her way out.

Leaving the Big Hen, she spotted Rhyker up the street and picked up her pace to meet with him. Nearly closing the gap between them, she went to call out to him, but another voice caught both their attention.

"Captain!" A woman dressed in simple, yet elegant robes waved to the captain from further up the street. Her silky brown hair was tied back into a long braid. Large brown eyes, speckled with gold flakes, lit up as they met Rhyker's gaze, and shifted curiously as she caught sight of Avery behind him.

Realizing it was too late to abandon her route, Avery gave a subtle wave, dreading what was sure to come.

A lovely smile fluttered onto the woman's face, and she looked over Avery favorably.

"Oh! You must be Avery! I don't think I've ever had a chance to meet you. My name is Mindy." She reached her hand out to shake Avery's, giving the captain time to take Avery in. He gave her a puzzled look, as if he did not expect her to catch up to him.

Avery maintained the friendly composure. "It's a pleasure Mindy, I have seen you once or twice in the guild meetings."

"Yes, Rhy told me-" She paused abruptly and blushed, correcting herself. "I mean Captain Adler has told me all about you. Leah also tells me great things! It's a shame it's taken this long for us to finally meet," Mindy spoke quickly, reminding Avery a lot of Leah. "The church was so worried when we found out you had been a part of that explosion in the ruins. I'm glad everything worked out for the best."

Avery tried not to wince at the mention of the incident. "Yes, I'm grateful for how understandings both the church and the guild have been." She kept smiling at Mindy but was suddenly feeling the urge to disappear. She could see the corners of Rhyker's mouth threaten to grin.

"We are actually getting ready to go out for another mission now," he added, causing Mindy to return her adoring smile back up at him.

"Yes! I heard and I came straight here to wish you luck."

A sliver of irritation ripped through Avery's body from an uncomfortable stirring she felt standing there. "Well, I better help Milo prep our gear," she said, trying to excuse herself from the small gathering. "It was a pleasure to meet you, Mindy."

Mindy dipped her head with practiced grace, maintaining her flawless composure. "And you! Travel safe, and may the goddess bless you!"

Avery felt a pit in her stomach as she entered the guild hall, her mind trying to rationalize why she felt so envious of Mindy. The High Priestess' protégée had been nothing but welcoming, yet Avery felt part of herself wish they had never met. Perhaps it would have been easier to dislike her that way. She managed to convince herself the thought was not worth her time and tried to shake it from her mind, focusing on the task at hand.

"Avery, is this really going to be our last mission together?" Milo crossed his arms and sent wide eyes her way in a fake pout. They finished gathering the last of their gear and were seated around one of the tables in the commons, waiting for the captain to return from a meeting with the Guild Master.

"I'm afraid so." She gave him a sympathetic shrug. "The Guild Master already agreed after this mission, my community service will have been served."

Reya threw her pack on the table in a huff. "Well, you could at least act like you'll miss us! It hasn't been that miserable."

They continued to jest with Avery until the captain returned and gave them the all-clear to head out, promising they would all get some time off upon their return.

Deploying the beacons had become a routine operation for the Blitz Team, occasionally disrupted by an unusual horde of mechoids drawn to the signals. Despite these interruptions, the team moved with a focused energy that kept them ahead of schedule, completing each objective in just under a week. On their last night out, Reya and Avery took on the patrol while the others wrapped up the last of the catalogs and set up camp. Other than a few roaming Prowlers, the approaching night remained clear as they walked with purpose toward the camp. There was an unusual agitation in Reya's movements, unlike her typically smooth and controlled manner.

Avery learned of the guard's own story over the course of the many field missions they ran together. Reya's family was from a long line of guards that served throughout Arcadia. She grew up with three older brothers, all of whom she had to learn to out match or endure their teasing and torment. Her grandfather was an accomplished blacksmith, forging steel for many renown knights and guards throughout the kingdom. This included the short blade that Reya wielded, which gave off subtle hints of magenta when the blade caught the light just right.

Reya shared stories of her siblings and how she

missed them but confessed she would not have traded the opportunity to work with Rhyker and the guard for the world. Her goal was to one day become a captain of her own team. Avery thought the position suited her well. She had a sharp eye for anticipating situations and handled her responsibilities well from what Avery gathered from her time working with her.

The guard always managed a calm demeanor whenever they were faced with challenges, which was also why it was apparent that something was on her mind when she anxiously kept eyeing Avery nervously along their patrol. When they finished their sweep around the camp and made to join the others, Reya suddenly cornered her.

"Listen Avery," she said, a slight urgency in her tone. "How long are you planning on staying in Farewell?"

There had been a taboo on the topic of Avery's departure from her community service set by the captain after they first set out on the mission. It was clear Reya and Milo were not happy to lose Avery as their travel companion, and Rhyker was tired of hearing about it.

Avery sighed and answered Reya truthfully, "I don't know. That's what I'll be working on figuring out with Harvey once I'm done with my time owed to the city."

"Right, I get that." Reya dismissively waved it away. "But I really do think you would make a great addition to our team. You already fit in so well."

Avery held her hands up showing the situation was out of her hands. "Thanks, I appreciate that, but I can't. Besides, I don't think your captain feels the same."

The excuse did not register for Reya, she pressed the issue. "I think he is warming up to you, it's been nice having the extra capable hand, and I'm sure he's starting to realize that."

Avery turned to face Reya, finding the guard imploring

her to consider it. "Really, Reya," she did her best to give her an apologetic smile. "I can't settle down in Farewell yet. I have some personal matters I need to resolve before I'm able to do much of anything."

Reya sighed, but after a moment of recognizing that Avery was not wavering, she nudged her arm. "You realize how ominous that sounds?" The guard laughed and shook her head, letting the matter rest.

They traveled back to rejoin the others with Avery's mind weighing significantly heavier. The unspoken truth of the matter was she enjoyed working on the captain's team. Reya and Milo had become friends, and Farewell was starting to feel like a place where she belonged. Except, she knew she could not slow down, and the end of her community service meant she would soon need to make the trip overseas to seek out the mage council in the capital.

Reaching the camp, Milo stopped messing with the part in his hands and eagerly looked to Reya. The guard shook her head. "It's a no go, she wouldn't budge."

Avery laughed but subsided as Rhyker curiously eyed her. Since their last mission, they had not exchanged more than a few words. The captain seemed to not care that she would no longer be accompanying his team, and he probably would have been more vocal about it if it would not earn him push back from his team. Avery reminded herself the needless tension would go away after they returned to Farewell.

The group returned to town eagerly awaiting to see what new decorations and stalls had been set up while they were away. Many more people filled the streets, enlisting a new wave of anxious energy that seemed to strain her aura. Milo and Avery wrapped up the remaining work from their trip, processing the collected parts as if it was just like any other mission. The only noticeable difference was the presence of the Guild Master, who was there to shake her hand before they left. He thanked her for being true to her word in repaying her debt. The glint in his eye told her he would not be a stranger while she remained in Farewell.

After taking the time to wash up, she sought out the comfort of the bookstore, prepared to pick up another book and discover what it was Leah had been up to while she was gone. To say Leah had been busy was an understatement. Upon Avery's arrival, Leah closed the shop early and hurried Avery up the stairs to look at what she'd procured since they last spoke. Leah could not contain nor hide her own excitement, refusing to hear of any of the details of the mission until Avery tried on the dress she found.

"I figured blue was the best color to go with your eyes." She ushered Avery into a room where she could change, shoving the fabric into her arms. Finding that arguing would not get her anywhere, Avery slipped into the dress, admittedly having difficulty figuring out how to work the ties in the back. Securing it in place, Avery took a look at herself in the mirror, her heart dropping at the sight. The dress overall was a beautiful blue that matched her eyes perfectly. The fabric spilled down her hips and hovered just above the floor. A small gap created an opening for her leg to slip out of, adding to the stunning shape. Yet, her eyes were not focused on the dress at all.

The strapless cut meant her exposed chest displayed the dark grey lines that cracked beneath her skin. The deep marks were much darker and spread slightly further along, beginning to reach for her shoulders. A slight gasp escaped Avery upon hearing a knock on the door. Her friend's unmistakable energy on the other side of the door. "What do you think Avery? Did I do good?"

"It's amazing, Leah," she called at the door, but she stared back in the mirror frowning.

Leah let out a happy squeal. "Well come out! Let me see!"

There was silence as Avery thought about it. "Leah," she started, speaking directly to the door. "I need to show you something, but I would like you to promise you won't say anything to anyone."

Avery could feel her friend take in the weight her words. She stopped shuffling outside the door. "What do you mean Avery? Is everything okay?"

"Leah, you have to trust me," she pleaded, hoping her friend would understand. "It is important they don't know. Mal, Harvey, Harris, all of them."

"Okay, I can do that," Leah reluctantly agreed. "Please just tell me what's wrong!"

Avery opened the door, and Leah's concerned eyes gave her a quick up and down before spotting the marks on her chest.

"Oh no!" she gasped. "How did that happen?"

"It happened after I took that blast from the Dozer. I hadn't used that much magic before, and my vessel didn't handle it well."

"Who else knows?"

"I think Harvey has an idea. He could tell something was wrong right after it happened."

"Does it hurt?"

She shook her head. "Not anymore, it did for about a week after I first noticed it."

Leah took in the rest of the dress on her, the concern on her face melting into a frown. "It really does look lovely on you."

Avery managed a smile, even as a wave of sadness washed over her. "I'm sorry, Leah, it is an amazing dress, but I can't go like this, Harris and Malcom will be anxious about it, and I don't have time to slow down. They already-"

"What if I could fix it?" Leah interrupted, her eyes skimming the dress again.

"What do you mean?" Avery asked, stunned by the sudden determination overtaking Leah.

"What if I added a top to it?"

"You think you could do that?" She looked down at herself, unaware of whatever possibilities Leah had in mind.

"Of course!" She beamed, her eyes taking the dress in as if it were a new challenge to be conquered. "Leave it to me. I think I know just how to fix it."

Avery obliged, and changed out of the dress so Leah could get to work. Deciding some tea was in order, Avery left her friend engrossed in the work to seek some out. On her way to the kitchen, she found Malcom at his desk tinkering on a strange black object that sparkled in the light. Upon seeing Avery, he looked startled, tossing the mysterious object into a drawer and closing it hastily, a few loose gems still scattered on his desk.

"Ah, Avery! Good to see you're back! Your last mission go well?"

"Yes, we couldn't have asked for better conditions," she responded, trying not to seem the least bit curious about whatever it was he was attempting to conceal.

"Good, good," he said gruffly, clearing his throat. "Sounds like you're ready for some much-needed rest."

"We shall see. I'll be working with Harvey more now that I'm not required to be at the guild hall."

"Well, I hope you can enjoy the festival with Leah. Really, it's time for the town to take it easy and celebrate."

Avery nodded. "I'll keep that in mind."

"Avery!" Leah called from the other room, "I need to take some measurements!"

Both Malcom and Avery shared a chuckle from Leah's enthusiasm before Avery grabbed the tea pot and headed back to oblige her friend.

In an effort to help Milo and Reya cope with her departure from their team, Avery promised to spend one of their days off exploring the festivities together. The town was alive with activity, boasting numerous booths offering everything from local crafts to exotic goods, drawing attention from both residents and tourists.

It was refreshing to spend time with the two of them outside of the field missions, free from the constant need to stay alert or pore over catalogs of mechoid parts. The vibrant atmosphere, filled with laughter and music, provided a welcome break, allowing them to simply enjoy each other's company, and the lively spirit of the celebrations.

Around lunchtime, they acquired an assortment of foods and sweets to share and found an empty table to enjoy the delicious bounty. As they chatted, Reya sat up right in a sudden moment of remembrance.

"Avery, I received a letter from my grandfather while we were away. I wrote to him about your sword. I was right, it's from his forge! He said Harvey asked him for a favor."

"Oh!" Avery marveled at the news, struggling to find the right words in her astonishment.

"I didn't realize he had it made specifically for me."

Reya enthusiastically bobbed her head. "Yeah I had no idea my grandfather was friends with Harvey."

"It's surprising that old man has any friends," Milo managed to say with a mouth full of candies he bought from the last booth they visited. "He's basically a hermit!"

Avery laughed and looked down the way where the Big Hen sign stood on the other end of the town, a soft smile spreading across her face. "He's not all that bad. He means well."

Milo shot Avery a skeptical look, not buying her assessment, but he did not voice his doubt.

A sharp tug on her aura alerted her to the captain before he took the empty seat next to her. He sighed as he sat down. "The team at the research facility is swooning over the amount of progress we made these last few weeks. The High Priestess was there to make sure they didn't try to set up any more missions until after the festival is over."

"We have set up beacons all around Farewell. What more do they want us to do? Set up beacons inside the dead zones?" Milo whined, batting away Rhyker's stray hand who was trying to steal from his plate.

"Or goddess knows what else," Reya added.

"That's the general idea." Rhyker grinned triumphantly, managing to snatch a biscuit from Milo. "The High Priestess was not too happy. The church is starting to get more nervous, but it was already approved by the council, so I don't see much they can do."

Milo slumped behind his plate. "Well, at least we can enjoy the break while we can. Sounds like we will be heading out right after they close up the festival."

"Some of us." Rhyker remarked, throwing a teasing glance at Avery. From across the table, Reya shot her captain a warning look, which only seemed to deepen his amusement.

"So," Avery started, wanting to avoid the topic, "do you all attend the masquerade?"

Milo perked up from his soured mood. "Yes! One of the advantages of working out in the field; we don't get stuck on patrol duty during events."

"Will you be there, Avery?" Reya asked.

"Yes, I promised Leah I would go. She's supposed to teach me some sort of traditional dance."

Milo nudged Reya. "See! I told you we should practice! Got room for two more?"

"Sure, I don't think Leah would mind. We are going to practice at the Big Hen courtyard this evening."

"We will be there!" He turned and frowned at Rhyker who managed to steal another biscuit. "How about you, Rhy?"

Rhyker shook his head, a satisfied smirk planted on his face as he took a bite. "Can't. I'm meeting with the Guild Master this evening."

Reya raised her eyebrow at Rhyker. "What are you meeting the Guild Master for?"

"Not sure, probably about our next steps once the festival is over." He shrugged, but his eyes flickered onto Avery long enough for her to register the hint of irritation they held. Both of them tore away from the glance, and the captain continued to speculate with his teammates on possible locations for more beacons in the next set of field missions.

Leah was overjoyed to have Reya and Milo join them for the dance lesson at the Big Hen. Harvey rolled his eyes when Avery asked if they could use the courtyard to practice, begrudgingly allowing them all through.

Thanks to the book Leah loaned her, Avery learned the masquerade itself was originally a tradition created in Astoria. Allyen Silivus, the Former King of Arcadia, was known for his dedication to all those who lived within the Arcadian boundaries. He created the masquerade and invited both mages and non-mages alike to attend, in a time when certain factions deemed non-magic wielders to be less than that of a mage. Neighboring kingdoms were already seeing a massive siege of power from different conclaves of mages, with the aim to restructure society to better accommodate the magic wielders' needs.

Arcadia was different. Even in her allotted teachings under Theodore, Avery learned of the many battles the Arcadian's fought to purge that mindset from within its ranks. Despite being a magic wielder himself, the former king was against any notion that would render the non-magic user a lesser being. This led to him creating the masquerade, requiring all guests to wear masks, with a thin mesh covering the eyes so it was not known whether one was a mage or not.

The event marked the end of the weeklong celebration of the new season and became popular among other cities outside the capital after the passing of Allyen Silivus. Of course, the tradition has taken on many alterations over the years. According to Leah, most of the masks no longer used mesh coverings as too many children – and many more intoxicated adults – were prone to accidents with their vision obstructed.

Farewell had its own unique addition to the tradition: a special dance performed toward the end of the event, encouraging the whole town to come together. Avery was given a demonstration of the dance, which involved only a few repeatable steps. The charm of the dance lay in the frequent changing of partners, creating a lively and communal atmosphere. Jaune even took a break from the kitchen to join in, admitting he could not attend the event the next night. He jokingly blamed it on Harvey needing a hand with the other sorry folk who would rather haunt the tavern instead.

Soon enough, Avery was comfortable enough with the process to fumble through it, and worst case, she could laugh about whatever mishaps occurred with her friends. She almost missed having the captain around, knowing he would have plenty of fresh insults and jabs to delegate out to her and his team. It was almost worth putting up with his brooding.

♦ ♦ ♦

The next evening, Avery stared at herself in the tall mirror, wondering if it was actually herself she saw in the reflection. The blue dress was on again, this time with the addition of a top made from a black mesh material embroidered with black leaves and flowers that cleverly hid away the dark cracks beneath her skin. Half of her hair was down in long blonde curls while the rest was pinned up in neat braids. Left over embroidered petals were pinned throughout the braids, mimicking a wreath.

Leah had outdone herself, even adding a touch of makeup to seal off the transformation. Avery concentrated on the mirror, trying to determine why she looked so out of place. It was not that she was unrecognizable, but rather, it was the fullness in her smile, and the faint light in her eyes that shined ever so slightly that made it hard for her to believe it was really herself she saw. "You look amazing!" Leah appeared in the mirror, smiling equally as big as she took in her handiwork.

Leah wore a dark green dress that reached the floor and brought out the hints of red in her hair which was pulled back in a decorative bun.

"You both look stunning," Malcom's voice called to them from across the room. He stood proudly as he took them in, his eyes threatening to embrace the sentiment. He cleared his throat and held out his hands. "You'll be needing these!"

Avery reached out and took the black mask he offered her. Beautiful silver swirling lines decorated the edges, and a few blue gems were strategically placed, creating a stunning contrast.

"I made one just like this for your mother when she

was a bit younger than you." He went on, "Her gems were purple though, to match her eyes of course!"

Avery admired the mask and the care that went into creating it. "Thank you, it's beautiful!"

"No need to thank me, I'm just glad to keep up the tradition!"

Leah already had her mask on. Hers was a white mask with a leafy red design that even further complimented her. Following suit, Avery slipped her mask on. It hugged her cheekbones, and the slits for the eyes were not covered, letting the piercing blue eyes show they matched the dress.

Malcom escorted the two ladies to the guild hall where the event was set to take place. As they approached, Avery could see a steady stream of people already making their way inside. The entire second floor had been cleared out and transformed for the occasion, adorned with shimmering decorations in a kaleidoscope of colors. Glittering streamers hung from the ceiling, catching the light, while elegant drapes framed the windows. Among the attendees, no two masks were the same, each one a unique piece of art. The variety of shapes and sizes made it challenging for Avery to discern who was smiling behind the intricate designs.

After they took time to scope out the scene, Leah pointed out Reya and Milo, and they made their way to join them. About halfway across the room, Avery was halted when the Guild Master called for her.

"Ah, Miss Avery!" She turned to find James, dressed up for the occasion and wearing a maroon mask. He was accompanied by another man she did not know, despite the fact he was not wearing a mask at all. The Guild Master, seeing her confusion, made the introductions.

"Avery, this is Arthur Stonewell of the Lunar Knights." The title caused her to do a double take. While she had never met a Knight before, Arthur would not have been what she had come to expect. He was much older, probably nearer to Professor Colleymore's age and a bit disheveled in comparison to the clean-shaven look she had grown accustomed to of the guard, or Harvey. No real aura emitted from the man, although she could not really be sure with so much interference on her vessel from the other mages in the room. His light brown eyes seemed to drill into her, showing an interest despite only nodding to acknowledge the introduction. A shiver erupted in her spine, and she fought to keep a polite smile.

"Miss Avery is currently training to be a Knight," the Guild Master boasted as if she were his own pupil to be proud of.

"So I hear," the man said in a rough voice. The faint smell of whiskey lingering as he spoke. "Heard the ol' general came out of hiding to do it."

With every word she liked him less and had a hard time picturing him being able to best the captain. He seemed to read into her mistrust, a crooked grin finding his lips. "Strange thing to be hearing these days."

The Guild Master laughed, but Avery found no humor in it, and hoped the conversation would end. She became aware of how vulnerable she felt with the absence of Lightbringer, a fight she lost when getting ready with Leah. The knight seemed to relish in her discomfort, his eyes fixed on her own. She was granted relief when Milo and Reya called to her, inviting her to join them at the other end of the room. The Guild Master looked eager to continue introducing the knight to other members of the guild and politely excused their departure. The knight gave her one last look, as if he was trying to memorize her features, before he trailed off to follow James.

As the evening progressed, the atmosphere grew more relaxed and jovial. It was not long before Leah was enthralled in the retelling of Avery's first Leveler encounter, curtesy of Milo's exaggerated reenactment. She could not help but join in the laughter when Milo reached the bit about saving the captain's life, swearing he had never seen such a look of shock and fury from his captain. At the mention of him, Avery let her eyes scan the crowds of people, wondering where the captain was lurking or if he even bothered to attend the event.

Laughter erupted again from the group, pulling Avery back into the peaceful moment. A warm belonging enveloped her as she glanced around her friends. She found herself caught up in the moment, asking herself why she could not keep living like this. She toyed with the fantasy of formally joining the guard. Rhyker made it clear he did not want her on his team, but the Guild Master seemed to like Avery. She imagined he would be able to find her a suitable position.

Truthfully, she enjoyed the work, even in the slow times she enjoyed helping Milo with inspecting the mechoid parts for the research facility. Patrolling the border of Farewell may not have been as exciting as going out on field missions, but at least she would still see Milo and Reya from time to time.

Leah squealed loudly as the band switched to a different song. "This is it; let's go!"

She grabbed her hand, nearly dragging Avery to the dance floor. Others were already lining up in rows, everyone looking slightly uncomfortable, except Leah who stood across from her and waved encouragingly. When the cue played, they all joined together, Avery taking Leah's hand as they all moved in unison. Just as they practiced, Avery followed the moves, counting down the beat until the first change in partners arrived. Milo reached her, his enthusiasm and encouragement matching Leah's as he praised her footwork. She danced with two strangers next, doing her best not to mess up the moves as they all danced across the room.

When the twist came again, she glided into step with her next dance partner. He towered over her, his hand gently pressing into her lower back as he pulled her closer.

"With eyes like those, that mask is useless," Rhyker's familiar voice came from behind his black mask. She laughed, letting her fingers intertwine with the captain's. A sudden weightlessness overpowered even her darkest worry, her expression brightening as she met his gaze.

"With all that brooding you do, I'm surprised you had time for this."

He gave a small chuckle, spinning her around, then placing his foot between her own so she was forced to hang onto him as she tripped. Rhyker effortlessly pulled her back up to him, grinning childishly. "I see you're just as reckless on the dance floor as you are in the field."

Her face burned. She was thankful to have the mask covering it.

"You did that on purpose!" She narrowed her eyes at him, but his infectious smile tore through it, and another laugh managed to escape.

"Good luck proving that." His arms seemed to draw her in closer, a warmth encompassing them both like a flame feeding off kindling, growing stronger with each passing moment.

Time melted away as they danced. Silently, she wished she could hang onto the moment a little longer and embrace the warmth she felt staring into the green eyes. A hint of uncertainty lingered in the way Rhyker studied her from under his mask, showing her a depth she wanted to explore, but before she could say or do anything, the time came for her to switch partners again.

Following the melody, Avery moved to take the next hand that reached out for her. As her fingers brushed against a new partner's, she felt every inch of her body freeze. The warmth she shared with the captain was violently stripped away without warning, replaced by the chilling void of dread. Staring back at her from behind a blood-red mask were familiar, piercing yellow eyes. Her heart nearly stopped as she took in the cold gaze that could only belong to one man.

"Well, isn't this captivating?" Theodore forced a sickeningly sweet smile. His long black hair was tucked behind his ears, accentuating the narrowness of his face. The black dress suit he wore was fitted with red accents to match his mask, where his sunken eyes remained the only feature that ever changed with time, drained from decades of dark magics. Lord Sinclair looked down upon her, savoring every moment of her fear.

Avery could not move or even think for that matter. Although her body *was* moving, following along with the dance only because he kept her there, locked in step with him. "Oh, don't let me spoil your fun." The demonic eyes drilled into her, seeing the contempt register in hers. His lips formed a venomous frown. "It's a shame to see that bright smile of yours turn so cold." His fingertips tightened at her side, making her aware of the magic he channeled. The flow of magic trickled throughout her body, flooding the expanse of her vessel, like a wave of water seeping into every possible crack.

"I see you've kept plenty busy." He tilted his head slightly, as if the magic he used on her was probing her vessel, feeding him information. "You've managed to change the terms in this game of ours entirely." The magic tightened sharply, causing her to stiffen, the familiar pain slowly squeezing her body. Theodore's lip twitched – his version of a smile – the power he wielded around her threatening to break her if he felt like it.

Inside herself, she felt her own power struggling to hold up against the forceful constraints he was putting into place. The pain in her chest returned as it burned to fight back, but Theodore's power was stronger, and stifled out the flames, leaving her to feel the strain on her body. She could not run. There was no fighting back.

To the right of her, behind Theodore, the captain came into view. He was dancing with someone else, in conversation with them as they moved around the hall. Perhaps the captain and the guild could help her, but would they be able to? Would the captain come to her aid if she called for him?

Theodore read her contemplation, merely glancing over his shoulder at the captain. He reinforced his hold on her, straining her further. She tightened her jaw, enduring the wave of pain while Theodore let his eyes lazily scan around the room. "I won't be causing a scene tonight, Avery. I want you to enjoy this while it lasts, because it will make a much more valuable lesson that way." He leaned in closer, whispering his promise, "Every single individual who has helped you and all you have gained? I will enjoy taking it all from you. All their lights will be extinguished, and you will be responsible for bringing the darkness upon them all." He spun her around as the music died down, the pain struck her nerves as she attempted to stabilized herself.

In the daze, she frantically searched for Theodore, but she could not find the red mask in the crowd of people who cheered in honor of the song ending. The band dove straight into another song. She stood frozen where Theodore left her, until Leah came to her side and tugged cheerfully at her arm. "Wasn't that fun! How'd you do?"

Leah's expression changed to concern when she saw

the panic on her friend's face. "Avery?" Leah quietly called to her, but Avery could not break away from her stupor. "Avery, Are you alright?" The distress in her voice sent the nearby captain looking in their direction.

It was Rhyker's concerned glance that forced Avery to snap out of her momentary daze and regained control of herself. With a strained smile, she led Leah away from the crowd. "Yeah, I was a little lightheaded there toward the end." When Leah did not seem convinced, she quickly added, "And Rhyker tried to trip me when we danced."

Leah's eyes widened in a mix of indignation and jealously. "He *didn't*!" she breathed. "I wonder if I danced with him, it's so hard to tell with these dang masks!" She looked around at the people left on the dance floor. "I'm going to go grab a drink, want to come with?"

Another wave of pain washed through her, not a physical pain, but the icy sense of dread for making Leah such a valuable target for Theodore.

Avery shook her head, fighting to keep herself together. "I think I need to step outside for some air. I'll find you after."

Leaving Leah, she made her way out one of the doors, slipping out onto the terrace that looked out over the training yard. She walked to the edge and leaned on the rail to steady herself, her body beginning to tremble. She could not believe how foolish she had been. How could she think she was safe in Farewell? Why was it not until now that she realized how much danger she was putting the others in the longer she stayed there? It was not a coincidence he showed up tonight. He had planned it, which meant that Avery did not know how long he had been watching her. He probably already knew where she was staying and exactly who she had been spending her time with. Theodore was collecting all his intel, and she was there dancing at a stupid festival.

Her grip on the guard rail tightened and she fought to regain herself. Slowly she stopped shaking and forced herself to run through her options. An alerting pulse on her vessel came from behind her, and she heard the noise from the festival leak out of the door as it opened and shut. Half expecting to see Theodore waltzing out, she whipped around to face the approach, only to find a startled Rhyker. He aimed a confused grin at her and walked over to join her at the railing. "Partied out, Blue Eyes?"

When they danced, she did not have the chance to take him in fully. He was in a black uniform that suited him well. Small medals glistened on his chest next to the captain's badge. Behind his black mask she could tell he was clean shaven again, and his deep green eyes fixated on her. Feeling her pulse spiking again, she turned to look over the railing, "Crowds aren't really my thing."

He laughed, letting the concerned look fade away. "Yeah, I'm starting to realize I think I prefer patrol over attending the event."

Avery scoffed. "I was just thinking I'd rather take on another Leveler then have to dance with you again." She could not help but laugh as she finished.

The comment amused him, and he leaned on the rail to considered it.

"I'd take one now for sure. Sometimes being out in the field seems less complicated than normal civilian life." He stared out into the night aimlessly, telling her there was something on his mind that brought more substance to the thought. Without looking at her, he spoke more quietly. "Mindy sought me out tonight and confessed her feelings for me."

Avery turned to look at him, her smile fading as she registered the sudden seriousness in his voice. Knowing he had her attention, he continued, "We've always been friends.

She likes to listen to stories about the guard and my team, but honestly, I've always seen her as a little sister. She's an extremely warm person and cares a lot for other people. I guess that's why I wonder if I'm meant to settle down and start something of my own here." He sighed taking his mask off and let his shoulders drop slightly. "At the same time, we both live in different worlds, I don't necessarily share a lot of the church's ideals. I really don't think it's fair with the work I do to leave someone here who is always worrying about me."

Avery quietly listened as Rhyker went on, feeling entirely unqualified to hear the pestering thoughts tormenting his own mind. In that moment, he was not the Farewell champion. He was simply a man – perhaps one of the most stubborn she had met – who needed to air out the noxious thoughts plaguing him.

Avery pulled her own mask off and looked up at him. "You know Rhyker, I have always admired your instincts and your sense for doing the right thing. I think you'll make the right decision for both of you, as long as you continue to trust those instincts." She paused to let it sink in and reflected on her own demons. The captain watched her now, both unwilling to break away from their shared gaze. "I don't have much experience with this," she confessed, "…but I believe that when you're given an opportunity to do the right thing, you should take it, even if it's more challenging."

He stared at her more intently, making her aware of how fast her heart pounded. She lost herself in the deep forest eyes once more, forgetting entirely what stirred her out onto the terrace in the first place. Realizing herself, she let the moment pass, giving him a soft laugh to break the silence. "Then again, what do I know? I'm just some reckless civilian."

He grinned, rolling his eyes, his body sinking closer to her. "You know for a whole second there, I thought we were going to have a serious conversation."

"Well, I guess your instincts aren't always that great," she said, joining him in the shared laugh.

They resumed watching out into the night, the silence creeping in between them until the captain shifted his gaze down to her, suddenly donning a playful grin. "You still owe me an answer to a question."

The notion confused her, and she took a moment to trace the callback from their first mission. "Are you really still on that?"

"Absolutely!" He moved so his back now leaned against the railing, a better angle to watch her try and avoid his question.

With a sigh she surrendered herself to the interrogation. "Alright, what would you like to know?"

He studied her a moment, then seemed to settle his mind on it. "Where do you see yourself in the next few years?"

She stared at him with wide eyes, taken aback by the question. A short laugh escaped her while she shook her head. "I can't answer that."

It was his turn to glare at her. "Come on, Blue Eyes! You can't honestly continue to resent me after all this time."

Avery smiled at his indignation, causing him to turn away from her to look back out at the training yard. After a moment he looked over his shoulder, a slight seriousness returning, his eyes intentionally searching her. "How am I supposed to take you seriously if you never give me a straight answer?"

Avery caught the moon peeking out from behind the clouds. A pang of guilt festered in her chest – after all, the captain was being genuine with her. She sighed, "Rhyker, I can't answer that because I don't know the answer. I can't figure out my past let alone plan that far into the future."

He fully turned toward her, studying her as if to make sure she was not trying to pull one over on him. When Avery stared back at him unyielding, he humored the possibility. "Does that mean you're an orphan or something?"

Avery thought about it before she responded. "Yes, something like that."

He continued to stare at her, untrusting. "Then, what brought you here to Farewell? Was it Harvey?"

She went to respond, but stopped herself, not ready to test that boundary. Not willing to risk his life.

"If I recall correctly, I only owed you one answer." She felt the crushing weight of her troubles become even heavier when the captain's curiosity turned to annoyance.

He swore under his breath, shaking his head slowly. "I've never met someone more frustrating to talk to." Despite his irritation, he gave her a soft smile.

She shrugged, letting a smirk take over. "The feeling is mutual, Captain."

The sound of the festival leaked out of the hall as the door opened behind them.

"Avery?" Leah asked as she peeked out the door. "There you are! Oh," she stopped when she took in Avery's company. Even from under the mask, Avery could see she was taken by surprise. Awkwardly, Leah found her voice again. "Captain Adler, Mindy was looking for you over by the refreshments earlier."

Rhyker pushed himself off the railing and let out a breath. "That's my cue." He tossed her a wink before throwing his mask back on and returning inside. Avery tried to look unfazed by it as she followed behind him, meeting up with Leah at the door. Her friend pulled her mask off, smiling devilishly at her.

"What's that look for?" she asked as they filed back into the hall pulling their own masks back up.

"Don't you dare give me that!" she teased. "You know exactly what! You've been acting strange all night, and then I find you off talking with the captain *alone*. Are you feeling okay?"

Avery, attempting to dissuade any thought of peril, looped her arm with Leah's as they walked to provide her with some reassurance. "I'm fine." She managed to say, almost convincing herself despite feeling as though all the walls were closing in. "I'm just not used to this many people, and Harvey pushed me pretty hard at training this morning."

"My feet are killing me," Leah added and the two made their way out of the guild hall after saying goodnight to Milo and Reya.

Back at the bookstore, Avery changed back into her normal clothes and set the dress on the end of Leah's bed, laying her mask on top of it. "Do you mind if I leave this here and grab it later?"

Leah dramatically fell onto the bed in fake exhaustion, murmuring an okay. Avery grabbed her pack and headed for the door, stopping as she reached it. "Leah, thank you for everything… tonight and always. I had such a great time."

Leah propped herself up on some pillows and beamed back to Avery. "Thanks for going with me, this was by far the best harvest festival I've ever attended!"

They said their goodbyes, but Avery's smile faded as she descended the stairs and exited the bookstore. The chime of the bell above the door reminded her how much she cared for that shop and the people within it. She took a deep, shaky breath, and made her way back to the farmhouse.

22
THE MISSING AURA
Rhyker

Rhyker struck the training dummy with such force that the steel pipe holding it in place bent sideways from the combination of the heat and force. Milo and Reya looked over at him from across the training yard where they were helping move furniture back into the building. The guild hall was in a state of disarray, tearing down the festival decorations and planning for the upcoming council meeting.

His teammates paused in their task to stare at him curiously. Distracted within his own thoughts, he momentarily let slip a sliver of the pent-up force that needed to be worked out. The result of which meant the training dummy stared at him lopsided. The small group of recruits all stared in awe, giving him the over-the-top reactions he was growing sick of. His dislike for demonstrating to the newest reinforcements did not stop James from volunteering him for the task. He was just glad Avery was not there to witness it. She would chalk it up to him trying to show off, and he would be hard press to deny it.

He took a breath and put his sword away, realizing it had not helped clear his mind anyway. He turned around to see Milo and Reya still staring at him, each holding the end of a table. The look he sent them was enough to instantly send them on their way through the open guild hall doors. With that settled, he dismissed the group, instructing them to help with cleaning up the event and following them in to check on the progress of getting the guild returned to normal working order.

"Captain, good to see you and your team are looking well. Seems some rest did all of you some good." The Guild Master stood beside him, clapping Rhyker on the shoulder with a large heavy hand.

"Yes sir, we are ready to get back to it whenever the research facility has more trackers for us to deploy."

"I see." James nodded, not taking in what the captain was saying because he was clearly more interested in asking his burning questions. "…and have you had a chance to think over the other matter we discussed?"

Rhyker avoided James entirely since their last meeting for exactly that reason. He finally gave the Guild Master a surrendering sigh. "Yes sir, I was just about to take off."

An unavoidable grin spread across the Guild Master's face, and he clapped his hands together. "Excellent, I'll be looking forward to hearing the outcome, let me know once you're back."

Rhyker agreed to do as much and was relieved to break away when another guild member stole the Guild Master's attention. He nearly made it to the front entrance when the Guild Master called to him. "Captain, one more thing!"

Rhyker stopped to hear him out, finding he was joined by Leif Corwin, the nosiest of James' advisors. The man manifested perpetual concern, always rambling on about something or another but never willing to get elbow deep into fixing something if it called for action. Leif's eyes shifted nervously from the captain to the Guild Master.

"Have you seen Arthur this morning?" James asked.

"Can't say I have," Rhyker called back, grateful for it.

Out of all his experiences working alongside the knights, dealing with Arthur was among the worst. Which was saying something since there had been a number of those occasions where he nearly died.

The knight showed up after Duke Vanguard caught onto some strange activity linked with the Traconian empire. Since his arrival, Arthur has kept the guild and guard in the dark, providing very little to account for what happened to the team that never managed to come back. Not to mention he would not take any of Rhyker's suggestions seriously or give him the courtesy of showing up for meetings to discuss how they would proceed with the investigation.

The captain briefly entertained the idea of asking General Carter about him, but dealing with Harvey was not any easier. In fact, since Avery showed up, it had become even harder to converse with the tavern owner.

"Strange…" The Guild Master pursed his lips, a genuine look of concern over the knight's absence. James waved away the worry, returning to his usual optimism. "Well, we were supposed to take a look at that sword with Harris. I suppose it will have to wait for another time."

"I'll let him know you were looking for him," Rhyker offered, and the Guild Master seemed to accept it, thanking him before going off with Leif.

Rhyker made his way out of the guild hall, figuring there was no use in continuing the delay of his task. He could not pinpoint why he kept postponing it, but an unfamiliar nervousness settled over him as he navigated through the plaza and down the streets of Farewell. Unwilling to confront his own feelings on the matter, he forced his mind to divert his attention elsewhere.

The first thought that came to mind was far from pleasant. As he passed one of the benches beneath the pioneer statue, a pang of guilt surfaced. He recalled the disappointment and hurt in Mindy's eyes there on the bench after they left the festival dance and Rhyker had to address her feelings for him. Mindy was incredibly smart and the most caring person he knew, but she did not always see the world for what it was. Her perception of reality was filtered through a smaller, more defined lens, and Rhyker realized it was probably for the best she found someone with a less dangerous lifestyle. He hoped the confrontation would not strain their relationship or cause her to treat him differently, but he knew it might be unavoidable. As surprising as it was, he agreed with what Avery said the night before. He needed to trust his gut, and honesty was necessary, even if it risked Mindy resenting him.

His mind bridged the thoughts over to Avery. During their short talk on the terrace, he felt like he had been given a small glimpse into who she was behind all the banter and mystery. He could tell something was bothering her; for a brief moment, she had looked frightened, both after the dance and on the terrace. Even in the worst of situations, Avery always maintained her composure, and it was unsettling to think of what could have startled her. But she seemed to brush it off as they chatted. She even laughed and played off his words in her usual clever manner, keeping him on edge. The more he got to know Avery, the more questions he had about how such a mysterious mage ended up on Farewell's doorstep.

His mind shifted back to his current task as the Big Hen came into view. It was early. Avery would be well into her training session with Harvey. It was no wonder she was excelling with her sword fighting with how hard she had been training, and despite her constant attitude, she did take direction from Rhyker to improve in the areas he suggested. While he would never admit it, he was impressed the last time they sparred. It was rare to find a sparring partner that could keep pace with him.

As he neared the door of the old tavern, he squinted at the closed sign prominently displayed in the window. It struck him as odd since he had never seen the sign there before. Through the fogged glass, he could see people gathered around the bar. He tested the door and found it unlocked, so he pulled it open. The heads around the bar quickly turned to take in his arrival.

"Can't you read? Were closed!" Harvey barked at him with narrowed eyes. The old man sat on a stool in the back with his arms crossed. Both Professor Colleymore and the bookstore owner were seated at a table nearest the bar. Malcom's arm was gently placed on Leah's back. She looked at the captain with red, puffy eyes.

Seeing the state of them all, he felt anxious for suddenly intruding on the scene. "I apologize, General. I was looking for Avery." His words prompted a simultaneous intake of breath from the group.

The professor looked up frantically at him. "Has something happened, Captain?"

An increasingly uneasy feeling crept over him and only worsened as he realized he could not feel Avery's aura. "No, is everything all right?"

"What do you want from her?" Harvey demanded, and he was not alone in the curious look he shot at the captain.

Rhyker searched them all again, not expecting the cold reception. "We are getting sent out on another field mission-" he began, but Harvey quickly cut him off.

"She finished her service with the guild, James told me she wasn't required to go anymore."

"I'm aware, General. That's why I am here," he managed to say, keeping a cool head despite his thoughts racing. Harvey glowered at him behind the smoke of his cigar, the old man was reading the intention all over Rhyker's face, so he spoke honestly. "I came to see if she would join my team on a permanent basis."

He kept his eyes locked with Harvey but could see Leah suddenly jerk her head in his direction. She looked the least like she wanted him to go.

The doors to the kitchen swung open, revealing an older woman whom Rhyker knew well. Cecelia came in from the back with a tray full of tea. She caught sight of the captain, and her frown deepened.

"She's not here, Rhy."

"Where is she?" Rhyker asked becoming aware of how they were all looking at each other.

"She left Farewell," the professor started, finding a strain in his voice.

"She's being hunted," Harvey cut in, keeping his eyes trained on Rhyker.

Rhyker took a step forward. "Hunted?"

"Harvey, you can't!" Malcom broke his silence and jumped up to face Harvey.

A rage poured out from the General. "The guild is going to want to know what happened. We can't expect people not to ask questions. She hasn't even been gone a whole day, and they are already looking for her." He swore loudly and aimed the frustration back at Rhyker. "You heard of Theodore Sinclair?"

Rhyker nodded. "Of course, I know of him."

"Well, that son of a bitch has been trying to track her down for months. He apparently made an appearance last night at the party and spooked Avery real good."

Rhyker stood dumbfounded, sifting through his memories in a desperate attempt to find anything that would make sense of the situation. "I don't understand, what does he want with Avery?"

"It's a long story, kid, and we don't have time to catch

you up on the details."

Leah stood up and handed Rhyker an envelope, her hands shaking. "She left this for me this morning."

He opened the document. Leah's name was written on the envelope and inside was a short letter. He recognized Avery's neat handwriting from all the reports and catalogs of hers that he reviewed.

Leah,

Theodore was there at the masquerade, and I've decided I can't risk staying in Farewell. You and the others have done so much for me, I would hate to repay it by bringing him straight to your door. I promise when this is all over I will came back and see you. Please tell Harvey I'm sorry. I'm sure he will think I'm being reckless. You all have taught me more than you know, and I will be forever grateful for everything.

-Avery

When he finished, Leah was in tears again. They all watched him silently, except the General, who glared at the floor, muttering, "She should have come talked to me."

"Where would she have gone?" Rhyker asked handing Leah back the note.

Malcom and Harris exchanged glances before agreeing it was too late to withhold anything. It was Malcom who supplied the information. "The plan was to get her overseas, further away from Lord Sinclair's territory. She needs to get in front of the Mage's Council in Astoria."

The professor nodded, adding onto the explanation, "As I'm sure you noticed, Avery has some complications with her ability to use magic. Call it a curse for lack of a better term. A courtesy given to her from Lord Sinclair."

The captain's mind worked quickly to arrange the mess in his head.

"Thank you," was all he said, giving them all a single nod before heading back out the door.

"What the hell are you going to do, Captain?" Harvey called after him, but Rhyker ignored him and exited the Big Hen.

23

THE ILLUSIONIST

Avery

The mechoid crumpled at Avery's feet as she withdrew her sword from its core. She had been doing her best to avoid the creatures, but the three Prowlers nearly managed to get a jump on her. She swore at herself for letting them get that close and not spotting them sooner. The exhaustion was going to cost her everything, and she had to remind herself of that as she caught her breath and surveyed the area for any other lurking danger. The encroaching darkness threatened to make her journey even more treacherous.

Without wasting any time, she quickly salvaged the mechoid parts and stuffed them into her bag. She could sell them for a few credits when she reached Dawnhaven, where she could resupply before heading back toward the Solstice City dead zone. This route would take her alongside the perimeter of the dead zone – a calculated risk designed to add confusion to her path. The detour would add a few extra days to her journey, but she hoped it would make it more difficult for Theodore to track her, especially since he had already found her once. She couldn't be certain how much he knew of her plans or how closely he was monitoring her movements.

From there, she would aim for Port Stevens, the only

port along the Arcadian sea coast capable of crossing the treacherous waters beyond. The port was the only viable crossing point because of the phenomenon known as the Void Tides—a powerful and unpredictable force that stretched along much of the coastline. Avery knew that, despite the detour and the added danger of traveling close to the dead zone, getting to Port Stevens was her only shot at reaching the other side of Arcadia and, ultimately, the capital.

Farewell was already two days travel behind her, and based on the maps she memorized, she had a long, arduous journey ahead. Besides the daunting distance, she needed to rest at some point and without others to keep watch, it was difficult to come by. Since leaving Farewell, she had only stopped for a few hours at a time, and per her usual struggle, sleep had been nearly impossible. She hoped that rest would come easier the further she got from Farewell.

Thoughts of what she was leaving behind lingered in her mind as she traveled alone. A heaviness weighed upon her chest. A crushing weight had settled there since Theodore's threatening words sunk in. She was not sure when she had decided to leave, nor did she allow herself to dwell on the decision for long. She knew she could not face the others, especially not Harvey, who would know something was wrong the moment he saw her – as he always did.

It was fortunate Cecelia had already gone to bed for the night when Avery returned to the farmhouse after the festival. Somehow, Avery felt that the old woman would understand. There had always been an unspoken respect between them, and Avery was grateful to have stayed with her. However, the guilt of vanishing in the night was too much, so she had prepared a note for Leah before stepping out into the late night. Harvey would be pissed, more so than usual, and no doubt he would have tried to stop her, just like the others.

There was nothing any of them could do, and that thought drove Avery further and further away from Farewell. Theodore would have to focus his attention on finding her before he could make good on his promise to hurt the people she cared about. Hopefully, by then she would have reached Astoria, and gained the protection of the Arcadian Mage's Council.

Finally giving in to her aching muscles, Avery stopped for the night to allow herself time to rest and warm up. She started a small fire and silently ate a meal. All the fieldwork she had been doing with Rhyker's team prepared her for this. Another ache wedged itself into her already shattered mind. She wished it was just another mission; sitting at the fire with Milo and Reya as they recounted their previous adventures. She would even tolerate Rhyker's brooding in the corner, critiquing all the missed openings she had in a previous encounter.

Smiling to herself, she wondered if Rhyker and his team knew she was gone. She imagined they were already preparing for another mission, given how impatient the research facility was getting. Milo and Reya were probably already giving their captain a hard time about not changing his mind on letting her go with them- Not that she could have gone anyway, but it was nice to know they wanted her there. Maybe when this was all over, she could return to doing work like that.

Avery's mind snapped to an alertness as a faint pulsing nipped at her aura, warning her of something approaching in the distance. With a quick wave of her hand, she extinguished the fire, hastily kicking dirt over the charred remains for good measure. Grabbing her bag, she moved slowly, backing away from her small camp. Clinging to the darkness, she found a sizable tree to hide behind, where she stopped and waited, listening for any signs of life. Every twitch in the forest set Avery further and further on edge, until finally enough time passed that she became increasingly aware of how much time she was wasting.

Adding further to her exhaustion, she pressed on, her mind racing through all the likely scenarios of what could have caused the disturbance – including her mounting paranoia that caused the phantom tugs on her aura just to keep her awake. Once she put enough distance between herself and the camp, she diverted her route, heading further away from the road, her gut telling her to stay vigilant and keep moving.

The detour led her to the ruins of what must have been a small town in the distant past. Buildings that once resembled homes were now torn apart by nature, and Avery had to watch her step to avoid tripping over the concrete that jutted out from where walls once stood. The stumps of trees, long since butchered for lumber, depicted the scars of a civilization that once thrived in the thick of the woods.

The air was thick with the scent of damp earth and decaying wood, and the faint rustle of leaves added to the eerie silence. She walked further in, finding a larger building that housed heavy machinery. Saw blades and chains, now rusted from generations of neglect, littered the ground, their metallic surfaces reflecting the faint moonlight that seeped through the gaps in the canopy above. The cold air bit at her skin, as she silently took in the bones of the lumberyard. The creaking of the old building adding to the unsettling atmosphere, while she was determining if it was a safe place to pause and rest.

After a few moments of surveying, she plopped her bag against one of the ruined walls and eased herself down, leaning against the structure to rest. She closed her eyes, forcing her mind not to wander down dark paths.

The snapping of brush sounded in the distance, tearing Avery's eyes open. From within the forest line, the red eyes of a mechoid trailed along the trees. It was peculiar finding another defected mechoid, unable to switch to the green lighted night vision. Despite the defect, the mechoid needed to be eliminated, and she rose from her position to meet it head-on. Avery pulled out Lightbringer, watching as the red eyes locked onto her and slowly stalked toward her. Keeping focus on the mechoid, she quickly scanned for more. To her surprise, no other eyes followed it. She thought it might have been a Stalker, hunting alone, yet the mech emerged from under the tree line, revealing itself to be a Prowler. Standing her ground, she let the mech close the distance. The beast leaped at her, and she readied her sword to pierce through it, but her steel met nothing. The mechoid vanished. She staggered forward, stopping herself from tumbling, as she frantically searched around for it. Somewhere within the darkness of the forest, she heard a slow, ugly laugh.

"I must say, I'm a little impressed," a voice called from another direction. Her eyes scanned the forest again for the source.

"I didn't plan for you to be hard to pin down after you left that town," the same voice continued, seeming to come from yet another direction. "...but you sure made it a long way in a short time."

A broad-shouldered man stepped out of the shadows into the moonlight. He looked rougher than she remembered, as if he had also spent the last two nights in the forest. Without a cloak, the moonlight glinted off the few blades he carried. His light brown eyes appeared as black voids, watching her hungrily. Theodore must have used his connections to tip off the Arcadian authorities, hoping they would do his dirty work for him. Once they killed her, word would get back to Theodore, and he could rest easy knowing his loose thread had been taken care of.

"What do you want?" she demanded, tightening the grip on her sword.

"Well, for starters, I'd like to be in a nice cozy inn rather than out here." He laughed, humorless. "But it doesn't seem like that's in the cards for me until I get you back to Tracos."

Confused, Avery held her sword slightly higher. "What's a Lunar Knight doing working for Theodore?"

Arthur laughed, this time genuinely. "Thanks for the compliment. I wish I could say it was my idea, but Lord Sinclair was the one to arrange it. Glad I was convincing enough."

The realization hit Avery: he was not a Lunar Knight – mentally, she gave herself credit for not liking him from the start. Of course, that also made things far worse for her.

"Theodore hired you to collect me, then?" she asked the obvious, needing time to think things through.

"Yes, and you'd be flattered to know you're worth a lot to him. Honestly, I've never taken on such a delicate job… even from him." Arthur tilted his head. "What is it about you that makes the Blood Tyrant travel all the way to some nowhere town to deliver a message?"

"How did he find me?" she demanded.

"I happened to be at the right place at the right time. I was pissed when you tore into that old base, blowing up half the damn place in the process. Thought I was going to lose out on finishing the job. Then again, it wouldn't have landed me this holy grail of a bounty." He forced a toothy grin. "I'll tell you all about it on our way back to Tracos."

"I'm not going." Avery said coldly, leaving no room for doubt.

"Come on," Arthur took another step toward her, flashing his teeth. "Just be a good little lady and come quietly with me."

She raised her sword, resolute in her silence.

He held out his hands in an attempt to show her he meant no harm. "Listen, you've got one more chance; this doesn't have to get ugly."

"I'm. Not. Going. Back," she repeated, keeping her eyes on him, knowing the encounter was inevitable. She could not feel any aura from him, which would play to her advantage.

He laughed as he stood there, pulling out his own short sword. "Good, I knew I liked you."

Avery's heart raced, and she prepared herself as he slowly started walking toward her.

When he got close enough, Avery lunged at him. He caught the attack with his blade and pushed back on her. They traded a few hits, and when she almost nicked his ear off, he raised an eyebrow at her blade.

"You're not even gonna try to kill me?" He groaned, sounding almost disappointed like some deranged lunatic. "Now that's a mistake." He reached behind his back and pulled out a dagger, driving it toward her. With her sword already guarding against his, she created a shield with her other hand to block the incoming dagger.

Irritated, he attempted to come at her from various directions, but she countered them, looking for another opening. When she finally found it, she pushed forward, knocking him back. She pulled herself back, creating space between them and preparing for his next advance.

"Not bad," he assessed her. "I gotta admit, I was excited when I heard you were being trained by the ol' general." He swung his sword around, driving more power behind it to force her on the defensive.

When Avery pressed her advantages, he seemed less interested in talking in order to regain his lost ground. She felt him calculating each strike to deflect her blade. His eyes narrowed in concentration, indicating he had underestimated her skill. After losing more ground than he was comfortable with, he forced enough strength into one of his strikes to force Avery away. He backed into the forest, where the trees embraced him in darkness. Avery did not follow, knowing it was an attempt to lure her closer. She remained within the clearing, scanning for signs of him among the trees.

"I had to find out more about you, so I hunted down your sparring partner." His voice seemed to come from right beside her, but she remained alone in the field. He was projecting his voice. "Found him and his team out scavenging some mechs. He didn't know much about you either. Mentioned Harvey's gone soft on ya. I was disappointed with how easy it was to kill them." Avery's heart dropped. He was talking about Logan, whose death the guild and knights were investigating, or so she thought.

Arthur appeared from the tree line, running with his blade ready. She prepared to catch his strike, but there was no contact. Another ominous laugh echoed from within the forest as her blade swiped the air and the illusion of Arthur shimmered away.

"Glad to see you're more skilled with a blade. I was beginning to think we weren't gonna have any fun with how easily the others fell to my sword." He mocked her from behind, running at her again. She prepared to receive the blow, and again, there was no contact. Avery could not understand—there was no trace of magic in the air, yet he was able to create these illusions.

Two more of him came at her. Not knowing if they were real, she guarded against both, watching as they disappeared on contact. Thinking fast, she sent out a large radius of light magic that shredded through three oncoming illusions. At the edge of the light, she spotted Arthur within the woods, hiding as he sent the mirrored men after her. She took off in a sprint, sending her blade around to meet him, and feeling the satisfaction of making contact. However, it was not him – instead her blade was implanted within a tree.

With force, she yanked out the blade just as a blow struck her head, knocking her against a neighboring tree. Her sword fell from her grasp as she slid to the ground. Arthur walked up to her, kicking Lightbringer aside. "Such a shame," he boasted. "I hoped all that time with the General would have made you more of a challenge. But you're too inexperienced to know better."

Avery got back to her feet, feeling a warmth trickle down the side of her face. She reached up to touch it, finding the dark red liquid on her hands courtesy of the fresh gash on her temple.

Arthur watched her, amused. "Little something to remember me by." He gestured for her to start walking. "Come on, let's get moving."

"I'd rather die," she said in a shockingly calm voice.

He held his sword out to point at her chest. "Look, you really aren't in a position to decide."

Avery quickly reached up a hand and fired a blast of light at the flat part of his blade, hoping to stagger his arm back or knock the blade out of his hand. Before she could see the outcome, she dove and rolled behind him, picking up her sword in the process. She sprinted back to the abandoned site where the crumpled ruins of the building were, forcing him to fight her in the open.

When he emerged from the darkness, she shot hard blasts of light that sailed through his mirrored phantoms, slamming into the trees behind them. As the multiples of him gained ground, she felt the slightest pulse tug at her aura from behind. Whipping around, she focused all her energy into a powerful blast, hitting him square in the chest and sending the real Arthur crashing into the ruined structure behind him. The illusions dissipated.

Part of the structure collapsed, and she heard rustling from within, indicating he was still alive. She hoped no nearby mechoids had heard the commotion. She had enough to deal with without Prowlers taking advantage of the chaos. He pushed away the fallen debris and stood, bleeding from several cuts.

"Alright, now I'm pissed." He spat, blood lingering at the corner of his mouth. He pulled out another hidden dagger. The tug on her aura was more noticeable now, and she prepared as he lunged at her. A chill emanated from his blade, now laced with ice, as they traded blows again. His aura grew with each strike. Arthur was creating fake arms with blades to throw her off. She countered each, trusting her instincts to identify the real strikes. It took all her concentration, leaving no room for mistakes or an opportunity to regain the advantage.

He slammed the hilt of his dagger into the side of her hand, forcing her to drop her sword. His elbow drove into her side, sending her stumbling to the ground. She scrambled to turn and face him as he aimed his sword, directing an icy blast her way. Quickly, she created a shield, repelling the blast back at him. The light blinded them both, and she fought to get back on her feet. Her body shook, and she could feel her chest burning. Scanning around, she spotted him charging at her. She prepared another shield, but as he made contact, the illusion dissipated, and another blow knocked her to the floor, plunging her into darkness.

24
A BATTLE OF TRUST
Avery

Avery's eyes stung, adjusting to a bright light, which turned out to be the sky showcasing the start of morning light. She lifted her head off the ground, a deep burning came from her chest as it throbbed. In fact, all her body ached. She heard a groan, and realized it was her own voice. She attempted to sit up, but when she moved her arms, something weighed them down, binding them together in front of her. She turned her head so she could see them. A thick rope tightly bound her arms. She had to use all her core strength to lift herself into a sitting position

"Well good morning, princess, did you have a nice nap?" the man's voice oozed with sarcasm. Sitting next to the fire, Arthur was helping himself to some of the food she packed. His arms were badly cut, and a bruise was forming around his left eye. "Some neat tricks you learned out there," he said, picking up Lightbringer to examine the blade. "Makes more sense how you took out that Conductor." He lifted an impressed brow at the blade. "Lord Sinclair was interested to know you were training with a blade, and he wanted to know how it was you stumbled upon those ruins. He had me pivot bounties the moment he learned of you." He tossed Lightbringer aside, picking up her bag as he spoke. "Not that I'll be hurting much, I'll be heading back to recover that crescent sword after I deliver you back to Tracos."

"What does Theodore want with that sword?" Avery asked, knowing how fruitless the attempt was.

He gave another humorless laugh. "Doesn't matter to you." He eyed her momentarily. "Besides, what I'd like to know, is what makes you so valuable."

When she said nothing, he shrugged, continuing to rummage through her bag, emptying the contents onto the ground. Finding nothing else significant, he stood up and walked over to her, taking a good look at her head. Her temple pounded, and she reached up to feel where the gash on head was trying to heal.

"You should be fine to make it back to the Lord Sinclair's place. I can't have you dying on me before we get there." He reached down and grabbed her by the ropes, ungracefully raising her into a standing position. Her body rioted as she stood, everything blurred as she tried to stand straight.

Avery waited until her vision cleared before she spoke, her words frighteningly calm despite the adrenaline in her system. "You might as well kill me here. I am not going back."

"Oh no, you won't be getting off that easy." He reached down to pick up the last of her rations. "Lord Sinclair made it very clear you were to be alive." He downed the rest of the meal and tossed the container into the fire. "And if you start trying to use magic," he tapped the side of his head, "I'll open that wound of yours again." He picked up her sword from the ground and kicked the rest of her bag to the side on his way toward her. "Let's go."

Avery did not budge, calmly watching him as he indicated the way forward. He groaned loudly. "Seriously, are you gonna make this difficult? My instructions were not to kill you, but that doesn't mean I can't use force. Get the idea?" He nudged her forward. "Let's go!"

"Am I supposed to find that threatening?" Avery asked. A powerful surge of energy suddenly crashed over her, pulling at her vessel and flooding her senses like a tidal wave. The unexpected shift was so intense that she nearly stumbled, a sharp dizziness setting in as her body reacted to the heavy, invasive presence. The air seemed to thrum with a force that wrapped around her, pressing against her skin and making every nerve tingle. She blinked, confused and disoriented—how had she not felt it creeping up on her before?

Arthur eyed her with a raised brow, surely wagering if she was going to vomit or something. She fought the disorienting effects to think quickly. Evading the man was useless, unless she could break out of the binds. Seeing her stubbornness, he did his own contemplation and groaned again loudly, taking an aggressive step toward her.

"Well, I did expect some compliance after I just kicked your ass! Do you really want me to knock you out?"

Avery shrugged. "Sounds more ideal than following you back to that estate willingly. It'll save me from hearing you prattle on."

He laughed, reaching out and grabbing her by the shirt. He pulled her close enough to him that she could smell whatever whiskey he last drank. "You really don't know when to stop, do you?"

She glared back at him, muttering in a bored tone. "So, I've been told…I'm sure it's something you can relate to, given your drinking problem." She crinkled her nose as she finished.

Resolving to silence her, the man pulled out his dagger, raising it above her head with the aim to drive the hilt down at her temple. Avery braced herself, feeling the magic stirring within her once more… but the blow never came.

Arthur's arm slashed through the air as another reached out in time to prevent the contact.

"How do I always find you in these situations, Blue Eyes?" a familiar voice called out.

Arthur stepped back in alarm, hastily releasing Avery to free himself from the newcomer. Not having her hands to catch her fall, she fell, hitting the ground hard.

"Rhyker?" She gasped, taking in the captain as he pulled out his sword, putting himself between her and the false knight. Her captor groaned again, taking in the new problem.

"The *hot shot* Captain. I knew you were going to be a problem."

"That's an understatement," the captain replied, his voice menacingly dark and ominous.

"Right, well I've got a job to do. It'll complicate things if I let you go back and tell your Guild Master that his knight was never really coming." He fluttered a hand in the air. "The knights don't take kindly to imposters, you know."

Flames slowly danced along the blade of Rhyker's sword. "The way I see it, the Knights are the least of your worries at the moment."

Arthur's eyebrows shot up, and he smiled in delight. "Oh, really, now? Are you planning on-" Without warning, Rhyker dashed forward, engaging the sword fight. The two clashed back and forth, and within mere moments, it became clear that Rhyker was forcing Arthur to lose ground. Avery felt a chill run down her spine as she saw the dangerous focus in the captain's eyes. He effortlessly countered each of Arthur's attempts to strike him, returning each with a force the illusionist could not contend with.

Realizing his disadvantage, the man quickly reverted to the tactics from the night before, losing himself among the trees. The illusions swarmed out toward Rhyker, flanking him from all directions. Avery pushed herself up off the ground, trying to get free so she could help eliminate the mirrored men. Rhyker was already moving before she could manage to stand. A soft channeling of magic stirred moments before the captain sent out a column of fire that tore through the forest. It was as though the fire itself came from within the ground, destroying everything in its path until it met the intended target. The captain, somehow, could see through all the mirrored men, causing the remaining illusions to vanish as their source was forced to protect himself from the fire eruption.

It was only as the fire started to fade that Avery could see the shield Arthur mustered together in time to prevent the devastating force from overtaking him. Just as the shield shimmered into nothing, Rhyker was on the man again, forcing him to counter blow after blow with his sword. Finding it hard to look away, Avery forced herself to focus on trying to work off the binds. Her wrists throbbed as she tried to pull her hands free of the rope, stealing quick glances of the fight as it continued.

Arthur, clearly outmatched by the captain, changed tactics in his desperation. He waited for Rhyker's next strike, deliberately sacrificing his chance to block. As Rhyker's blade tore into his arm, Arthur raised his other hand and unleashed a burst of power through the opening. The energy surged past the captain, cutting through the air with lethal precision, and hurtling directly toward Avery.

Instinctively, she created a shield to protect herself, but a sharp pain hit her chest like a dagger, and the disruption caused the shield to flicker until it collapsed from the force. The remaining blast was enough to knock Avery back into the ruined building, taking out a corner of the rotting wall. The momentum sent her rolling until her shoulder collided hard against the thick wall. Combined with the earlier destruction from Arthur being forced through it, the sudden lack of supports spiraled the remainder of the building in unrest. The sound of metal scrapping came as parts of the building came down around her.

A bright red shield formed above her, preventing the debris from burying her. In seconds, the captain was at her side and slipped his arm under hers, helping her get to her feet. When they were clear from the collapsed debris, Rhyker dissolved the shield sending the rubble crashing behind them. He held on to Avery, stabilizing her while he did a quick scan of the area.

It was clear the man resorted to attacking Avery with the intention of distracting the captain, allowing the chance to slip away. Catching her breath, Avery scanned the forest, wondering if the man took the opportunity to flee or if he was awaiting another chance to strike. Her gaze clashed with Rhyker's, who assessed her. His breath was heavy, eventually his eyes fixed somewhere above her temple. Her own breathing was evening out, just as her eyes rested on the captain sigil upon his chest, reminding her exactly who she was with.

Avery pulled away from Rhyker abruptly, fuming as she took him in. "Why are you following me?"

He looked relieved to see her glare and smirked while he fought to catch his own breath. "You know, people are usually far more grateful when they've been rescued."

She did not return the grin, instead she kept her eyes narrowed at him, taking a swift step back when he tried to reach out for her again. The guarded behavior caught the captain by surprise, and he halted in place.

"Why are you following me?" she repeated. Perhaps she was not wrong in thinking Theodore tipped off the Arcadian authorities. Did they send the captain to retrieve her?

Rhyker glared at her, reading into her distrust. "I think I've made it more than clear I'm here to help."

Avery shook her head, deciding it best to concentrate on getting her hands free. Her heart was still racing, and she could not begin rationalizing how the captain stood before her.

"I have so many questions about why you are here," she muttered and attempted to use magic to break the binds. The sharp pain hit her chest again, and a pathetic whimper escaped her as the pain abruptly stopped her ability to channel the magic.

Rhyker sighed and took a step forward. "I can say the same thing. Hold still." The captain pulled her to him again, despite her protest. Carefully, he pulled apart the binds until she was able to slip her hands free.

Rhyker turned his attention to the forest, calling over his shoulder, "What do you say we take turns answering questions after we establish your *friend* is no longer a threat?"

Avery said nothing, moving to her sword on the ground.

When they decided the man fled, Avery hastily repacked her bag with what little remained from the man's rummaging. Rhyker returned from his search of the area with a bag he must have abandoned somewhere along the way to intercept the false knight.

Before the captain had a chance to regroup, Avery was already off and walking in the direction of the road. "Come on, Blue Eyes. Farewell is this way," he called from behind her, but when she did not stop or acknowledge him, he called out to her again. She continued to ignore him, set on her path.

Not deterred, he picked up his pace so he could step in front of her, placing a hand on her shoulder. "Whoa, Avery, hold on!"

She attempted to move past him, but he remained

firm, not giving her room for another step. Frustrated, she pointed aimlessly into the forest. "That man is probably going straight back to report that he was intercepted. I can't waste any more time-" She stopped suddenly, hearing the panic in her own voice. She forced away a shudder, keeping her thoughts from spiraling.

He shared her frustration plainly, still determined to stop her. "You need to go back to town where we can protect you!"

"I'm not going back to Farewell. I can't go back!" She returned his glare, managing to brush off his arm. She took a step back, finding a way to slip past him. "I'm only putting the town in danger the longer I remain there."

"Avery," Rhyker started to say, but when she continued to ignore him, he swore aloud reaching out for her once more. She tried to dodge it, but instead she collided with a tree. Seeing the opportunity, Rhyker pinned her against the trunk. "You're only going to get yourself killed."

He towered over her, blocking the way out as he held her there.

She glared at him venomously. "Seems like the consensus either way."

Rhyker did not respond right way, frustrated by her stubbornness, his eyes studied her while he must have been making up his mind. "*Fine…*" He let her go, taking a step away from her. "Then we will get you to Astoria."

"*We?*" Exasperated, she shook her head. "You can't be serious."

He was glaring at her now, the annoyed tone in his voice returning. "Yes, I will go with you until you make it to the council." He turned and without waiting for her, he started walking toward the road.

She sighed impatiently. "You're not going Rhyker; you can't just drop everything and go with me." He turned around to face her, the imposing glare on her. "I'm already here, it's a good thing too. Seems like you *really* had the situation under control with your friend back there."

Avery ignored the jab, returning the glare. "Rhyker, you don't want to do this, you don't understand what you're getting yourself into."

He forced a laugh and shook his head. "I'm pretty convinced you don't know either."

She paused at the comment, finding herself in disbelief both at his frankness and the ever-complicating situation. The captain had a point...and the most frustrating way of getting under her skin. Still, she brushed aside the notion and remained adamant. "You are not going with me."

The captain grinned, adding to her frustration as he proceeded to keep walking. "What...are *you* going to stop me?"

Avery waited, contemplating her options as she watched the captain continue on her path. She let out a groan before she started following him, knowing she did not have time to waste trying to convince him to go back to Farewell. The threat of her pursuit still lingered, and she needed to start getting as much distance between her and Theodore's hired help.

For miles the two walked in silence, both on high alert and straining to find any sign of a pursuit against them. Upon finding a small creek, Avery took the time to wash off the dried blood from her hair and along her face where the man struck her the night before.

"Let me take a look at that," Rhyker said, his eyes scanning the wound as he kneeled beside her. She ignored him, straightening from where she was bent over the small stream. Using her cloak, she patted her face dry while Rhyker continued to protest behind her. "Seriously, Blue Eyes. You're going to need to trust me at some point."

"I'll be fine, let's keep moving."

"Avery," he tried again, this time using the commanding tone she only heard when he needed it. Out in field missions, it was Rhyker's signal to the team when he needed swift and immediate action. However, Avery's mind was far too preoccupied processing the events since the previous night to concern herself with what the captain wanted.

"What, are *you* going to stop me?" she mused over her shoulder, pulling on her hood as she continued to walk away. He did not respond, but his footsteps crunched softly behind her until they were once more walking together on their set path.

As the sun set, Avery fought shivers as her body processed the various areas that hurt. Pulling her cloak on tighter, she pressed on, wondering how much more ground they should gain before resting. Rhyker, noticing Avery's slowing pace, scanned around in search of an ideal area where they could set up for the night. Grabbing Avery's attention, he pointed to a spot where rocky hills and abundant overgrowth cradled a small clearing.

"If we set up there, we would have enough coverage to have a fire without someone being able to spot it."

Avery eyed the selection and ultimately agreed it was a safe bet. The two proceeded to survey the surroundings, ensuring no mechoids lurked nearby and there were still no signs of being followed. A small fire was made and the two shared a meal from the quick rations the captain threw together before leaving Farewell. Avery was becoming increasingly aware that they would need to make a trip into a town to resupply before they would make it anywhere near Port Stevens.

It was a contingency she prepared for, but not so early in her journey. Port Stevens was still several weeks of travel and detouring to one of the nearest towns would only add to that. She knew she would have to discuss her plan with Rhyker. In all the time planning for the trek, she never imagined someone would be with her – least of all the captain.

He sat across the fire from her where he seemed to be lost in his own thoughts, absentmindedly inspecting his sword in the light of the fire. Other than the necessary callouts, they both were incredibly silent as they travelled throughout the day. Surprisingly, the captain refrained from asking any questions, but she often felt his questioning glance as they walked together.

The short time they spent alone together on the terrace came to her mind. The memory already feeling like it was ages ago rather than just the few days. Still, she struggled to understand why he decided to confide in her about his personal conflictions. Perhaps Reya was right in thinking that the captain was warming up to her. Even if the captain proved to be unpredictable, she could not understand what would have compelled him to follow after her or how he managed to track her down.

To make matters worse, Theodore would learn of the captain's involvement in her escape. While she was grateful to be freed of the capture, she could not help but feel guilty for Rhyker's aid, knowing how Theodore typically dealt with his obstacles.

The side of her head throbbed as she continued to feel the weight of everything coming over her. Avery let out a surrendering breath, eyeing the captain, "How did you find me?"

Stirred from his thoughts, he set his sword aside and leaned back to take her in. "I was wondering if you were just going to avoid conversation until we got to Port Stevens."

Avery kept her eyes on the captain warningly. "Why are you here, Rhyker?"

He must have taken her unamused glare as a sign and spoke plainly to her. "We were about to be assigned out for another set of field missions. I went to the Big Hen to find you, but instead I found a small army gathered and they tensed at the mention of you. I learned you gave everyone the slip after the festival."

Avery aimed her gaze away from him, glaring at nothing in the night. It was not hard to imagine how angry Harvey must have been. She had to remind herself it was all for the best with every step she took away from Farewell.

"Harvey told me you were being pursued by Lord Sinclair and mentioned a bit of your plan to go to Astoria," Rhyker continued, watching her from behind the fire. "So, I decided I would try to catch up with you before you got yourself into trouble."

Avery eyed him, not withholding her suspicion. "You just left town and tracked me down?"

Rhyker shrugged, not taking it personally. "I stopped by and told James I was going to step away and left Reya in charge. Once I set out, I knew the general route you would take to get to the Port and ran into the remains of a few mechoids that told me I was on the right track. Last night, I caught a glimpse of your battle with Arthur. I could see your light magic flashing in the distance. By the time I caught up, I found him there with you, heard bits of what was said..." He trailed off, apparently recalling an annoyance as he shot her a narrowed look. "Your turn, who was he?"

Avery leaned back and shrugged. "Someone hired to find me and bring me back to Tracos." She hesitated a moment, not knowing how to interpret the captain's gaze. "How much did the others fill you in?"

"Not a lot, just that Lord Sinclair was hunting you down, and you were seeking out the Mage's Council in Astoria. I figured you would clue me in once I caught up to you."

Avery sat up abruptly, starring at him incredulously. "You seriously only had that to go off of, and you came following after me?" She raised a hand to her head and rubbed her temple that throbbed slightly from the rushed movement. "Goddess, and you call me reckless...I could be some wanted criminal from Tracos for all you know."

Rhyker laughed. "Well, I've never doubted that you were trouble since I met you, but someone told me I have good instincts and something about always doing the right thing even if it isn't easy." He paused unable to withhold a grin and shook his head. "Or in this case, if it isn't easy and *extremely* unclear."

Avery reluctantly joined in the laugh, feeling a slight warmth overtake her. The sound of her own laughter made her aware of how grateful she was for Rhyker's company. Their laughter subsided into the surrounding night until only the quiet crackling of the fire could be heard.

"Well," Avery gave in, deciding it was only fair for her to be plain with him. "If you are in this for the long haul, I should probably give you some context to work with."

Rhyker inclined his head, agreeing. "It probably would help our chances of getting you overseas if I had some idea of what is going on."

She took a breath, intending to start from the beginning, but realized she no longer knew where it all began. Over the last few months, she learned so much and yet still knew so little about herself or how to truly be free of Theodore. "It's complicated..." she found herself saying as she decided which thread to start on. "To sum it up quickly, yes, Theodore Sinclair is trying to find me. I managed to get away from him and Tracos after living under his false guardianship for over eighteen years."

Rhyker's gaze sharpened, a hint of suspicion creasing his brow. "False guardianship?"

"Yes, he killed my mother when I was two and took me to Tracos claiming that my mother owed him a life debt, and I was to take her place."

The vision of her mother's death played in her mind. The determined violet eyes facing Theodore often appeared in her dreams. It was strange for her to feel so connected to a woman she would never meet. All Avery knew of her mother was from what little Theodore mentioned over the years. He would make passing comments regarding Amelia's natural abilities wielding magic and how eager she was to learn from him. From the little that he did bring her up, Avery knew Theodore was fond of Amelia, which made it all the stranger for her to see the hatred he held for her on the night he killed her.

"So, he just raised you?" Rhyker's voice pulled her from her thoughts. He was watching her intently, resuming the stoic nature she had become all too familiar with.

The manner set Avery on edge. "Yes, he decided he was going to train me to be his successor. He acted like it was some sort of honor, but I didn't want anything to do with managing his operations."

She hesitated; Rhyker seemed to be growing colder with every passing moment, but he waited for her to continue.

"Theodore's reputation isn't from being a well-mannered Lord. He works under the Traconian empire and has been playing the Arcadians for decades. Over time, he managed to corrupt Arcadia from the inside out."

The captain did not receive this news well, his face darkening. "Then why are you trying to get in front of the Mage's Council? Why not go to the Lunar Knights or the Queen with what you know?"

Avery tensed at his icy tone. She matched it, narrowing her own eyes at him. "Before I do anything, I have to figure out if there is a way to remove Theodore's hold on me."

Getting defensive would not help the situation, and she reminded herself that the captain was working with very little information. Not to mention his allegiance was with the same people she was tasked with thwarting during the time she worked under Theodore.

Contemplating her next words, she faced the green eyes that continued to assess her. He was right, she was going to need to trust him if he was insistent on helping get her to Astoria. "Theodore has an affinity for demonic magics," she started, pulling her cloak a little tighter around her as a chilling wind blew through. "When he took me in all those years ago, he found a way to separate my soul and kept it for himself."

The quick gut-wrenching feeling of regret set in as the captain stared blankly at her, his eyes narrowing further. No matter how many times she went over it in her head, or all the ways she could say it, none of them ever sounded sane to her.

"I can't tell you how-" she quickly added, "because I don't know, and so far, nobody does. If I truly want a chance of living through this, I need to figure out if it's even possible to get it back."

When the captain's glare became too much, Avery stared into the embers of the fire, letting him process the information. There was a long pause before Rhyker finally spoke.

"Well, I won't lie to you, and say this isn't a lot to take in." His voice was not sharp, but it carried a coldness, like the winter breeze slipping through a crack in a window. "I don't understand what it all means, but I know we have a lot of ground to cover." He stood up, not looking at her as he grabbed his sword and slid it into the sheath at his side.

Walking away from the fire, he called to her from over his shoulder, "I think you should get some rest. I'll take first watch."

Stunned by his sudden departure, part of her wanted to stop him and help explain the situation, but she could think of nothing that would help any of it make more sense. The captain could not understand, and Avery could not blame him. She wondered what she would have done in his shoes.

"Rhyker," she called to him quietly. "I wouldn't hold it against you if you want to go back to Farewell. You don't have to do this."

The captain did not stop or face her. Faintly she heard him sigh heavily as he called back to her. "Get some rest."

She watched him walk away, searching for some spot to settle into his watch. Avery waited a bit longer, her mind still grasping for the right thing to say. There was so much she still needed to know, part of her not feeling any closer to getting out from under Theodore's grasp. The aches in her body reminded her how poorly her encounter with the Illusionist went. Unknowingly, she closed her eyes, letting her aching body succumb to the weariness.

Her journey to the capital had only just begun.

ACKNOWLEDGEMENTS

Avery's story wasn't something I initially planned to share with the world. It exists today, in your hands, thanks to the encouragement and unwavering support of so many people. This story has been shaped not only by those mentioned here but also by countless others who have, in their own way, contributed to Avery's world.

First and foremost, I owe so much to Scott, Thomas, and Janisse, who were the first to read the book and fall in love with the characters. Your genuine enjoyment and unyielding determination breathed new life into this story and gave me the momentum to keep writing.

To Ash and James, I owe both thanks and a bit of an apology for enduring endless hours of brainstorming and idea-dumping. Your willingness to workshop concepts and offer listening ears during my chaotic creative process was invaluable.

A heartfelt thank you to my sister Cassie, who took on the heavy responsibility of social media and marketing, lifting that burden off my shoulders and handling it with far more diligence than I ever could.

To the early readers—Rachel, Jen, Bran, Chrisi, Jenna, Jessii and the many beta readers—thank you for your insightful feedback during the early stages.

A special thank you to my mom, Reneé, who has been my biggest cheerleader since the beginning. My Dad, Russ, for modeling what hardwork and dedication looks like.

Lastly, to you, the readers: thank you for taking a chance on Avery's story. Your excitement and feedback drive me to continue her journey.

I can't wait to share the rest of her story with you!

ABOUT THE AUTHOR
@AlyH4x

Whoa dearest reader, I did not think you would get this far. I assure you, Avery's Story is far more fascinating than that of the author, AlyH4x. Still curious? Well, she can often be found slaying dragons amongst her friends in weekly Dungeons and Dragons sessions. If not found there, than perhaps she can be found hiking in the Pacific Northwest. Of course, if all else fails, you can try searching in the darkest and coziest of corners in local bookstores, engrossing herself in fictional worlds. It is there that she finds solace from her tiring day, as a defender, warding off cyber criminals.

www.ingramcontent.com/pod-product-compliance
Lightning Source LLC
Chambersburg PA
CBHW050530110726
47899CB00005B/1659

* 9 7 9 8 9 9 1 9 8 5 7 1 0 *